DEVIL'S

Clark Lohr

DEVIL'S KITCHEN

CLARK LOHR

Oak Tree Press   Taylorville, IL

Oak Tree Press

DEVIL'S KITCHEN, Copyright 2011, by Clark Lohr. All Rights Reserved. Printed in the United States of America. No part of this book may be used or reproduced in any manner whatsoever without written permission except in the case of brief quotations used in critical articles and reviews. For information, address Oak Tree Press, 140 E. Palmer St., Taylorville, IL 62568.

Oak Tree Press books may be purchased for educational, business or sales promotional purposes. Contact Publisher for quantity discounts.

First Edition, June 2011

Cover by Lewis Agrell

Devil's Kitchen road sign photographed by Clark Lohr

Devil's Kitchen road sign photograph enhancements by David Siddall

Interior Design by Linda Rigsbee

This is a work of fiction. Names, characters, places and incidents either are the product of the author's imagination or are used fictitiously. Any resemblance to actual persons living or dead, events, or locales is entirely coincidental.

ISBN 978-1-61009-012-4
LCCN 2011901012

DEDICATION

For Audie Buffington Lohr,
George and Karen Cowie,
and Jayne Kyl.
Teachers all.

ACKNOWLEDGEMENTS

Pima County Sheriff's Department
Tucson Police Department
The Marksman Pistol Institute
Arizona Mystery Writers

Pima County Forensic Center:
Michael Downing
Ronald Penning

Mobin Qaheri: Economist, State of Arizona
Michael Conway: Arizona Geological Survey
Jeffrey G. Buchella, Attorney at Law.
Craig Wissler and Jim Malusa: desert vegetation.
Sunny Frazier: crime writer, OTP editor.

Thanks to:
Keiko Matsui's music.
Charles Bowden for *Killing the Hidden Waters*
and all the rest of his books.
Susan Cummins Miller, crime writer,
who found Oak Tree Press for me.
Camille Rose Garcia, artist.
Paul E. Fouliard, author and teacher.
Dr. William Heywood
Dr. Takaharu Saito
Doug LeMond
James Romenesko
Scott Seckel
Jim Sullivan
Gina Dessart Hildreth
Sharon Christiansen-Broz
Grayboy, the cat.

Celina Enriquez
Diane Tarpinian Schaller
Jan Mike
Kathryn Lance
Lester K. Jennings
Kristina Kjolhede
Greg Martin for Two Bar Road
Santa Cruz County Library of Boulder Creek
Rainbow's End, Boulder Creek
Barbara O'Brien
Ron Gardner
Elliot Hendricks
Linda Fugate
Gregory Stephenson
Birgit Stephenson
Dick Trout
Steve Cohen
Daryl Parks
Lisa Coan
Pete Slater
Craig Childs

Thanks to the creative people at The Orphanage and 804:
Dr. Craig Blurton
Sean Patrick Kelly
Robert S. McGowan
Bill Harris, Jr.
Sandra Demarest
Charles F. Hadd, Jr.
Dr. Richard Fridena

CHAPTER ONE

MANNY AGUILAR DROVE into the landfill without stopping. A young woman's white face shone in the guard shack, a blonde cowgirl. She's excited, he thought. Murder's more fun than garbage. Parking next to a sheriff's cruiser, he planted his boots on the dirt and walked toward two men framed by mountains of refuse and upturned earth, birds wheeling in circles above them.

A bulldozer still roared, the operator watching out of the corner of his eye. Manny kept walking, lifting his badge case over his head and drawing his free hand across his throat. The operator cut the engine and the silence expanded in Manny's ears.

A deputy named Carver, his pale eyes half-visible behind sunglasses, nodded and pointed at a human head that lay wreathed in plastic in a nest of lumber and broken sheet rock. Manny stood there for a minute, looking through the plastic at the face of an aging white man who had worn his thin hair plastered to the left. The eyes were locked to the right in a frozen stare, eyes that had been gray to begin with, now grayer still, the corneas clouded in death. Manny started looking at the tracks around the scene.

"The boot prints belong to a scavenger," Deputy Carver said. "He found the body part." Carver pointed with his chin at an unbarbered old man in blue jeans who stood twenty feet away, waiting.

The scavenger was apologetic when he said he'd rolled the head with his boot. He'd understood what he was looking at, he said, after he'd done that.

Carver was taking the yellow crime scene tape out of the trunk of his cruiser when a white SUV rolled in, the words KQUD Newsplex plastered all over it. Martina Escobar-Hudspeth hopped out and came straight for Manny. A videographer got out behind her, wrestling a camera.

Here's Martina in her little black suit, Manny thought. She's flashing those tombstone teeth and her cha-chas are climbing out of that pushup bra. The woman in the guard shack probably called her.

"Martina," Manny said, making a stop sign with one large hand. "This is a closed crime scene. Talk to our Media Information Officer."

"You can't comment at all?"

He smiled the cop smile, conveying hostility, and recited a law enforcement mantra in a voice that was deadly soft. "It may jeopardize the investigation if I comment under these circumstances."

"Is it a man's head or a woman's head?" Martina asked. "Do you think this murder is connected with the one last year?"

Manuel Aguilar had been lead investigator on last year's landfill head discovery and he'd solved it. Some drunks had cut their buddy up in pieces. People were just starting to stop calling Manny "the dump cop." He knew he'd never live down a second head.

"Back off, Martina," Manny said. "Do it now."

Martina and the camera operator backed off. She began scribbling notes while her partner put his camera on a tripod. Deputy Carver made a big circle with yellow crime scene tape. Other detectives began arriving, along with a van loaded with forensic equipment. The vehicles did a pincer around the news truck, stopping between it and the crime scene.

Manny turned to his work as other detectives joined him, giving the cameraperson a good action shot. Martina was checking her makeup. In a moment she would be staring soberly into the camera and telling Tucson that another head had been discovered at the county dump. The sun, now only a few minutes from setting, would put crisp, golden highlights on her rich black hair.

The team called it quits at ten o'clock that night and Manny started home, driving southbound on Interstate Ten toward Tucson. He enjoyed the ride, glancing at the silhouettes of the mountains west of town— the Tucson Mountains. He'd walked into them, many times, when he was a kid in Barrio Hollywood.

Manny's mind drifted to his older brother, Luis, killed in Iraq, years before. Then to his Yaqui grandmother, the *bruja* or *curandera*, or whatever she was. What a nutcase, he thought. And she smelled bad, too. He was grinning when he took his exit at Saint Mary's Road.

When he stepped inside his little house on 15th Street Manny was tired, but about as happy as he got. Nevertheless, the head in the dump was a problem. His team had looked all over the landfill and hadn't found the body. He hoped one lead and then another would turn up. If it didn't, he'd still be employed, even if he had to listen to more jokes about being "the dump cop." Manny snapped on one tiny light beside a sagging green club chair, sat down, and parked his boots on a near dead footstool.

Reina, his girlfriend, gave that chair a dirty look every time she showed up at his place but he liked it too much to throw it out. He glanced at the red light on his ancient answering machine. No calls. Reina and Manny called each other, when they could, at the end of every day. Being lovers had worked for over two years. They weren't restless, or mistrustful, much, anymore. It felt good. And Reina had to be the world's most sexually driven paralegal over forty. His cat, a big tom he'd named Grayboy, yowled for food in the kitchen.

His cell phone rang.

"Poor Yorick, I knew him well."

"What do you mean?"

"It's Shakespeare, dummy," the voice said. "Hamlet is holding up this clown's skull and talkin' at it. Ain't that a hoot?"

"You got bad grades in English, Randy. I remember. What about the skull?"

Randy Rogers, the curly headed blond wild man with the crazy blue eyes. Women loved him. Randy wore a baseball cap, scruffy jeans, and a baggy Phoenix Suns T-shirt to cover a thin Smith and Wesson automatic.

Randy, the narcotics cop from the Tucson PD, a character Manny had known since they'd played football at Tucson High in what, Manny reflected, was getting to be a long time ago.

"Well, Man-well Augie-lar," Randy said, "I have a clown in custody who wants to talk to you about a head in a landfill."

"Why me?"

"Why not you? Landfills are in Pima County and Pima County has county sheriffs and you are a county sheriff, my man. You even a detective in the murder police."

"Do you have this guy right now?"

"Is there a Picture Rocks Road in Anytown, Arizona?"

"What?"

"Damn, I gots to go real slow for you, goober. Yeah we got him right now," Rogers said.

"Where is he?"

"He's where we keep scumbags, Manny. Come on down."

CHAPTER TWO

TEN MINUTES LATER Manny walked through the main entrance of the Tucson Police Department, Downtown Division. Officers directed him to an interview room where he joined Detective Randy Rogers, who was sitting and grinning, his arms folded and his chair tipped back against the wall. A skinny man with greenish skin sat across the table. Manny took in the big jailhouse tattoo squatting on the prisoner's neck. The ink had run together, blurring an image of a Mexican eagle carrying a serpent in its claws. Wet black eyes popped out of the man's face, looking as if they'd been stuck there by a sloppy baker making a gingerbread man. Manny made the guy for a junkie in a nanosecond.

"Perez, this is the detective you need to talk to," Rogers said.

Manny sat down directly across the table from Perez. Manny's eyes were large, dark, deep-set, and they were fixed on Perez in a way that said they were there to stay.

This guy's an Indian, Perez thought, sizing Manny up. He's real brown and he's got that Indian look. Perez kept evaluating, junkie mind skittering, looking for an opening, for a chink he could fill with lies.

Manny was big, six feet tall, two-hundred pounds, with neatly trimmed black hair. He was handsome, but not pretty. His nose had been broken, Perez noticed, and it had healed crooked. Manny looked like a boxer who'd played a lot of football. And he looked smart, scary smart, as cops went.

Perez had been thinking that these cops would be eating out of the palm of his hand. Now his convict's instincts told him he'd made a crown out of tinfoil. Fear and self-pity grabbed him like a whore grabs a mark's elbow.

"I'm in trouble," he said.

Randy Rogers leaned forward, letting the two front legs of his chair smack on the hard floor. He stood up and looked down at Perez. "Yeah, you are," Rogers said. "You're in trouble. I caught you dealing heroin and using it too. And you murdered an idiot just like you ten years ago—

over a heroin deal. You ain't been out of Florence a year, not one year. And now you're back in my face, Perez, you murdering hose bag, and I'm gonna throw your ass all the way under the jail unless this man hears the most wonderful story from you."

"How can I help?" Manny asked quietly. "What do you have to tell me, Mr. Perez?"

It was the tough cop and the con cop routine and all three of them played without even looking at the script. Only Perez had something to lose.

"That body you found in the dump, I know who it is," Perez said, looking hopefully at Manny.

"Who is it?"

"It's a guy named Harper, old guy, used to drink downtown a lot."

"Thanks, Perez," Rogers said. "You just gave us a dead drunk. We really wanted one of them because we ain't got enough of 'em already, you lyin' sack of squancho. What about him?"

Perez looked embarrassed and kept talking. "Yeah, and he told me something one time, but what can you do for me, can you get me out of this? This bust, I mean, it ain't nothing, I was just dealing to friends—"

"That depends on what you have to tell me, Mr. Perez," Manny said. "You know we can't promise you anything, but if you can help us out, we'll do what we can. Were you a friend of Harper's?"

"No, man." Perez was almost shouting. Sweat sizzled on his green junkie skin.

"Are you afraid of something, Mr. Perez?" Manny asked.

"You know what," Perez shifted uncomfortably, "these handcuffs are really tight."

"Perez," Rogers said, "you done all this time in jail and you complain about the cuffs and now I got to use the world's oldest joke on you, man. I got to."

The junkie squirmed. "Ah, please, sir, these cuffs are very uncomfortable."

"You did it, you prissy piece of crap. Now I got to go and tell you those cuffs are real tight because they're brand new, man. I just bought them yesterday. They'll loosen up after you wear them for a while."

Perez decided to forget the cuffs. "I knew him, like downtown, bars, just on the streets," he said to Manny. "It's not like we were friends or nothing like that."

"Where?" Manny asked.

"The Bar Nine."

Rogers leaned forward in his chair. "The Bar Nine. We never bust that place because nobody big time hangs out there. I laugh when I go by the Bar Nine."

"Tell us the truth," Manny said suddenly. "How do you know the dead man's name? You never heard his name on TV because law enforcement has not made that information public. Do you have a crystal ball? If you don't, then I can only think you had something to do with this. Tell us what you know or we stop this conversation right now and charge you with murder."

"I just knew the guy, in the bar," Perez whined.

Manny waited.

"And he'd get drunk and talk sometimes. He told me once he come from this rich family back east and he knew people out here, rich people who did land deals and things. He said they knew the governor. He said he knew things about the governor, like they was all working together, doing illegal stuff." Perez twisted his feet on the cement floor.

"Perez," Rogers said, "I'll bet when you didn't do your homework, you told the teacher a big bird ate it, am I right?"

"I finished high school in prison," Perez said, sudden pride showing in his face. For an instant there was someone in Perez's body who wasn't a junkie. Then that person was gone.

Something made Manny want to ask for specific names, for more information. But he and Rogers both knew how longtime drunks talked.

Rogers sat back, crossed his arms, and began talking. "What else did this drunk tell you, Perez? Did he tell you he was in the Navy SEALS and then the next night he was in the Special Forces, and he'd say to anybody who didn't know him, hey, it's my birthday, buy me a drink. You're all liars, Perez. That's what addicts do."

"His name was Harper," Perez continued. "He had a street name, like everybody in there. He went by Barney, but his name was Bernard Harper. I saw this old ID he had once when he was showing me pictures of his kid. I'm telling you, he was cool, sometimes. He didn't lie all the time, he just drank a lot. He said he knew Patrick Dollanger, the big real estate guy. He said he knew stuff about him, stuff from back east and out here, too."

"What did he know?" Manny asked.

Randy Rogers cocked his head in mock reflection. "Barney. That's a kiddie show, Perez. It's on TV."

Perez ignored Rogers. "He knew where the bodies were buried."

"What bodies?" Manny asked.

"He said this guy Dollanger snuffed this old guy who had horses on a lot of property Dollanger wanted, and this old guy got his neighbors to help him stop Dollanger from building on these pieces of land they all owned out there—"

"Where?"

"New York," Perez said.

"What was this old guy's name?" Rogers asked.

"He's dead, man," Perez said, as if that mattered, "and Barney never told me his name. But they killed him, for sure."

Manny nodded, staring hard at Perez. "Where in New York?"

"Saratoga. Like where the racetrack is."

"Perez," Rogers said, "you got to remember how much we hate liars down here in these rooms."

"No, he told me," Perez sniveled, drawing the words out like a four-year old.

"Dollanger," Manny said. "This is the same Dollanger we have here in Arizona right now?"

"Yeah, that's right, that's what Harper told me. Dollanger, the guy who knows the governor."

Now Rogers was watching Perez intently. "Which governor, Perez, here or in New York?"

"Here. Governor Vinette."

Manny and Rogers glanced at each other in disgust.

"How about Mickey Mouse, Perez?" Rogers asked. "Is he in this story too?" Rogers stood up, playing the mad dogging cop, and shoved his handsome wild man's face at the junkie. "Where's Mickey?"

"Hey, officer, I am telling you—" Perez began.

"Shut up!" Rogers yelled. "You know why I like talking to heroin addicts? I like talking to heroin addicts because you never stop lying. Street drunks are just a bag of crap that mumbles. Coke addicts and speed freaks got all this nervous, stupid energy. But heroin addicts I like because you people are utter filth. You never stop trying to suck somebody into your lies. You never shut up, never." He'd moved as he spoke and he was behind Perez now.

Perez knew Rogers was a narcotics cop and narcotics cops got away with hurting people. He put on a defiant junkie sulk and stared at the wall.

Manny gave Perez the evil eye, the way a supervisor looks at some clerk who's screwing off.

"Where's Mickey?" Rogers continued, turning toward the door. He ducked his head sideways, looking under the table. "That little *pendejo* ain't under there." Rogers walked away, singing the Mickey Mouse Club theme song.

"Say Donald Duck, Perez," Rogers said as he opened the door and yelled, "One to go." Perez suddenly started up, as both Rogers and Manny knew he would, babbling about everything being true.

Manny got to his feet and stood, looking down at the junkie. "Perez, you're already a convicted murderer and you've already done time. If you don't tell us about this murder, we'll prove you did it, you'll go up to the road to Florence, and they'll execute you by lethal injection. Now what do you want, cooperation or execution?"

"I can't say nothing unless I get a deal and witness protection," Perez whispered, shrinking down in his chair.

"You're a lying sack of crap," Rogers said, getting the last word. "Officer," he called after the cop who was leading Perez away, "hold him at the desk, we'll be right there."

Rogers shut the door and turned to Manny. His voice was calm, indifferent. "Okay, charge him with murder?"

"Tomorrow, probably. After I check out the name he gave me—Harper. I know where I can find him, right?"

"Damn right," Rogers said, "Perez ain't leaving jail any time soon."

They both started out the door. It was getting close to midnight.

"One more thing," Manny said, as if it were an afterthought, "let me show him a picture."

When they reached Perez and the officer who had him in tow, Manny slipped an 8x10 photograph out of a thick manila envelope and held it up in front of the prisoner.

Perez squawked, then slumped forward and hung there, suspended by the burly officer who had a grip on his cuffed wrists.

"Who is this?" Manny asked, still holding up the evidence photograph of an old white man's severed head.

"It's him," Perez moaned. "It's Barney."

"You know what," Rogers said to the slobbering junkie, "for a murderer you ain't got a real man's hair on your ass."

CHAPTER THREE

AFTER PEREZ WENT to county jail and Rogers went back on the street, Manny got a TPD officer to do a check on Bernard Harper.

"Here it is," the officer said, scrabbling his fingers over a keyboard, "Bernard Harper. Two weeks ago TPD picked him up as a walking drunk. He was cooperative and officers drove him to detox. Harper gave his address as a rooming house down around the Miracle Mile. I'll write it down for you. An officer named Thomas Bennett wrote the report. Bennett took him in to detox."

"Did Harper have a phone number?"

"No phone."

"Does he come up in NCIC?"

The officer punched the keyboard some more. "No."

Twenty minutes later, Manny was standing behind a TPD officer and Daryl Trainor, another sheriff's detective. Trainor was pounding on a door on the second floor of a white building with thin walls. A couple of miserable looking white women who were mumbling together just inside the entrance had gone dead silent and melted away when they saw the cops.

There was no answer from the room. Manny and Trainor spent half of the next hour getting a telephonic search warrant. Nobody was around to let them in when the warrant came through so Manny pulled out a credit card and slipped the flophouse lock by sticking the card between the door and the doorframe and pressing the latch bolt backward on its springs.

The room had a hot plate on a dresser in front of an unmade bed. The sheets wore a sickening yellow patina. A chair was jammed in next to the bed, covered with clothing. The bathroom had no door and offered only soap, a razor, and an unflushed toilet. There was no television, but there were empty pint vodka bottles and several worn paperback books. A dirty pan sat next to the hot plate. Four unopened cans lay on the counter, still in a plastic grocery bag. Manny pulled a can out of the bag and read the label.

"Wolf Brand," Trainor said, looking over Manny's shoulder. "The right chili at the right price."

"I'm just shooting in the dark here, Daryl, but you live alone, huh?"

"Yeah, and since the divorce I can eat whatever I want."

Manny started rummaging through the dresser, lifting up the mattress, going through filthy trouser pockets, looking under the bed, looking in the toilet, in the toilet tank, and looking behind the toilet tank. There was nothing in the room to confirm or deny who lived there. No names in the books, no papers. Somebody went over this room, Manny thought. Somebody did it carefully, disturbing little or nothing, and almost certainly leaving no prints.

One of the city cops called in an ID tech who dusted for fingerprints, bagged some of the junk for DNA testing, and photographed the room. Manny and Trainor knocked on adjacent doors and told people they were sorry to disturb them, but that they very much needed to know who had lived in the room. Somebody told them it was somebody named Barney. It was after one a.m. when Manny got home. Grayboy the cat was growling about the poor meal service.

Manny started his day again at eight the next morning, calling the jail to check on Perez. Manny's fellow officers passed him around for awhile. Then somebody who knew him had the balls to admit Perez was dead. He'd overdosed in his cell that night, they said, and his death was under investigation.

Manny hung up the phone and sat back, about as shocked as a murder cop could be. The Pima County Adult Detention Complex had few prisoner deaths of any kind and a death from a drug overdose was almost unheard of.

Still, he couldn't help but like it. He knew Randy Rogers would love it. It meant a murder suspect was dead—a career junkie who'd already done time for another murder. And Harper, if that head in the morgue was what was left of Harper, had been a professional drunk who lived one rung above the streets.

Manny poured himself a giant cup of coffee and forgot about how simple it might be. Perez wouldn't be granting anymore interviews and the head in the morgue wasn't going to identify itself. Harper had no Arizona driver's license and no state ID card. Manny checked with the public health service and drew a blank.

He put a social security number into his computer, the social security number officers had taken from Harper when he'd gone to detox, and got a hit with the Social Security Administration. Harper's card had been issued in New York. Harper, if the head now in the morgue was Harper's, would have died at age sixty-eight. Manny picked up the phone and called the police in Montauk, New York, Harper's place of birth, and requested a check for any next of kin on a Bernard Harper.

"When can you get back to me?" Manny asked the Montauk contact.

"Later today, tomorrow at the latest."

Montauk was doing fine, they were cooperating. He called the Tucson Police, reaching Desk Sergeant Riley, a long time acquaintance.

"I need an officer named Thomas Bennett to meet sheriff's detectives at the Forensic Science Center to help identify a John Doe. We believe he picked up our deceased person a couple weeks ago…yeah, Riley, when the deceased person was still alive—and they say you people at TPD aren't funny—and you aren't. One hour? Fine."

Manny met Bennett at the county morgue an hour later, instantly disliking the young officer, who radiated a preening officiousness that didn't crack, at least this time, when the pathology assistant pulled the drawer open. The assistant wasn't as lucky as Bennett. He opened the small, white body bag and threw up his breakfast at the sight of the head sitting inside, face up.

"I always wondered when this would happen," the assistant said cheerfully and went to get a mop and a bucket. Both Manny and Bennett had jumped sideways. They looked down, eyeballed their pants and shoes for vomit, and got back to business.

"Is this the guy you picked up?" Manny asked. Bennett took his time, partly to be sure he remembered and partly to savor the moment.

"Yes, that appears to be the same man," Bennett said, running a pale hand over his shiny hair.

This guy talks like a robot, Manny thought, probably stores his billy club in his butt and sleeps with his badge.

"You took him to detox. Is there anything you can tell me about him, other than what you put on your incident card when you picked him up?"

"Mr. Harper was slurring his words. I believe he said something about feeling safer in the patrol car than on the street. He said he knew things about people. He said he knew the law from the other side, or words to that effect."

"So Harper indicated he felt threatened. Did he say anything more about that?"

"No, he did not."

Bennett has a good memory, Manny thought, but it doesn't go anywhere. Except that now he had a name a dead man gave a cop. He had a social security number with the same name, but the head in the morgue could still belong to anybody—even though Perez, after a fashion, identified Harper's remains. Manny hoped somebody would have something from Montauk by the time he got back to the office. Meanwhile, he was headed for The Dark.

DARC, the Drug and Alcohol Rehabilitation Center, was known as The Dark to everybody who had anything to do with it, including the Pima County Sheriff's Department and the Tucson Police. Both agencies paid a monthly fee to keep a couple of bunks available for drunks and drug addicts.

The law enforcement philosophy was simple: If you were drunk, and probably loaded on whatever else you could get your hands on, and if you didn't give the officers a hard time, and you didn't have illegal drugs on you, or any warrants, you wound up in The Dark in one of the reserved suites they called Wet Rooms. You then slept it off and checked out the next morning—unless the alcohol and whatever else you'd been taking crept up on you in the night, via your bloodstream, and killed you by way of overdose. Aspirating your own puke was another option. Either way, you either died in a Wet Room in The Dark, or you survived.

The complex was almost invisible from the street and there were no signs to mark it. Manny's boots crunched on the gravel as he headed for the entrance. Daryl Trainor pulled into the parking lot as Manny pushed a button wired to the chest-high metal gate. Daryl joined Manny and they waited while the minimum wage detox techs peered out the doors. For these guys, it wasn't hard to figure out Manny and Daryl were cops, there for some sort of cop business. The techs buzzed them through the gate.

"Hi, fellas," one of the techs grinned as the detectives approached the counter. "How's crime?"

"Same as it ever was," Daryl Trainor said, producing a flat badge with a picture ID.

"Do you have a September 15th admit for a man named Bernard Harper?" Manny asked, watching the tech through a pair of sunglasses.

The tech started going through 3x5 cards while Manny and Daryl stood there with their arches falling. After awhile the guy looked up and gestured them around the counter to a couple of spare chairs. They sat and watched another tech search the luggage of an incoming client, the client being a blond male with needle marks on his arms.

The client didn't like being searched. "If that was a crucifix instead of a medicine bag, would you poke around in it? It's a religious object."

"I understand," the tech said, "but do you understand how I might interpret this small leather bag containing, among other things, a leafy green substance, as something we might consider contraband here in The Dark?"

"Here it is," the tech said. He handed Manny the card. Sure enough, Bennett from the TPD had brought Harper in. Harper had checked out the next morning. He'd given his address as the rooming house the detectives had searched.

"What did he look like?" Manny asked.

"I wasn't here, but she was," the tech said.

He gestured at a gray-haired woman who was stepping into the office. "Hey, Lucinda, remember a guy named Harper from two weeks ago?" The tech was grinning again.

"Hell," Lucinda said, "I don't remember them from yesterday."

But she did remember. A registered nurse, she'd been the shift leader who was working the morning Bernard Harper took his leave. Manny got enough physical detail to be pretty certain the detoxed Harper was the same guy now partly residing in a drawer at the morgue.

"Anybody pick him up or did he just leave?"

"Somebody picked him up," Lucinda said. "The guy came into the lobby. Had a big tattoo on his neck, looked Hispanic."

"What kind of a tattoo?" Trainor asked.

"Looked like an eagle, like the one on the Mexican flag," Lucinda said, "the one with the snake."

Daryl Trainor looked a question at Manny. Manny nodded and said softly, "Perez, had to be."

Manny's cell rang while his boots crunched gravel on the way back to his Crown Vic. He listened, then jerked his notebook out of his shirt, threw it on the car hood, bent over, and started writing. Daryl Trainor waited. After awhile Manny straightened up and stuffed his notebook and cell phone in his pants. "Montauk police got us the next of kin. There's an ex-wife and an adult daughter named Carole."

CHAPTER FOUR

MANNY AGUILAR AND Daryl Trainor stood with a uniformed airport cop and watched Carole Harper stride out of Gate 19, awestruck plain folk falling away on either side of her like kids watching mommy serve a birthday cake.

Manny already knew she was thirty-five years old. Other than that, he was just standing there getting his ass kicked like every other man in the room. Carole had thick, elegant blonde hair and large blue-green eyes—motionless eyes—staring directly ahead, the only part of her that wasn't moving.

Her straight black skirt broke below the knees, appearing modest, even chaste—except for the way it gathered in at the bottom, hugging those knees, and rhythmically rubbing itself over a pair of glistening, muscled calves, gone the color of copper from an early morning spray-on tan. Three-inch heels with straps mounting the tops of her ankles bludgeoned Manny's mind with a flurry of bondage fantasies.

She wore two sweaters, both the color of cream, the inner one smooth, lightweight. The outer sweater, a crocheted, fisherman's net of peek-a-boo holes wrenched together with a thin tie, worked ceaselessly to corral two perfect D cups, swaying in their own rhythm above a thin waist and a pair of undulating, no nonsense, killer hips.

Manny saw her glance at him and then continue walking, lifting her head slightly, almost as if she'd been caught looking at an attractive man. Then she stopped and let him take in her profile for just the second that it took to do it.

"Officer," she said to the uniformed airport cop next to Manny, "are you here to meet me? I'm Carole Harper."

Her voice was gracious, gentle. She seemed vulnerable, someone who'd welcome protection. Was it an act? Was she a doormat or a manipulator? Both? Neither? Manny didn't know—yet. He wondered what her job was, who her man was. She would have a man. If she didn't, she'd have men working their butts off to date her.

She had no luggage and Manny and Daryl walked her to the car. It was unusual for detectives to meet a relative at the airport to make an identification of the deceased, but this was an unusual case. Everybody in Tucson knew about the head in the dump.

"The mountains are looking good today," Manny said, making small talk. "Sometimes we get dust storms out here. Other times, it's smoggy."

Carole glanced at him and nodded. Nice mountains don't make up for dry air that smells like burnt metal, she thought, dropping her gaze to hide her expression.

The Pima County Forensic Science Center, like the airport, was on the south side of town. It stood by itself near the grounds of a hospital, half surrounded by scrub desert. The place was new, Carole Harper realized, jarringly new.

The lobby was all pastels and warm wood trim. Magazines lay in neat rows on the end tables. The receptionist put them in a dim conference room with track lighting and orange-pink walls.

"Funny walls," Carole muttered. "I thought they'd be white."

Manny and Daryl made eye contact, thinking about the old cops who joked about the old morgue, the one downtown, gradually dwarfed, over the years, by high rises. The old cops said it got so too many people could look down and see a field tech from the medical examiner's office wheeling a stiff on a gurney through the door of the autopsy room. That didn't sit well with a crowd that made a living wearing laundered shirts and pushing pencils. Nobody wanted to smell formaldehyde on their lunch breaks.

When the secretary told him the next of kin wanted a look at Harper's head, Brady Pogue unfolded himself from behind his desk and glided down an empty hallway. A dark haired man in his fifties, Pogue wore black horn rimmed glasses and cowboy boots. He had the look of both a funeral director and a cop, the cop look being a carryover from his detective days with the Tucson Police. He stopped at a half open door and pushed it all the way in.

"They're ready, Doctor Storm."

Storm sat with her feet propped on her desk, legs crossed at the ankles. As Pogue watched, one ankle twitched. She held a newsletter in front of her. Pogue could see the title: *Forensic News Odontology*. A black and white photograph of an older man with frighteningly large hands sat in the center of the page.

Storm's skin was the color of old china, carrying a faint patina that could never have come from the sun. Her fuzzy gray hair matched her sweater. She wore an ankle length black skirt and a white lab coat that hung to the floor. Pogue guessed that the air conditioner in her office was set at fifty degrees. His chest tensed from the blast of frigid air.

"Um." she said, and ripped through another paragraph.

A cup of instant soup stood on her desk, smelling like a sodium broth in which someone had preserved the yellow skin of a dead chicken. A muggy odor of ancient noodles provided a blurry olfactory base line to the mess.

"I never see you eat anything else, Suzanna," Brady said.

She swiveled her head toward him, coming out of the love affair she was having with the newsletter and recognizing what Pogue meant at the same time.

"Slim says I never eat anything else." She swung her chalk white legs off the desk.

Brady nodded. He could never figure out who Slim was. He had to assume Slim was her partner but he knew nothing else, not even Slim's gender.

"Let's do it," she said, blowing past him on her way down the hall. Pogue could never figure out what size she was, either. Her energy made her seem bigger, like a puffed up cat. She was slightly built, weighed 100 pounds, tops, he thought. She never wore shoes with heels and the grayest bits of her hair always stuck straight out from the sides of her head. He followed her, feeling like a large, clumsy troll. She was already in her own world again, casting her eyes up at a forty-five degree angle to help her think. She sometimes muttered aloud, and always about teeth, as near as he could tell.

Brady Pogue and Doctor Storm exchanged greetings with Carole Harper and the detectives. The secretary stood by, a clipboard under her arm.

"Ms. Harper," Pogue said, "we need a photocopy of your driver's license or state identification for our records."

Carole produced a New York driver's license. The secretary thanked her and left the room, returning a moment later to hand the license back.

They all took seats in the pinky-orange conference room. Carole mentally compared the scene to a corporate meeting, or a dinner party with no food. They've even got their own mad scientist, Carole thought, taking in Doctor Storm. She almost giggled. Giggling is the last thing you want to do right now, Carole told herself.

"We thank you very much for coming, Ms. Harper," Brady said. "We do believe, as the police in Montauk told you, that your father is dead.

We are asking for a positive identification. We received Mr. Harper's dental records today, via email. Thanks for putting us in touch with his dentist from back there in Saratoga. We'd like to show you a photograph of the deceased—"

"Thank you," Carole said, "I'd rather just do the viewing."

"I have to tell you that the body has been traumatized," Brady said. "We are sorry, Ms. Harper, but, so far, we have only been able to recover the head of the victim."

Carole Harper looked away. No one could see her expression. When she faced them again she was very pale. "It doesn't matter," she said, "I can do it. I have to be sure."

She stood up, staring over their heads, and waited for them to get off their haunches. They're all watching me, watching and waiting, she thought. She would give them nothing.

Pogue led the way to the Forensic Center's second building. Carole wondered why they were going outside.

"This is where we do our viewing," Pogue said, holding the door for her.

Carole got it: Living people in one building, dead people in the other one.

Now they were inside, stepping to the left. Pogue nodded to a small man who wore his glasses crooked on his face. Carole read the words stitched on the man's cap: Medical Examiner's Office. He carried a sign that read Viewing in Progress. Carole understood that he was going to hang it on the door.

They came to a small room with a couch, chairs and a curtained four-by-two foot glass window in one wall.

Curtains, Carole thought, over the window. When it's curtains for them, it's curtains for us. The big one's been watching me—they both are, but he's good, he's on my wavelength, somehow—handsome, sort of, with his large eyes and crooked nose. He's thinking curtains for curtains, too. Don't be silly, she told herself, he'd never have a sense of humor.

She heard faint conversation and the curtain floated away. A man in a white lab coat stood in sourceless fluorescent light on the other side of the thick glass.

The man unzipped a small white bag and Carole saw her father with his eyes frozen in a contorted, sidelong look. All frost in his gray eyes, she thought. And there is his hair. Dad's tousled gray hair.

She knew too much about her father being there and not there at the same time—being a drunk, someone who was present only in body. She had been born into this. Now her father was, again, there and not there. How can he do that? she wondered. How can *they* do that? The Dead. Then she was staring into Manuel Aguilar's eyes and knew that, despite his experience with death, his question, at that moment, was the same as hers. "That's my father," she said.

Carole Harper signed the papers in the conference room. Then the detectives went to work, hoping she'd know something.

"Can you think of anyone who might have had a reason to hurt your father?" Manny asked.

"No," Carole said, staring past his shoulder at the pink-orange walls.

Manny leaned forward, looking directly at her. "Did he ever mention having problems with anyone?"

Carole kept her gaze on the walls. "No, I hardly knew my father, you see, so I can't say whether he made enemies or had problems—other than alcoholism."

"When was the last time you saw him?"

She gave Manny a cold look. "I haven't seen him since I was a teenager."

"What was your father's background and what kind of work did he do?" Manny asked.

"He was a real estate agent. He went to college when he was young. Never graduated. He drank and my mother divorced him when I was thirteen. As I've said, I hardly saw him after that. I think you know that my mother lives in New York, Detective Aguilar. I came out to spare her the trip."

"Do you know when your mother last saw Bernard Harper?" Daryl Trainor asked.

This Daryl guy is too short and bald to take seriously, Carole thought. He looks so alert, like a pudgy little tuning fork. She wondered if he would vibrate when he heard a lie. "It's been years since my mother saw my father," she said. "He made no real effort to keep in touch. If he telephoned at all it was when he'd been drinking."

"Did you ever try to contact him?" Manny asked, looking up from scribbling a note.

"No," Carole said, "I talked to him when he called. That's all."

"Was he ever violent?" Daryl asked.

Carole shifted her hips on the hard conference room chair. "No, not very. He broke things, mainly by, well, falling on them when he was drunk."

"Why did he move to Tucson?" Manny asked.

Carole stared at the tabletop in front of her. "We don't know. Neither my mother nor I know much of anything about him anymore. He was a very dysfunctional man."

Manny and Daryl circled through the questions again. Then they asked about Carole's life. She said she was single and working as a real estate agent.

"How long have you been in working in real estate?" Manny asked.

"Almost fifteen years," Carole said. Fifteen years of being at the beck and call of the general house buying public, she thought to herself. Surely that's long enough.

Now it was late afternoon. Manny offered a ride to her motel. She declined and the receptionist called a cab. Carole said she would fly out the next day.

"What are you going to do?" Carole asked, finally. "About this? Do you have any idea who murdered my father?"

"There's enough information to actively pursue an investigation," Manny said.

His language is so very stilted, nondisclosive, and smug, she thought. She wondered if he practiced it in a mirror.

Everyone thanked her and expressed their gratitude and sympathies. When the cab arrived she got into it gracefully and left.

The forensic dentist, Suzanna Storm, had Harper's jaw pried open when Brady Pogue let Manny and Daryl Trainor into the autopsy room. The men stood there while she leaned over the steel table and began wrestling with the head. Its gray eyes still looked to the side—like an uncomfortable dental patient. Brady Pogue excused himself and left the two detectives to watch the show on their own.

Manny watched Storm eyeball every filling in Harper's teeth, sometimes stopping to peer at the x-ray images sent from the last dentist Harper had ever seen. Finally, Manny saw her face relax and glow with satisfaction. Her pupils were dilated. He knew she was seeing the match, recognizing the shadowy shapes.

Storm did a thumbs-up for Manny and Daryl without looking at them. Teeth were children, prey, and religion to Suzanna Storm—her jewels and her favorite board game. Manny thanked her and Storm's eyes shifted up to him, a glimmer of violet. Her pupils were contracting now, but still smoky from their dream of teeth, and barely visible under heavy lids.

"Oh come back anytime," she said. "We'll be waiting."

She put her arm around Harper's head as if she were putting it around the shoulders of a playmate. Then she stared at them and smiled. Manny and Daryl headed back to the conference building, looking for normal people and sunlight.

CHAPTER FIVE

MANNY PICKED UP a phone in the Forensic Center conference room, dialed, got no answer, and left a message for TPD Detective Randall Rogers. Daryl and Manny lingered there, waiting for a call back.

"What'd you think of Carole Harper?" Manny said.

"She does a lot to a skirt and sweater," Daryl said. "I think she doesn't like us, but it hurt her to see her father like that. What'd you think, Manny?"

"She's shut down—she's guarded. She was upset, who wouldn't be, and you're right about that skirt and sweater." Manny picked up the ringing phone and Rogers' voice came on the line.

"Hey, headhunter," Rogers said. "What's up?"

"Who are the associates of our deceased friend, Perez, and where can I find them?"

"Call you back in five," Rogers said.

Manny waited. Daryl stepped out and got a root beer from a vending machine in the break room.

When Rogers called back, offering a couple of names and some mug shots, Manny and Daryl drove to TPD, Downtown, where they listened to Rogers make jokes about heads and headhunters, and walked out with the names and the mug shots. Now they had the last known address for Perez: a house in Tucson's Pie Allen neighborhood, two blocks from the Bar Nine, Harper's old hangout.

Ten minutes later, Manny and Daryl parked the Crown Vic and walked toward the bar. The windows were covered with plywood and painted with murals of the denizens of this place, regulars, many of whom, Daryl and Manny knew, had fallen by the wayside years before.

A pool table sat just inside the door and a player pulling back for a shot narrowly missed Manny's crotch.

"Let's go back to the forensic center," Daryl muttered. "It smells better there."

A shaky white man with long brown hair hovered over a machine tucked in a corner, trying to pick up a stuffed animal with a miniature crane, its hooks dangling like a silvery metal spider from the ceiling of a glass case.

Graffiti covered the brown walls on all sides. *Time flies like an arrow*, someone had written, *Fruit flies like bananas.*

A brace of heavy television sets stood on shelves near the ceiling in two corners of the room. The sound was muted but the screens were alive with the movement of basketball players.

The bar had seen an upgrade since the last time Manny had been there. That time a drunk named Thurman McGinnis put his head down on the bar to rest for a minute and died on his lips instead.

A cigar case sat behind the bar, cigars being a current cultural interest, associated with sports and movie stars. Aging cowboy prints hung on the walls.

The shuffleboard was still around but a tiny automatic teller machine now sat next to the jukebox. A customer could walk out with no money in his pocket or his bank account. Pint and half-pint bottles of package liquor waited in a small, backlit case on the wall behind one corner of the bar. The bottles looked like holy relics, generating their own light.

Manny signaled the bartender, a woman in jeans who aggressively patrolled up and down, smiling and stuffing drinks in front of the customers. Her manner of moving cued the clientele to keep drinking, fast, as if drinking were a life's work. For many of them, Manny knew, it was. He introduced himself, asked for her name, and got down to business.

"Have you seen this man, Bernice?"

She glanced at the mug shot of the late Mr. Perez. "Yeah, he used to come in here. I don't know his name. I remember the tattoo," she said, tapping her neck.

"Did he have any friends here?" Daryl asked.

The woman didn't know.

"How about this man?" Manny asked, and showed her a photograph he'd gotten from Carole Harper.

The woman nodded.

"That's Barney," she said. "I think."

"When was the last time you saw him?"

"A week, I guess." She dropped her voice. "Maybe Robert knows. He'd talk to you." She pointed with her chin to an unshaven barfly ranting at two men who gaped and nodded. Robert's pale eyes were flung open, staring into space. Greasy curls of black hair sprang from his red baseball cap and coiled down the back of his neck.

Manny began to watch and listen, expecting nothing. He knew

Bernice was trying a diversion. She moved away fast, escaping the smell of cop. He'd come back to Bernice and her cold little heart when he was done with Robert.

"So we're goin' down this two-lane somewheres around Charleston—Highway 90—that's it. And I remark upon this stinkin' desert and these bare ass hills—the Tombstone Hills, I guess, was some of 'em. This is some stinkin' desert I says to Hendricks and he says 'Know how it got this way?' And I says somethin' about the Taylor Grazing Act of 1934, or somethin', so as not to look stupid. He just stares at me. 'By then it was way too late,' he says."

"Waay too late." Robert said again and his two disciples bent heads to glasses, thirsty from the thought of it.

"Well, so Hendricks says the Americans come in after the Civil War. By 1891 they was a million and half cows in Arizona Territory—and sheep. Sheep will eat grass, root and all, and they'll bunch up and kill the ground with them sharp little hooves—but it was the million cows that mostly done it. Overgrazed it and there was nothin' to hold the water when it rained. Nothin'. Erosion sets in, all these arroyos opened up, goin' nowheres. Lost the water. The San Pedro dried out, leavin' nothin' alive but some weeds Hendricks was callin' whitethorn acacia. And the mesquite and the creosote took over the country around it, and what it didn't take turned into bare desert like that stuff out by Charleston. Hendricks says she'll never come back. The grass is gone. It's gone. Now it's people. Millions of 'em." Robert took a long pull on his glass and Manny stepped in with Daryl right behind him.

"He drank here," Robert said, when he had looked at the photograph. "I knew his name. We'd have a few laughs down the bar. Now I know he's dead and that's all I know."

"How do you know he's dead, Robert?" Manny asked.

"You're here, ain't you? Can't be about nothin' else. Barney, he wouldn't hurt nobody."

"Why not?" Manny asked.

"It just wasn't in him. Tell you what, though."

Manny waited for the other shoe.

"You keep on. Find out who got him. You do that and it'll make a difference in the way the wind blows around here."

"We'll do the best we can, Robert."

"You know why them Indians piled bighorn sheep bones around the waterholes?" Roberts was asking the disciples as the detectives stepped away. "To keep the wind from leaving the country."

It was time for Manny to circle back to the bartender.

"Bernice," he said, "you spend a lot of time here. So do heroin addicts. They drink at your bar and they loiter out in front. The Tucson Police don't come here but that doesn't mean they don't know about it. We need your cooperation. Have you seen these men?" He showed her two mug shots. One was a white male named David Granger. The other was a Hispanic male named Paco Corral. Manny looked at Bernice with a hopeful, sympathetic expression.

"Yeah, they come in here," Bernice said.

"Do you think they might live near here?" Manny asked.

"I seen them in here, but I don't follow 'em home."

It was plain she didn't want cops coming around, making a point of busting her customers. It was also plain she probably knew more than she admitted knowing. And, finally, it was plain that she knew her rights and that the cops in front of her didn't have anything on her. Manny thanked her for her cooperation and the two detectives left.

Manny dug out the keys to the Crown Vic. "Think Bernice knows anything else?"

"Probably," Daryl said.

"What about Robert?"

Daryl didn't answer until he was inside the car, pulling on his seatbelt. "He's just a drunk, but it's true."

"What's true?"

"Livestock turning grassland into desert back in the 1880's. It's Old West history."

Manny turned the key in the ignition. "I thought the first liar didn't have a chance in that dive."

"Robert was probably buying. That makes anything he said the truth."

They drove two blocks down the street and turned right. It was getting near the end of the day. The sun threw bright golden light from its perch on the Tucson Mountains. Manny thought he'd have to take a walk out there sometime. They parked a half block from the junkie house, walked up the steps, and knocked.

If David Granger hadn't been stupid enough to rack the action on his shotgun before he blew a toilet bowl-sized hole in the door, Manny and Daryl wouldn't have had a chance.

CHAPTER SIX

THE PIMA COUNTY Sheriff's Department issued Glock handguns but authorized personally owned weapons. Most detectives carried .40 caliber automatics with short barrels. Manuel Aguilar and Daryl Trainor chose to carry heavy .45 caliber automatics with five-inch barrels. The design dated back to 1911 and that design's purpose hadn't changed: Knock down determined attackers, whether they could feel pain or not.

Manny and Daryl stepped sideways just as David Granger fired and drew their .45's before the splinters hit the ground. They glimpsed their target through the hole in the old door—a white man's hand, gripping the wooden forend of a 12 gauge shotgun, the muzzle pointing out through the blasted door. They started shooting, sweeping their guns in an arc across the door. Leaving one last round in the chamber, they dumped the empty magazines, drew loaded ones from their belts, and slipped them into the guns, glancing sideways to see if anybody was coming at them from another direction.

Daryl was on the left. He blew the old lock out of the rotting door with three rounds and Manny kicked it open. Manny went in high, Daryl went in low.

David Granger lay on the floor beside his shotgun. He was in pretty good shape for a man who had just had a flock of squat, nasty copper jacketed bullets fired in his direction from ten feet away. He'd been hit in the left side as he turned to run. The bullet had cut a channel through the edge of his hipbone and sailed into a wall, dumping Granger on his backside, out of the line of fire.

Daryl kicked the shotgun all the way into the bedroom and followed it, keeping a two-handed grip on his weapon. Manny cleared the kitchen in the same way, with his big 1911 Colt held out in front of him like a cross to ward off vampires. Nobody was home but Granger.

Daryl called in to tell the posse, who would be arriving any time now, due to the volume of gunfire, to come in without their weapons drawn. Manny bent down to talk to Granger, a skinny punk with dirty green eyes and a pock marked face.

"Why did you shoot at us?"

"I didn't know, man."

"What didn't you know? You never asked. Why did you shoot?"

"I thought—" Granger began. He stopped and looked away, seeming to stare at some personal horror playing out in his drugged mind.

"What are you scared of?" Manny asked. "Who did you think was coming through that door?"

The junkie clamped his unshaven jaw shut.

"I'll ask you again. Who did you think we were? What are you afraid of?"

Granger stayed quiet, looking stubborn and hopeless at the same time. Aguilar kept asking questions. Granger would not say whether or not Paco Corral still lived there. The one bedroom house had two mattresses on the living room floor and two more in the bedroom.

Manny heard sirens and then footsteps. The wooden floor vibrated underneath him as the room filled with cops. Whatever this had been about, it was over for now. Manny and Daryl handed over their weapons to an Officer-Involved Shooting Team and started answering lots of questions. The Tucson Fire Department EMT's took care of Granger.

CHAPTER SEVEN

THE DEPARTMENT HELD the shooting review board four days after the incident. The conference room they used made Manny think of the conference room at the forensic center. He preferred the dark pink walls at the center. They reminded him of the way Reina had her house done. He preferred Reina's to both places, for that matter.

The sheriff's department had given a routine administrative leave to both detectives, pending their appearance before the board. Daryl Trainor used the time to sand a rifle stock and Manny and Reina used the time to have so much sex that even Reina was tired and ready to quit.

Daryl and Manny sat together in the hallway, waiting. They'd both been questioned separately and now it was time to go on stage as a duo. They were less than totally comfortable in their best and only suits and they'd been waiting nearly an hour.

Manny fantasized about Reina and half-listened while Daryl talked about padouk, a fine and truly red-colored wood that grew mainly in Asia. Trainor wondered aloud whether padouk would make a good rifle stock.

"Neither of you considered that there could have been innocent people in that house when you returned fire?" one of the sheriff's department administrators asked, one minute into the meeting.

"We were operating on intelligence from Tucson PD Narcotics which stated that the house was a known address of two male heroin addicts. No mention was made of anyone else," Manny said.

Daryl joined in. "We had a target. We fired at the shooter and at no one else. We saw the shotgun and we saw his hand on that shotgun through the hole he blew in the door."

"Can you be a heroin addict and have a child living with you?" the administrator asked.

"Yes," Manny said.

"Could you two have killed an innocent child, then?"

"We had information that only adult male heroin addicts were living in the house," Manny said again, knowing that wasn't good enough.

"Did you have the option of a safe retreat, in your opinion?" another board member asked.

"The street was open," Daryl said. "There were no trees. The nearest car was about forty feet away. We had no real cover, nothing to hide behind. Our car was at the end of the block."

"What about taking cover around the edges of the building?"

"We could have done that," Manny said, "but if whoever was inside chose to continue firing we might have drawn fire toward other houses. Those houses are very close together."

"Here's your biggest problem," a captain named Holbrook told them, finally. "You had a barricaded subject, gentlemen, and our procedures don't vary. We retreat and we call SWAT. Don't tell me you don't know that."

There was no doubt that Manny and Daryl had fired without being sure of what was around their target. It was true that they hadn't retreated—or called SWAT. It might have been as dangerous to retreat down an open street, which afforded a clear field of fire from the house, as it would have been to counterattack—but that didn't matter.

Manny and Daryl had done a brave thing, but they'd violated departmental policy. Both men wanted to keep their jobs. Their answers showed it. They did what they could to follow the time-honored principle of covering their asses. They hadn't lied. The street had been devoid of cover. They had acquired a target before they fired. Still, it was possible, very possible, that the shooter would not have fired again. He could have dropped the shotgun and fled after he fired. The board let them know that, too.

When it was all finally over, Manny and Daryl heard the department tell them they'd get a written reprimand. After the meeting Manny and Daryl looked at each other and shrugged, then went their separate ways.

Manny walked across the parking lot toward his Crown Vic. He looked west at the Tucson Mountains and thought about taking a walk out there. It was a small range, deceptively small from a distance, and he could be inside those mountains in fifteen minutes. He knew it would be quiet out there, except for noisy aircraft on the glide path into the Tucson International Airport.

There were deer herds in the Tucson Mountains and more than one mountain lion. He knew the stories the Tohono O'Odham people told. They said the mountains housed spirits, lots of them. He didn't believe it, but people had lived in those mountains for thousands of years. He asked himself why he didn't just take a walk out there. When he was a kid in Barrio Hollywood he would take off and walk right into those mountains. But he'd grown up and gone to work. He didn't have time for kid's stuff now. Maybe later, he thought.

"Am I speaking to that badass Manny Aguilar?" the voice on the other end of the line was saying. Manny had been sitting in his old green club chair. One 15 watt bulb in an aging lamp barely lit a side table on his left. His regular workday had ended when the review board let him out the door with a reprimand and the news that he could go right back to work on his caseload. That had suited Aguilar just fine. He'd been thinking about going up to the hospital that evening to have another chat with David Granger, in spite of the fact that he was off the Harper murder case, officially, having become part of it by being involved in a shooting incident with Granger.

"Hello, Randy," Manny said.

"Well, tell us what you've won for shooting the living hell out of a house and a junkie."

"Written reprimand and return to duty," Manny said.

"Are you getting a *head* on the Harper case?" Rogers asked.

"I am making progress on the case," Manny said, in a level voice. "I now have a positive identification on the victim—and when I try to ask your junkies about it, they shoot at me."

"Want to know where you can find more of them?" Rogers asked.

Manny jerked out a notebook and held it open under his 15 watt light bulb. "You mean alive or not in the hospital?" he asked, pulling a pen out of his shirt pocket with the same hand he used to hold the phone.

"Yeah. See, I figure I tell you and Detective Daryl where they are and you two soldiers just go out and light 'em up." Rogers laughed.

"Tell me about these junkies," Manny said.

"Well, I'd give you Paco Corral," Rogers said, "but he was found dead today, downtown, by the railroad tracks. Thought you'd like to know."

"And there is suspicion of foul play in this death?" Manny asked.

"Nah," Rogers said, "looks like an overdose."

"Can you let me know when they get an autopsy report?"

"Sure," Rogers said. "So how's life, gunslinger? How's Reina?"

"Life," Manny said, "is getting very full of dead people. And Reina is a beautiful woman. And I need another favor."

"What?"

"Find a reason to get up to Saint Mary's Hospital and interview Granger. Our guys interrogated him but they got nothing. I can't have contact with him."

"Yeah, it's too bad about them legal ramifications," Rogers said. "You could shoot him again and we'd be done with him."

"I think we can shake him up. Would you talk to him?"

"Sure," Rogers said. "When?"

"Tonight," Manny said. "Drop by my house. I'll give you something to show Mr. Granger."

"Hell," Rogers said, "I'm on duty anyway and I could ask him about Paco Corral. I'm on my way over."

Grayboy was the first thing Manny heard after he hung up the phone. The cat was pacing the kitchen and looking fearlessly at Manny. Manny fed him, then got out a briefcase and found Harper's photographs for Rogers.

CHAPTER EIGHT

THEY HAD DAVID Granger on a special, secured floor of Saint Mary's hospital on Tucson's west side. Department of Corrections Officers took care of the place and one of them escorted Randy Rogers down to Granger's room.

Rogers walked in with the DOC officer and they stood and looked at Granger. Rogers almost laughed, seeing the little junkie all tucked up nicely in white sheets on a narrow bed, looking pale and woebegone. No heroin left in his veins now, Rogers thought, just lots of painkillers for the gunshot wound.

"Mr. Granger," Rogers said, leering at the little junkie, "I'm Detective Rogers, Tucson Police. I work narcotics. Do you know why the nice sheriff's detectives dropped by your house the other day?"

"To shoot my ass?" Granger said.

"No," Rogers said, "to ask you if you know this idiot." Rogers held up an 8X10 photo of Harper's head. The severed neck was visible. Granger's eyes flickered with fear and shock.

"God." he said. "Talk to my lawyer."

"You don't have a lawyer, dick brain," Rogers said. "And you know what? I don't give a damn about the law right now, which means I don't care about your Miranda rights, which means I don't care about blowing a case against you for trying to kill a couple of cops. And if you get off on a technicality, Granger, that's tough because your life will be dirt on the streets in this town. And you know why? Because I got a thousand people in my gang and we all got badges. Now I'm going to show you another picture and you better talk to me about it."

The DOC Officer, now standing in the corner of the room, shifted uncomfortably to signal that he didn't like being a witness to a violation of the law. Rogers gave him a contemptuous look and turned back to Granger. Granger appeared unimpressed by Rogers' tirade. Being beaten and threatened by narcotics cops came with the territory for him.

Rogers held up a mug shot of Perez.

"See the tattoo on his neck, Granger?"

"I knew him," Granger said. "You know that."

"You *knew* him?" Rogers asked. "Is he dead or something?"

Granger's eyes flickered some more.

"Do you read the obituaries?" Rogers asked. "How do you know if he's dead?"

"I knew him one time, man." Granger said. "I don't know if he's dead."

"We have a murder victim here." Rogers held up Harper's photo again. "You knew Perez all along. Did he do this old guy? Because, if he did, we can close a murder case. But you know what, Granger, I think you and Perez killed Harper and that's what they're going to charge you with, alongside of the charge of attempted murder on a couple of sheriff's detectives."

"I didn't kill nobody," Granger said.

"Then what are you doing shooting at cops, man?" Rogers said. "And, by the way, did you know your *other* roommate is dead?" Granger was trying to control his breathing. He suddenly looked very scared.

"Yeah, buddy," Rogers said, thickening up his accent like a Mexican tough guy, "Paco Corral just died, homeboy."

Corral's death might mean that somebody was stalking and killing everybody who lived in the junkie house—and Rogers could see that Granger believed that.

Rogers decided to take a chance and lie to Granger about the way Corral died. "Yeah, your boy Paco Corral," Rogers said. "Somebody shot him a whole bunch of times and before that they cut on him awhile, just for fun. Was somebody going to shoot *you*, Granger? Save your own butt. This is attempted murder on cops that you're up for. You want a break? You got to sell me, man. You got to sell me on what you know and if you can sell me, Granger, you're going get a break. Who killed Harper? Who's after you? Come on."

"I need a lawyer," Granger said. "I got nothing to say." He was eyeing the DOC Officer. Rogers noticed he did that a lot.

"Give us a minute, will ya?" Rogers said to the officer.

The DOC stepped out of the room and shut the door.

"What's the matter, don't you trust that officer?" Rogers asked, stepping close to the bed.

"Perez got killed in jail, man."

"How do you know?"

"I just know," Granger said hopelessly. "It just makes sense. If you can get me protection, I'll talk to you. Protective custody first. That's the only way."

Rogers smiled. "I'll see what I can do."

CHAPTER NINE

"GUESS WHAT," ROGERS said.

Manny was holding the phone and listening. Grayboy the cat sat on a file cabinet in front of him. He liked to be at eye level with Manny so he could give him a commanding stare. But, this time, he wasn't watching Manny. He was watching the bubbles in Manny's beer glass.

"This junkie, Granger, wants protective custody," Rogers said.

"Perez wanted protective custody, too. I'm starting to wonder about these gentlemen," Manny said. "Did he tell you he knew who killed Harper?"

"He's not talking, but he knows something."

"All I can do is explain it to my boss and let it alone," Manny said. "How did Granger act?"

"He acted shifty," Rogers said. "He acted scared when I showed him the photos. I don't know what he's thinking. The little bastard could just be stalling. And, sure, he's scared. I'd be scared too if I tried to murder a couple of cops."

"Thanks," Manny said. "I'll talk to my boss tomorrow."

Manny left his house the next morning thinking about Perez, who had, almost certainly, been the man with the tattoo on his neck who came for Harper at the detox center. Grayboy jumped up on the gate to Manny's yard and watched him drive away.

At the sheriff's headquarters on Benson Highway he talked to his lieutenant about protective custody for Granger. The lieutenant said he'd talk to the captain and reminded Manny that he was off the case.

"Granger's being held without bail anyway, isn't he?" the lieutenant said. "If he's going to talk, he'll have a long time to think about it and we'll be there when he's ready."

"Who's on Granger's case now?" Manny asked.

"Gary Bang is doing the follow-up. Why?"

"Granger is the key to the case, to Harper's murder."

"You don't know that. And Granger, the wannabe cop killer, is a lot bigger deal than Harper. The pressure's off to solve Harper's murder, Manny. The head in the landfill is last week's ball game. Talk to Gary Bang if you want. Get him to talk to Granger. You know that's all you can do. You cannot have any more contact with Granger—that's the law. You've got other cases besides drunks in dumps."

The Lieutenant, Manny thought, is covering himself because Daryl and I shot it out with Granger. We made waves, violated procedure. And nobody cares if a drunk gets killed. Manny knew that, somehow, he'd come to believe Harper's killing was different.

He went back to his desk and stared at the wall. He was waiting for the anger to subside and for the ideas to come. Anger isn't a nice friend, he thought, but it is a loyal friend. He knew it would tell him if he betrayed himself. He knew it would tell him when it was time to take action in his own best interests. When he did that, the anger would go away until the next time he needed it.

Manny wanted protective custody for Granger. He wanted to see if Granger could solve the Harper puzzle. But junkies were liars. He'd been sure Perez was lying when he'd started in about big shots and governors and land deals. What if Perez wasn't lying?

Manny called the sheriff's department in Saratoga County, New York, and asked about Patrick Dollanger, the land developer.

"Yeah, we know about him," a detective told Manny, "but not in any criminal connection. He was a local real estate hotshot. Got some bad press for aggressive business practices—not for crimes. Can't help you with your homicide. Sorry."

"Just checking out an allegation," Manny said. "Thank you."

Manny sat back in his chair. Barney Harper, the dead guy in the dump, was from New York. In life, Harper had been a drunk who inserted himself into stories he heard and then repeated them in bars. As a real estate agent, Harper no doubt knew of Patrick Dollanger from his New York days. At some point Harper realized Dollanger had moved to Arizona where he had become a prominent land developer. Harper put himself in the story.

Manny knew he could find out if Harper had any real connection with Dollanger, but there was only one apparent, probable key. That key being Granger, who, Manny thought, probably helped Perez kill Harper.

Manuel Aguilar finally said to hell with it, quietly left the sheriff's headquarters, and headed for Saint Mary's. He would at least ask about Granger, find out who visited him, if anybody. Find out anything he could from the Department of Corrections guards, or the nurses. He'd just sit down in the hospital cafeteria and see who would talk to him.

It was raining when he reached the Saint Mary's hospital complex on Tucson's west side. He pulled around to the entrance where prisoners were brought in and out from the secured ward upstairs. Someone was being moved out on a gurney. When Manny gave the guy a second glance he saw it was Granger. Manny shut down his Ford and flipped the keys into his pocket. He got out, keeping his eyes on the men with the gurney, reaching for his badge case with one hand, using the other to position his holster, unsnap it, and loosen his weapon.

He walked toward the men with his badge case open in one hand, picture ID displayed. The guys pushing Granger's gurney had The Look. They were carrying concealed weapons and they were ready to use them.

"Detective Aguilar, Pima County Sheriff's Department," Manny said. "I need to talk to Mr. Granger."

"I'm Petrocelli, Federal Agent," one of the men said. "We have custody of this guy and he won't be talking to you today."

There were three men facing Manny. They had an ambulance all right, but they were all wearing suits and none of them looked like the care giving type. One man's coat flared open in a little gust of wind. Manny saw an Uzi submachine gun strapped under the man's arm.

"I'm going to protective custody," Granger chirped, looking up from the gurney, his dirty green eyes shining like a child's. Manny put it together fast. Granger was high as a kite on something somebody had given him in the hospital, probably twenty minutes before these thugs in suits showed up.

Manny looked at the men. "Show me your identification."

There was no point in doing things the easy way, the way he liked to do them. He was going to be damned if he'd let these guys roll over him on any level. No cop of any kind could rightfully refuse to identify himself to another law enforcement officer.

"I told you, I'm Petrocelli," the spokesman said. "We're moving this prisoner."

"I just came from sheriff's headquarters and they refused to consider protective custody, Granger. Who are these guys?"

Granger looked back and forth from Manny to the men, his drug happy face collapsing in fear.

Manny on one side, Granger in the middle, the three goons on the other side. Manny heard the traffic go by on Saint Mary's Road. Ssshhhhhh, the tires said, rolling through dirty water that ran down the black, wet street. Soft rain still falling, soundless.

In the instant before it all began, Manny felt as much as saw his grandmother standing on his left. Then there were two of her, one on either side of him, identical long-skirted women wearing gun belts with rows of .45 caliber cartridges stuck in the leather loops like teeth, brown hands resting on the walnut handles of Colt Peacemakers.

With three prepared opponents facing him, Manny knew he'd have to start the fight or die. He'd probably die anyhow. Either way, this was the kind of situation that ended law enforcement careers—but better fired than fired on first. He dropped low and kicked the gurney, drawing his weapon and shooting as he crouched. Granger, strapped in the gurney, became a blocking device. The man calling himself Petrocelli reached under his suit jacket and the other two men did the same.

Two men fell. One managed to clear the Uzi from his shoulder holster as he rocketed backwards with the gurney falling on top of him. His hands clenched. The gun chattered and spat fire.

Petrocelli hadn't been in direct line for the gurney. A big, silver Beretta came out of his shoulder holster and he and Manny pulled triggers at the same time. Manny fired from kneeling position, double tapping the 1911 Colt. Both rounds smashed through the man's chest and blew him down. Manny felt heat tearing across his left side as he swung his gun on the others. The Uzi crackled again as the man using it took two hits from Manny's .45. A hot, invisible beehive snapped by Manny's head. The third man was down and out, hit by Aguilar's first two shots.

Then Manny was on his feet, bounding up like a panther. He looked down, swinging his weapon from man to man. The gunfire had deafened him. He was still in a trance, concentrated like a basketball player making a free throw, oblivious to the noise of the crowd. The men didn't move. They were out cold or dead. It was hard to tell, since all but Petrocelli were already on the ground when they'd been shot. Petrocelli lay in a pathetic heap with one ankle lying crossed over the other. A ribbon of blood ran from underneath his body now, parallel to the back side of his legs. The sad, classic pose of someone who'd died more or less instantly from a gunshot wound. The soft rain and the wet black asphalt surface of the parking lot could not wash away, nor noticeably dilute, the blood.

Manny became aware of the sound of ragged breathing. The gurney lay on the hard pavement, its legs facing Manny him. Manny dumped the magazine out of his .45 and let it clatter to the asphalt. He reloaded and came around the gurney in a crouch. Blood oozed from the sheet covering Granger's body but the little junkie was still strapped in. Manny was shaking now and his side continued to burn. He had to check the downed men. He was aware of voices and movement at the windows and doors of the hospital. An old man drove a white Pontiac into the driveway from the street and stopped, staring through the windshield in shock.

Manny held his .45 in one hand and went to each man, checking for pulse at the neck, touching the men as if he were touching snakes and watching the others out of the corner of his eye as he did. When he was satisfied there was no pulse in any of the three he backed around the gurney, still watching them, and found his badge case on the black surface of the parking lot. He held it over his head and yelled, "Police. Need medical assistance here." Then he dropped down, holstering his weapon, and concentrated on Granger.

"Hold on Granger," Manny said. "You're okay."

Granger was not okay. He'd been hit several times. Manny figured bullets from the sputtering Uzi submachine gun had struck him.

"Tell me what's going on," Aguilar said urgently. "Tell me what this is about. These guys tried to kill you, there's no need to protect them."

"Rico," Granger slurred.

"Who is he?" Manny asked.

"Dealer," Granger said. "Rico. Dealer, big time," Granger whispered. "I never seen him. Talk to Tony, I just knew Tony Cisneros." Granger was dying. It was lucky he was conscious, that he could talk at all, let alone talk sense.

"Who is Cisneros?" Manny asked. "Where can I find him?" Granger could not answer now. His eyes went glassy and his gaze became fixed.

The parking lot was filling with cops and medics. Manny knew he'd have a lot of explaining to do—and that none of it would do him any good.

CHAPTER TEN

THEY TREATED MANNY at the hospital and recommended he stay overnight—for psychological reasons as much as anything. The bullet wound, a neat pink groove in his side, was painful, but not serious. Manny went back to his house and his cat.

He barely had time to call his parents before the shooting incident broke all over the evening news. His mother spoke to him mostly in Spanish, something she did when she was upset. She told him his younger brother, Rigoberto, could get him a job selling Ford trucks and that she was going to tell Rigoberto to call him right away.

Manny's father got on the phone. "How you doing?"

"Fine."

"You sure you're okay?"

"Yeah, I'm okay."

"Don't worry about nothing. Your mother gets emotional."

"Right, pop. You know, the chances of this kind of thing happening again are less than zero. I'll probably go to retirement without ever drawing a weapon again. Goodnight."

The old man knows what it's like to feel lucky you're alive, Manny thought. He went over the history in his mind. His father, Jesus Aguilar, was not untypical of a lot of men from Arizona. He'd worked in Arizona's cotton fields as a boy and liked it. He'd never attended high school. His family needed the money he brought in by working. When the Korean War started in June of 1950 Jesus joined the United States Marine Corps.

Mexican Americans received more Medals of Honor in World War II, per capita, than any other ethnic group. Jesus Aguilar didn't get one of those in Korea, but he got two Purple Hearts, a Bronze Star for valor, and, Manny suspected, a lot of bad memories about a lot of dead friends.

When Manny's father came home he went straight to work in Arizona's copper mines. He would only talk with old buddies about the Korean War. To his children, he would say that it was a mess and that he was glad to be home. Manny had never seen his father cry until they sent Luis's body home from Iraq.

Manny glanced at his watch. Five o'clock. He had to call Reina fast. She would be hurt and angry if she had to hear about this from someone else—or, worse yet, see it on the news. She came to his little house on 15th Street, looking beautiful in her work clothes.

"They shot you, baby," Reina said. Manny was lying back on his bed and she sat on the edge of it, looking at him and the large bandage stuck to one side of his ribcage.

"Yeah," Manny said, "and I shot every one of them dead."

He was grouchy. He hurt, he'd been nicked by a round, and people had been trying to kill him. He was still half deaf from the gunfire.

But look at this woman in front of me, he thought. So pretty and so tall, red hair and green eyes. When he looked at her, when he was alone with her like this, he had no words. Have to watch my ass, he thought, she could be running my whole life. He noticed everything about her. He knew her eyes went yellow as a hawk's when strong light fell into them. He knew all the details. Whip smart and she could see way better than 20-20 with both of those eyes. How can she be this pretty, he thought, and still be this kind?

"Manny, do me a favor," Reina said, leaning forward and bringing her razor sharp pupils level with his. "Don't you ever do anything like this again."

Manny kept his gaze still. He couldn't come apart and start crying. He couldn't tell her he'd quit working homicides and go sell Ford trucks with his brother, Rigoberto. He couldn't tell her all he wanted, for the rest of his life, was to be in her arms, to look in her eyes. He knew he wanted his job as much as he wanted her. He wanted both.

"Somebody has to get the bad guys," Manny said softly. "That's what I do. When I'm not going after bad guys, I'm going after you, Reina. I only want a couple of things. I want my job and I want you—and I love you. It's real simple. Please understand."

They'd held hands, hugged, looked in different directions. Reina shed a tear or two and Manny held back a tear or two. Then she went home to get up early in the morning and go to work. He started to doze off. He would do records checks tomorrow, he thought, and he'd see if somebody named Tony Cisneros comes up—and somebody named Rico.

Dreams of his grandmother came that night, the *bruja* or *curandera*, or whatever the hell she thought she was. The old Yaqui woman was pacing back and forth in front of her shack in the desert. Herbs hung in bundles from the eaves of her porch. Then the dream shifted to memories. She scared Manny and his older brother, Luis. The woman smelled bad and she always made passes over them with her brown claws, like some crazy parody of a priest, muttering words in what she claimed was some sacred language. She argued with his parents, trying to make Manny and his brothers take tiny pouches of dried herbs, or drink bitter potions she made from plants.

Only Luis had been there when she'd talked to Manny the most. No other family in earshot. He wished he could talk to Luis about it, but Luis was dead. Nineteen forever. The kid in the green uniform, looking serious in the photograph on the mantel.

Manny dreamed the memory of swallowing some grainy paste she pushed on him. He felt well afterwards but later an image exploded in his head, a gloved hand, on a background of black sky. A gloved hand defined by beads of colored light. Manny was watching himself in the dream, trying to remember his age, when his grandmother suddenly straddled his chest and stood looking down at him, her hands resting on the plough shaped walnut handles of two Colt Peacemakers stuffed in a heavy leather cartridge belt.

Manny screamed his way out of the dream and woke up half-way across the room, soaked with sweat, the pain in his side bringing him fully awake. There was a blur of motion along the floor. The cat was leaving the room. A second later Manny heard Grayboy clawing his way over the back fence to leap into the alley. He's vowing never to sleep with a crazy person again, Manny thought.

His grandmother had been there, wearing guns, and there were two of her, when the fight started in the Saint Mary's Hospital parking lot. Now he remembered. How could he have forgotten that? The answer was simple, he thought. Stress. And seeing grandma with guns? A stress-induced hallucination. All law enforcement personnel heard about them in training. Hallucinations could occur and not be accompanied by gross psychopathology, as the docs liked to say. Funny. He laughed, got a drink of water, took a leak, cursed the scumbags who'd shot him, and went back to bed.

He fell asleep, but not before doing another round of thinking about the hallucination. What if she, or it, comes back? Not likely. What if she's somehow real? No way. What if it happens again? He would just make sure it didn't happen again.

Lying to the lieutenant and the captain was easy. Manny told them he was checking hospital records on another case when he spotted Granger by accident. After that, Manny knew, he was in for the ass chewing of his life.

"We're waiting to get sued," Captain Juvera began, sitting straight in his conference room chair and giving Manny a nut-shriveling look, "because you started a *gunfight* at a *hospital*. And now for the good news, Manny. The good news is you shot certified bad guys. These perps had well forged identification, the hospital bought it. The perps kidnapped a patient, probably because he was a witness—to what, we don't know—yet.

"Two of the dead perps are east coast hoodlums with long criminal records. The third dead guy is a Mexican national. Turns out he's a former member of the Federales, the Mexican National Police...." Juvera sank back in his chair and fixed Manny with a tired stare. "Now, I'll let *you* answer my first and only question. What's my question, Manny?"

"Captain, your question is why didn't I call SWAT," Manny said. "I didn't call for backup because it was too late. These guys knew I was a sheriff's detective. They knew I didn't believe their story. They would have killed me right there in that parking lot. They would have killed Granger at the same time. One of them had an Uzi. I saw it when his coat shifted away from his body in a gust of wind. They would have left in the ambulance they came in and switched vehicles a few minutes later. They'd have been gone before anybody could respond."

"And we'd have got them later," Juvera said. "You know that. Vehicle switch or not, we'd have got them—or not. Either way, we wouldn't have had a gunfight at a hospital. If you believed, in your best judgment of the situation, as it was when you first came on the scene, that there was a kidnapping in progress, you could have stayed in your vehicle and called it in. If you'd been wrong, you would have been wrong. You would have felt stupid, people would have complained about you, but that would have been the end of it. If you'd been right—and you were right—those guys might have killed Granger, but we would have tailed them and picked our own place to fight. As it is, Granger's dead anyway, so are the bad guys, and we don't know much more than we did before.

"I have a lot of respect for you, Manny. You won a gunfight against three well armed kidnappers. But that doesn't give you the right to make us look like a bunch of cowboys. You endangered a whole hospital full of people. You made that choice. You're responsible for every bullet you fired and your bullets apparently hit their marks. But what about the rounds from that Uzi? What did the other bad guys hit when they missed you? We've got three reports of vehicles in that parking lot with bullet holes in them. I'd advise you to buy another carry gun—*if* you still have a job after your upcoming meeting with the shooting review board. Your weapon is evidence and it'll be a long time before it's cleared. Like I said, we're waiting to get sued—and the psychologist is waiting for *you* down the hall. I'm requiring you to meet with her. You're suspended pending the shooting review board. We'll call you when we have a date for the review. That is all."

Aguilar headed down the hall where a smiling woman waited for him at the door to a conference room.

"I'm Gina," the psychologist said, shaking his hand. "You're Detective Aguilar?"

"Call me Manny. Everybody else does," Aguilar said. "Pleased to meet you."

She shook his hand and encouraged him to sit. Attractive woman. Wispy hair, little half-glasses, lavender eyes. She wore a tailored blouse and slacks, both in shades of gray. Manny could almost tell she had a nice body, but not quite.

"I heard you were shot and wounded in this incident," Gina said. "Where were you hit?"

"In the side, here." Manny pressed lightly on the bandage over his ribs.

"What would you say your pain level is on a scale from one to ten, ten being the most pain, one being the least?"

"It's about a three."

"You'll have a scar."

"It'll make me look like a tough guy," Manny said.

They both smiled.

"How did you sleep last night?" Gina asked.

The doc is a nice lady, Manny thought. He could tell her that he got some sleep right after he had a hallucination of his grandmother standing over him with two guns stuck in her belt. He could tell her that he'd hallucinated his grandmother during the gunfight, too. There were three of them, two of his dear old *nana* and one of him, shooting it out with the bad guys. He could tell her he thought she'd like to know that because he'd love some tea and sympathy. Then she'd make damn sure they stuck him in a desk job for the rest of his life—if they didn't just retire him as a nutcase.

"I slept okay," he said. "I felt anxious, but I got to sleep."

"Has anything like this ever happened to you before?"

"You mean a shooting incident? Only once, just recently. No one was killed in that one."

Gina cocked her head to one side and asked, "How do you feel about what happened, Manny?"

"Right now, kind of numb. I had to shoot. I did shoot."

"Numb is normal at this stage. Numb is okay. I understand you're very lucky to be alive, given the fact that there was one of you and three of them."

She'll keep talking until she knows I'm fit to walk the streets, Manny thought.

For a closer, Gina summarized the symptoms of Post Shooting Trauma and Post Traumatic Stress Syndrome.

"I'm asking that you attend some peer counseling sessions, Manny." She proffered a meeting schedule. "We both know you'll see some familiar faces there. Come back and talk to me anytime you want." They shook hands on it and he headed for the parking lot.

He automatically glanced in all directions on the way to the car. Martina and her news truck were parked on the curb, just off the property, and just by the exit. She had spotted him. She waved. He got in his Crown Vic and drove toward her. He could see her huge white teeth and he was sixty yards away.

"Do you know you're a hero, Detective Aguilar? How do you feel? Can you comment on the shooting incident at Saint Mary's Hospital?"

"I feel fine," Manny growled. "And I cannot comment on an ongoing investigation."

Martina asked him why the bad guys had done what they'd done and how Manny had gotten involved. He winced from the pain in his side as he raised his elbow to rest it on the window frame of the Ford. "Again, I cannot comment on an ongoing investigation. The department will release information when and as they see fit. I need to be on my way." Aguilar cruised off, leaving her standing there in her high heels, microphone in hand.

His cell phone rang. He held it up in front of him and glanced at the number. He'd never seen that number before so he waited for a message instead of answering. When no message came he pulled over and called back.

"Class Act Show Club." A woman's voice.

"I just received a call from this number."

"Who is this?"

"My name isn't important," Manny snapped. "You called me."

A new voice came on the line, "Hey, Aguilar."

"Rogers. Aren't you supposed to be working?"

"I am working," Rogers answered. "How you doing? Heard you got in a war."

"The psychologist tells me I'm fine. I'm glad you called. I need to talk to you about a couple of bad guys."

"Then get down here and I'll buy you a late lunch at the gentlemen's club, hoss. It's Friday night." Manny heard a woman giggle as he hung up the phone.

CHAPTER ELEVEN

TUCSON WAS TECHNICALLY a city, but it behaved like a town. And a town has to have a main drag for the weekends. In Tucson, the main drag was a street full of car lots, stores, bars, restaurants and nightclubs called Speedway Boulevard. A Tucson mayor had once called it the ugliest street in America.

Aguilar watched the scene as he drove toward the Class Act. Youth subcultures on wheels. Everybody had some kind of insignia that had to do with their cars and their clothes. The adults hung out in bars.

The police served as Tucson's weekend babysitters. They stayed a year or two behind the trends and styles, and this year they seemed to be deliberately mistaking anybody who had baggy pants and a baseball cap for a criminal.

The Class Act Show Club occupied most of a block of Speedway Boulevard. Manny spotted Randy Rogers in the parking lot, leaning against the trunk of a car.

"How you doing, Manny?" Rogers said cheerfully.

"You're working here?" Manny asked Rogers before they walked to the bar. "You're chasing criminals here?"

"Hey," Rogers said, "you spend too much time with dead guys in landfills. You should join the colorful and exciting war on drugs. How do you think TPD paid for all the toys the SWAT team uses? Drug money. You know that. It's the RICO Act, man. We bust people for drugs, we take any money they have lying around and tell the world it's money from drugs so it's ours now. And we take their cars, too. And their houses. I love it. By the way, you seen my new Corvette?"

Randy Rogers always had a Corvette. He'd had one in his senior year in high school, Manny remembered. Rogers' father was a partner in a garage that did body work. The old man got hold of a beat up Corvette and gave it to Randy. The new one looked new, indeed. It was long and slinky and of a metal-flaked, medium-hued blue that had been around forever. This year, the car salesmen were calling it Aruba Blue. The

Corvette looked just right sitting in the parking lot in front of the huge strip club with neon palm trees glowing all around.

"Nice car. So you're still a bachelor? That how you can afford these cars?"

"Yeah, I'm a bachelor. We're both going on twenty years in law enforcement, am I right? I've got the little condo and the car. It's easy as long as I never get married again. Hell, you never even tried marriage one time. You must do okay. What do you do with your money?"

"I save it. What are you doing here, Rogers? You can't enforce the RICO Act while you're looking at some girl's cha-chas."

"Yeah, I can, Manny. I'm here because narcotics cops have a standing deal with the girls. The dancers get around fifteen percent of any money we get out of a drug bust. Some dork comes in here that's dealing or just has a lot of drugs. He impresses the women with it. They tell him what a big shot he is and maybe take a toot of his dope. Then they tell us. It works like a charm. You surprise me, the stuff you don't know, man. Now, shall we go inside, Manny? Get your mind off all these serious matters you think about all the time? Relax for awhile?"

Rogers walked in with a grin, his curly blond hair sticking out from under his baseball cap. Manny followed. The woman taking money at the entrance and the bouncer standing next to her let them walk by without making any eye contact. Professional courtesy, shark to shark.

The interior of the place was a vision from underwater, a giant aquarium in dim blue light. The patrons covered the bottom of this ocean, weaving sluggishly back and forth like seaweed. The women floated around like colorful fish, soliciting table dances. The bouncers moved too, from time to time. A disc jockey sat high in a corner, playing music and announcing the fictitious names of the dancers.

Rogers and Manny were sitting within ten feet of the stage. Rogers got a waitress to bring them a couple of beers and they watched an athletic bleached blonde waltz out in six inch heels, a plaid miniskirt, and a top so thin it floated to the hardwood floor when she flipped it over her head. She dropped the miniskirt next and jumped at one of two poles mounted at center stage. She swung her legs to the other pole, bridging the two, creating a surreal picture of a woman lying sideways in the air. Her back was to the audience. Manny thought about late 19th century, when every cowboy bar in the west had a print of a reclining nude spread on the wall behind the whiskey bottles.

The woman flipped back to one pole, wrapped her legs around it, hung upside down, and slid to the floor of the stage without using her arms. Manny had to admire that.

Rogers turned on him and grinned. He tipped his face into Aguilar's and said. "Every man who comes into this place thinks one of these women is going see him and think he's different from all the others. Yeah," Rogers was laughing hard now, "yeah, one of these women is gonna' see the real me."

The next dancer up was another bleached blonde with large breasts enhanced in size and firmness by some material which had been shoved into a hole cut under her pectoral muscles. She writhed across the stage on her back to where a husky patron sat waving a ragged five dollar bill. Manny noticed Abraham Lincoln staring out from the money. Abe looked like he wanted to jump off the paper and run out the door.

The woman undulated to her knees and turned her implants on the man. She reached out and swiveled the brim of his baseball cap around until it was backwards on his head, then cupped her breasts from the outside, shoved them into the man's face, and squeezed. When she let go and drew back his face was crinkled up in a punchy grin, like a ten-year-old who'd just lost a round in a pillow fight. She threw him a hip and he stuffed the money in the strap of her G-string. She stood and rocked her torso at the audience.

"Maybe it's the scorpion tattooed next to her muff that makes me not want to trust her," Rogers said to Manny. Then he slapped Aguilar on the back and doubled up laughing, his teeth gleaming, his wild, handsome face a bluish-purple, a comic book color from the stage lights. Manny winced from the fresh bullet graze on his left side, a permanent souvenir of the gunfight at the hospital.

Manny and Randy Rogers spent an hour and a half in the timeless undersea world of the gentleman's club. Then Aguilar took a few minutes off to call Reina.

"Where the hell are you, Manny?" she said. "I can hear all kinds of stuff going on in the background."

"I'm seeing Rogers on official business," Manny laughed. "Ouch. Aie."

"Why are you saying Ouch, Manny? One of the girls pinch your butt?"

"No it's just my side," Manny said.

"Oh, now it's your side," Reina said. "How about your ass? How about you get your ass out of that bar and come home."

"I'll see you in an hour," Manny said.

"Yes, and you will see me tomorrow, too, for your niece's *quinceanera*. Am I right, Manny?"

He started back to his table, picking his way through the sea of male bodies slumped in the dim blue light. The Class Act Show Club, Manny decided, is like a forensic center for peeping toms. The bad guys could throw Harper's body in here and nobody would notice until the show was over.

He thought of Harper's head, cooling in the morgue—and the corrupt big shots Perez claimed Harper talked about. First, Governor Vinette, a sometime land developer from back east. Second, Patrick Dollanger, the governor's sidekick, said to be the richest land developer in Arizona.

The governor, as Aguilar and everyone else in Arizona knew, was currently fighting fraud charges. It seemed a lot of misrepresentation had gone on while the governor's development company destroyed various pieces of historic real estate in the capitol city of Phoenix, a town thought of by many environmentally conscious Tucsonans as home base for a legion of gleaming weasels who'd do anything for a buck.

The governor demolished the landmarks and had his campaign contributors in the construction industry build new collections of buildings which were supposed to function as centers, mainly for the activities of shopping, eating, and drinking alcohol. Trouble was, nobody came to these centers, the project went broke, and the owners falsified reports to show it as profitable. Then the truth came out.

Still, the governor had time to use a large, state-owned aircraft to fly his crony, Dollanger, down to Mexico, to meet with hugely rich Mexican businessmen and cut special deals out of the free trade agreements which were supposed to benefit working people on both sides of the border.

It's all lies, Manny thought, this junkie Perez and this drunken sack sucker, Harper. These sorry bastards having fantasies about politicians and businessmen. What motive could the governor and his friends have for murdering a wino?

As Manny and Rogers got up to leave, the dancers were giving two men a birthday party. The birthday boys were stripped to the waist and surrounded by dancers while the music played and the disc jockey kept saying "Happy Friggin' Birthday." The women used felt-tipped markers to write birthday wishes all over the men's brown, baby fat bodies. Their torsos looked like walls decorated with graffiti, Manny thought, like a ghetto with legs.

"Many happy returns of the friggin' day," Rogers said and swiveled his crazy blue eyes toward Manny. Manny nodded. Sleaze and general human folly always made Rogers laugh. Sometimes Manny had to laugh, too. Black humor. If you didn't have it, you didn't belong in law enforcement.

They walked to the parking lot. Aguilar's side still burned from the bullet wound and he knew it would burn for awhile. Rogers leaned on Manny's bulky Ford and crossed his arms, waiting.

"I have Granger's dying words that somebody named Tony Cisneros and some big dealer called Rico are the people I need to find. Granger fingered them as his killers," Manny said.

"Yeah," Rogers said, after a moment. He was looking down now. The cap bill, which he had carefully curved into shape, hid his eyes. "Tony Cisneros. Maybe I know the guy. I think he got popped for smuggling awhile back. The DEA might have something on this Cisneros dirtbag. I'll talk to those guys and check the computers. Those DEA guys can be pricks, though. They don't like to share information. I never heard of anybody who goes by Rico. I'd like to. Sounds like it'd make for a big bust."

Manny drove home. Grayboy the cat stared at him sternly from his perch on the gate that led to the little backyard. Manny fed him and headed for Reina's place.

"So how are the strip clubs these days, Manny?" Reina asked when he appeared at her door.

"Just like they used to be only with more surgery. And they put somebody in the men's room who wants a tip for handing you a towel."

"Great. And what about your case?"

"I learned that a bad guy named Tony Cisneros exists in law enforcement records," Aguilar said. "And Rogers might get me something on him."

"I think I've got something on you," Reina said, sliding a hand behind Aguilar's waistband and deep into his crotch. "Cooperate and you won't get hurt."

They stripped off in the bedroom.

"Let's burn the sheets and bust the slats," Aguilar said, flexing his bicep on the side of his body that didn't hurt.

"Oh, the subtle chemistry of your words," Reina said. She tossed her underwear in his face and he reached for her.

He was thinking about Harper as soon as he caught his breath. "Reina, what do you know about Patrick Dollanger?"

"You're the king of pillow talk, Manuel. We have sex and you bring up land developers."

"I got a murder victim, a common drunk, who may have tried to blackmail Patrick Dollanger. It makes no sense to me so I'm asking you because you know a lot of people and you read a lot about that stuff."

"I try to keep up. Rivers drop dead. The earth eats houses. Poisonous toads grow rich. I get curious," Reina said.

"What do you mean?"

"Killing the hidden waters. Fissures in the earth. Profit as god. An invasion—"

"What about Dollanger?"

Reina turned to him in the bed. "If you want to know about this stuff I'll have to take you back before Dollanger—if you'll go."

"Let's go," Manny said, unobtrusively pinching his thigh so he could keep a straight face.

"The water table around Tucson was twenty feet in the 1800's. It's two-hundred and fifty feet now, or more, depending on location. Rivers and riparian areas stolen. Gone, in one lifetime. The Santa Cruz River flowed right through Tucson, Manny. The natives used it for a thousand years and never used it up. That river is sand now. And the forests around it? Poof. The Tohono O'odham and the Mexicans farmed and ranched for hundreds of years but now we are all seeing Arizona broken in our laps—"

"Calm down, okay? Why'd the river go dry? Just drought, right?"

"Hey, forget calming down," Reina said. "And another hey: You're the Indian. Don't you know this stuff?"

"I'm one quarter Yaqui, three-quarters Mexican," Manny said. "And I'm good with that. Problem is, Reina, the history and culture of my ancestors will not help me solve murders."

"Yes it will solve murders," Reina insisted, her voice rising. "It will solve the murders of entire cultures—cultures we killed off and the knowledge killed, too. They had a culture that knew how to bend instead of rape and abandon. Oh, and the river? It went dry because the Anglo Americans sucked up all the water."

She shook a long finger at her lover. "You should read Chuck Bowden, Manny, it'd do you good."

Manny grimaced as if in pain. "What about the other story you started to tell me?"

"Okay, fine. The Covered Wells Stick, Manny, year 1912 of the white man's god—and I cannot pretend to be other than I am. My ancestors came from Europe, all of them, the Spaniards and the Anglos, too. I speak as if I were not, quote, white, so I can convey, a little bit, how it's got to feel. The Covered Wells Stick, a carved wooden stick, is a Tohono O'odham historical record.

"Anyway, the Tohono O'odham made their largest entry on the Covered Wells Stick in 1912, about a well at the Santa Rosa village, eighty miles from here. The natives opposed the well, knowing it would keep them from their old way of life. The Bureau of Indian Affairs drilled the well anyway. The whites broke a culture that had functioned *with* the desert for a thousand years and they did it with one well that brought up underground water—water which will not, repeat not, replace itself in this desert."

Manny frowned. "What do you mean it won't replace itself? Water runs underground when it rains. Rain replaces underground water."

"No, Manny. Water from wells is fossil water. It's been there for millions of years. Geologists call it 'mining water....'"

Reina stared at nothing, looking suddenly tired. Manny waited.

"We've run water out of the tap our whole lives, "Reina continued, almost whispering. "We hardly notice when a drought drags on for years—but the desert notices, and she's batting last in this ballgame. Anyway, settlers drilled wells all over the desert. Then they grabbed the Colorado River and ran a huge canal to Phoenix and Tucson. There are lawsuits, disputes with Mexico. We're stealing their water, too—"

"What about Dollanger?"

"Dollanger, and people like him, sell a fake Arizona. The state legislature did the same thing in the nineteenth century. They hired writers to lie about the desert, to sell it as a place with water and four seasons. They called it *boosterism*."

"We've still got water," Manny was caught up in it now. "We've got more people, but we've got a better economy—"

"As for the water, Manny, I heard the bottom line on that the other night—"

"From who?"

"From a hydrologist at the University of Arizona. The guy said that we'll always have water. The real question is: How much are we gonna' have to *pay* for it? Smoke that, Manny. How much is the water bill going to be when your water travels five-hundred miles from the Pacific Ocean by pipeline after it's been desalinized?"

"Okay, go on."

"The developers are destroying an ecosystem and flat out lying, I say, about how many millions of people the Sonoran desert can support. And Dollanger, since you asked, is their dark lord. The developers will be far away, living in mansions elsewhere, when the whole thing collapses. The rest of us might be around and we'll be stuck with it—"

"Stuck with what?"

"The desert is disappearing, we're losing an eco system, we're losing native species of plants and animals, and there's no timetable as to when, and if, it'll ever come back. And one more thing...."

"I need a drink of water," Manny said, shifting his body on the bed as if to leave for the kitchen. "Would you like some?"

Reina gave him a look that would have set paper on fire. Then she sprang up, mounted him, and leaned into his face. "No, Manny. I'm not done yet. Now, a lot of us who've lived here all our lives are already freaking dying, spiritually, from the aesthetics these guys dump on us."

Her breasts teased his chest. Her thighs locked on his hips. A big orange sun lit up in Manny's crotch. She straightened up, grabbed a couple of Manny's chest hairs, and pulled. The big orange sun went away and Reina went on talking. "We've got acres of cheap, crappy houses with weird architectural styles—and golf courses—the human boot on the throat of Mother Nature—shoved in between those houses. Scotland meets Santa Barbara in Disneyland is what we're talking here, and fitting in be dammed. Camille Rose Garcia should paint it. It's another Tragic Kingdom, another Saddest Place on Earth—with cactus."

Manny said nothing. He stared into Reina's eyes, hoping he could wait until she was done before he made a move on her.

Reina took a breath. "As for Patrick Dollanger himself I don't know all about him. Nobody does and he likes it that way. He's the most successful developer in Southern Arizona, which puts the guy, as far as I'm concerned, right up there with the little old god some folks like to call Satan. He bought up thousands of acres of land early on and stayed on a roll with it, buying more land, building more homes, buying politicians as he went."

Manny ventured a comment. "If Dollanger didn't buy and sell land, somebody else would."

"Be that as it may, Manny, developers are always doing what's barely legal and it's hard to catch them doing anything completely illegal, but you can bet they do whatever they can get away with. Dollanger is close to being an organized crime boss and organized crime can only function by corrupting local government—but he's legitimate until somebody catches him. Word is, he can be a personable guy and, like most really rich people, he's got a lot of friends. Best I can do for you, Manny. Wish I could show you his head on a stick."

Manny grinned. "But how do you really feel?"

"Shut up, wiseass." She twisted his chest hair again and he grabbed her wrist and held it while she went on talking. "There are two kinds of intelligence working here. There's the logic of profit, development, of lording it over the earth. But there's another kind of intelligence. You find it if you study Native American cultures. You find it if you study Asian cultures. Anybody who looks for it finds it in themselves. If we don't start working with the intelligence we've degraded and shoved into the shadows, we're going down."

"One more question," Manny said.

"What, dammit." She straightened up and he stared at her naked torso.

"Am I gonna' get laid again tonight?"

CHAPTER TWELVE

"IS THAT A *chupacabra* or is that your bulldog?" Manny asked his brother. Manny was in a rare mood. It was Saturday afternoon. He was loose enough to make a *chiste*, comparing his brother's ancient, ponderous bulldog, Beastie, to the mythical, blood-sucking monster of popular regional mythology. *Chupacabras* had been popping up in the states of Sonora, Mexico, and Arizona, USA, like visions of the cross, or retirees fleeing cold northern weather.

"How many beers you had, Manny?"

"Three or five. Why?"

They sat in Reggie's landscaped backyard by a swimming pool of a color the salespeople were currently calling Ecology Blue. Reggie's youngest children, a son and daughter, were splashing around like otters.

"Yes, this is my bulldog," Reggie said, affectionately massaging the ugly creature's head.

"So, Manny," Reggie went on, "you know that I have to make the pitch. I am going to make the pitch, too, and let go of the results like the wise person that I am."

"Okay," Manny said. "But you know what I'm going to say."

"I can put you in sales and in one year you'll be making thirty percent more than you do now. And it's legal, Manny, and it's fair. You won't be misrepresenting Ford trucks. You *drive* Ford trucks. I can put you to doing fleet deals, keep your floor time to a minimum, I can do other things like that—"

"Thanks, Reggie," Manny said, "but you know how it is."

"Manny," Reggie said, "I've got a better retirement plan for my employees than getting shot—great health insurance, too. We've both got our parents to consider, you've got Reina—"

"And you know what I'm going to say," Manny said, "when you start this stuff, Reggie."

"You've got, what, sixteen years with the sheriff's department," Reggie said softly. "That's a lot of time. You got a lot of bad guys, Manny."

I've seen you beaten up. I know you've been shot at before. This is the first time I've seen you shot—"

"Do you remember hearing about the pools?" Manny said suddenly, staring out over Reggie's swimming pool. "The public pools? After the war."

"Which war? First Iraq? Second Iraq? Vietnam? Panama? Kansas versus Iowa? What? I don't know."

"No, World War II. I don't remember them either, but the folks used to talk about it once in awhile. You know, the pools, the public swimming pools after the war. The brown kids swam at one time of day, the white kids swam at another time of day, and the black kids swam—I don't remember when the black kids were supposed to swim. I guess with us. And our grandfather and all the other Mexican guys came back from the war and they got those pools integrated. Our grandmother, too. They just made them quit that stuff. It was maybe 1962 by the time the last lawsuit got through court, right here in Arizona. That's justice. You work for it. Sometimes you get it, and sometimes you don't. There's that, Reggie. I work for justice. And, yeah, I like being a homicide detective. I like doing murder investigations. That's how it is, so let's not talk about it anymore."

Reggie grinned his graceful salesman's grin. "Just don't get shot again, okay?"

My older brother gets to be a raving idealist after a couple of beers, Reggie thought. Either he's a stuffy cop or he's Zorro.

"How is that daughter of yours doing in there in the house?" Manny asked. "Is she going to make her own *quinceanera* on time, or what?"

Reggie called to the children to get out of the pool and get dressed. The two men followed them through the pool gate and Manny watched Reggie lock it, knowing kids drown in swimming pools because somebody didn't pay attention. Manny remembered racing to a drowning call when he was still a patrol deputy. Nothing to do but stand around in the stark Arizona sun while the EMT's tried to resuscitate a child.

Once in the house, Manny followed Reggie to Celina's door. Reggie knocked and somebody opened it. Celina was sitting at her mirror, putting the finishing touches on her makeup and trying on her headpiece. Beautifully dressed young women of various skin shades surrounded her, helping her, or fixing their own dresses, makeup and hair. Their combined voices, mixing English and Spanish, were part parrot call, part lullaby. Giggles and whispers. They wove back and forth like kites in the wind, like *papalotes*.

Reggie told them it was almost time to go and respectfully pulled the door shut on his way out. He and Manny chatted with Maria, Reggie's pretty wife, for a few minutes until the girls trooped out. There were aunts and uncles sitting around Maria and Reggie's big living room, younger girls and boys, more girlfriends of Celina's, and some male friends, including a couple of blazingly handsome young men wearing the green uniforms and berets of US Army paratroopers. Less than a year before they'd been high school students.

Seeing the young soldiers always made Manny feel a dull sadness. Luis, the oldest Aguilar brother, killed on patrol in Iraq, long ago. Just another unlucky kid, Manny thought, sacrificed, while we tried to dominate a bunch of people who had their own stupid problems. But I'm no different, he thought. I joined the Army. I put my hands in the black work of military intelligence—and I liked it.

It didn't matter, he decided, we've got our lives to live and this is a good day. He headed for his truck. He was happy from the beer. His back was a little sore from sex with Reina the night before. This isn't bad, he thought, scuffing his newly shined boots down Reggie's paved driveway. His new 1911 Colt was in his glove box with his badge.

He'd hated spending the money for a new weapon but the .45 he'd carried for years was sitting somewhere in an evidence room. In any case, it felt nice to feel light, not to have several pounds of steel weaponry strapped to his ass. Behind him, Reggie and Maria were organizing Celina and her attendants for the trip to Saint Margaret's.

Once he'd cleared the Catalina foothills, he started down Grant Road. He planned to run Grant westbound, into the El Rio neighborhood, and then turn south, to Saint Margaret's church. He could take his time getting there. His brother's family was behind him. He knew Reina would be there in time to meet him and they'd go inside, sit down, and witness a long ceremony, wherein a smart and beautiful young woman would be formally welcomed into adulthood and informed of her responsibilities. Then there'd be a dance and a big feed and all the young men and women would do their best to forget what the priest said about those responsibilities. And Manny and Reina would leave early.

Manny was working on a pretty good fantasy about Reina when he reached the stop light at Campbell Avenue and Grant Road. Reina was screeching like a cat in his daydream when he noticed a white Mercedes in the southbound lane on Campbell. The S class sedan was a piece of prestige that would have paid for Manny's house, with a year's supply of cat food thrown in. The car was chauffeured and there were two people in the back. The side windows were heavily tinted, but he could glimpse the back seat through the front windshield of this rolling piece of high dollar tin. The man in back was tanned and balding, and seemed to be giving off a sense of relaxed personal power. It was the woman who caught Manny's eye. She had a full, beautiful head of blonde hair. It was Carole Harper, had to be. The Mercedes whisked by and was gone.

Manny popped his left turn signal and waited for oncoming traffic, craning his neck to watch the Mercedes turning into a flyspeck. By the time traffic cleared enough so he could gun his truck and make the turn, he was spitting curses in two languages. He flew south on Campbell but the Mercedes was long gone. He pulled into a parking lot, called sheriff's headquarters, and got a detective doing weekend duty to find Carole Harper's home phone number.

"No," the man who answered said, "she is not here. Who is this?"

Manny identified himself, said he needed to talk to Carole about some routine police business, and asked where he could reach her.

The man again said Carole was unavailable and added that he'd leave her a message and, when pressed, asked Manny to understand that, he, Rolf, who was just staying there, couldn't really provide specifics about Carole to someone who was, after all, just a voice on the phone.

"I'd appreciate it very much if Carole could call me," Manny said. "My number is—"

Manny heard a click. He hit the redial button again and then again. No answer.

What kind of name is Rolf, he thought to himself, sounds like something you'd name an attack dog. The guy sounded like a German—heavy accent of some kind. The snotty little bastard is probably just being protective of Carole Harper's privacy. But English isn't Rolf's first language. The guy might have problems communicating. Nevertheless, people got into trouble, even if they did not speak fluent English, by refusing to cooperate with an investigation. The problem is, he thought: What was he investigating? He had nothing on Carole Harper. If she had stayed in town after she had told him was leaving, was that a crime? Hell no. She could have changed her mind and stayed for any number of reasons. If you bully citizens, especially upscale types like Carole Harper, you could be up a creek. Law enforcement culture loved a Barney Fife story. Headlines reading, in essence, "Detective Aguilar Steps On Own Dick Again", were not the kind of headlines Manny needed right now, especially with another shooting review board coming up. He had run out of spare time. He was due at Saint Margaret's.

The ceremony had begun when Manny arrived. The priest was droning on. What he said had sentiment and meaning, but the sound of his voice could put anybody to sleep. Manny saw Reina, wearing a black dress, sitting in the third row. He started to sneak down the aisle while the priest continued to drone.

Manny was still in the aisle, just a few feet from Reina, just catching sight of her breasts under that black dress, and her bare shoulders. Manny was a shoulder man. He loved shoulders. He was feeling dizzily tender, looking at Reina's shoulders, and lustful, looking at her breasts, when he was caught, flatfooted and crazy with love, in the middle of the aisle, by a sudden call to prayer. Manny did an absurd but graceful right face out of the aisle and into a row, practically running into the young paratroopers he'd seen at Reggie's house as they stood, heads bowed, with their berets stuffed in the epaulets of their green jackets. Manny bowed his head as well and weathered the brief cloudburst of prayer, then made his way to Reina.

Manny sat down next to her, guarded and slightly flustered. She looked full at him, grinning at his discomfort, his lateness, and at the comedy of being lovers in church. And since it was Reina's nature to snatch some sensual, catlike satisfaction out of most situations—a trait that made her hated by some men and quite a few women—she admired Manny's looks, too, as a smart matador admires a strong bull. They turned away from each other and lifted their heads to watch the proceedings.

Celina had risen and was walking toward the priest, who was holding his arms out toward her and calling to her in formal welcome, when Manny's cell phone vibrated against his leg. He glanced at the number while Reina glanced at him. She knew what it meant to have a homicide detective as a lover. Her green eyes registered that she was ready to do the rest of the celebration by herself, if she had to, without throwing a huge magnitude of bitchery at him later.

Manny glanced up from the phone, telling Reina with his eyes that he had to answer this call. He got up and made his way outside.

Manny walked across the street to a convenience mart, thinking a package of breath mints might be appropriate after the beer he'd been drinking. A half-naked kid, a tattooed stoner with hair down to his nipples, was whining nasally into a pay phone outside the store.

Manny punched a number on his cell phone and Rogers answered.

"Rogers," Manny said. "What's up?"

"What's the wave, brother?" Rogers said, in his broken Spanish, "I got an address for you and it's the best one we can find for Tony Cisneros."

"Go," Manny said, and jerked a pad and pen out of his black Sunday trousers.

"Well screw you then," the guy at the pay phone yelled into the mouthpiece.

Manny was too busy scribbling down another druggie's address to care about the one on the pay phone. All that had to change when the kid started screaming obscenities and smashed the receiver against the call box, then jumped up like a monkey, braced his sneakers against the slump block wall of the convenience mart, jerked the phone out of the call box by its cable, using his full weight, and fell on his back, cockroach-like, with the phone and half the torn cable drawn up against his chest.

"Rogers," Manny said. "Hear that?"

"Yeah," Rogers said. "Send the men?"

"Yes," Manny said, and rang off, coming up on the stoner just as he leapt to his feet and threw the amputated telephone receiver at the call box. The kid had an arm like a cannon and the phone went airborne, arcing backwards off the call box in the direction of a wide-eyed matron who was trying to gas up her Dodge Aries.

Manny yelled, "Police!"

The stoner threw a roundhouse kick and Manny jumped him. They fell together and the shirtless man screamed like a banshee and tried to knee Manny in the groin while struggling to loosen Manny's grip on his neck. Manny used his extra weight, trying to press the kid flat and choke him out, but the guy slipped sideways and scooted backwards toward the Dodge Aries, pumping and windmilling his long, blue jean-clad legs.

Both of them landed against the front tire of the Dodge while the woman let the gasoline hose clatter to the pavement on the other side and backpedaled, thumping off the sides of the pumps as she went, and yelling "Aie. Aie."

Manny missed a second chokehold and the stoner spun and sprang to the hood of the Dodge, landing on one foot, then slamming face down on top of the hood as Manny jerked upward on his other foot.

The kid tried to pushup himself across the hood of the car while Manny dove on top of him. Manny finally got his chokehold and the guy was never getting loose. The perp had one more surprise. He rocked sideways and both of them rolled off the front of the hood like a couple of squabbling housecats and fell onto the pavement, right in front of the car. The kid was on the bottom and Manny held his elbows up so the kid, and not Manny's elbows, would smash against the pavement. It worked, and the guy's face smacked the concrete. He kept struggling until Manny choked him into submission. TPD cops pulled up and hopped out of their cruisers to stand over the mess.

Manny uncoiled himself and crouched, putting one knee in the middle of the guy's back. He kept the man's head pinned with one hand and reached for a set of proffered handcuffs with the other.

The two young TPD cops didn't know Manny so they didn't tell him he looked like hell. Besides, Manny knew he looked like hell. His only suit was ruined and there was blood on his white shirt. He went over the particulars with the officers after they'd escorted the babbling, handcuffed maniac into a cage car. Then the TPD cops allowed themselves a cheesy, satisfied grin and started to turn away to their cars when the woman started yelling, "*Maldita policia. Y que de mi coche? Cabrones.*"

The little lady was standing by the gas pumps and pointing at the scratched and dented hood of her Dodge.

"What's she saying?" the two cops asked Manny.

"She's concerned about her car," Manny said. "I'd get a Spanish speaking officer down here to deal with it. I need to go on other business right now."

"Okay," one of the cops said. "I'll call Carmen." He started talking into his radio while the woman continued to curse the police.

The nutcase screamed a string of maledictions and started kicking the inside of the squad car.

"I'm going now." Manny said, over the sound of the thumping and cursing. "Good luck."

The two macho cops stood there in their military haircuts and their sunglasses and radiated embarrassment and frustration. The woman kept berating them in Spanish.

Manny blew off a trip to a hospital emergency room. He knew he was supposed to get checked out, but he hadn't got any blood directly on his skin. He had a couple of sore spots, but he had no open wounds or abrasions. His clothing had all the abrasions. He thought about getting his next suit at a thrift store so he could save a little money. Manny drove home to shower and change clothes. When he got back into his Ford he pulled his 1911 Colt out of the glove box and holstered it inside his belt.

A half hour later, Manny was easing his truck through the Vistoso neighborhood of Tucson's south side. A lot of the houses looked trim and well kept up. Manny could see the red bougainvillea and the green lawns. He pitied the older people who'd lived in this neighborhood for forty years. The people who couldn't imagine moving, or couldn't afford to. Vistoso was a high crime area, in spite of its deceptively neat and modest single story homes. The worst looking piece of property in the neighborhood belonged to an Anglo who covered his back yard with wrecked cars and trucks. Manny watched a hound dog squat in the middle of the mess as he passed by. The man was out there too, peering at a rusty rear axle, a crescent wrench clutched in his hand.

Manny never went to the Vistoso, TPD patrolled it, but every cop knew about it. He passed a group of boys who weren't more than fourteen years old. Gang kids, he thought, probably members of the Southside Vistosos.

Manny rolled to a stop in front of the address he was looking for. The turquoise paint was peeling off the walls and the place looked deserted. There were no cars in the driveway. He knew that didn't mean a damned thing. Manny got out of his truck and started around it to go up the drive.

The Vistoso neighborhood had a street pocketed with little cul de sacs on its east side and Manny was parked in one of them. There was plenty of room for a seventies-vintage Buick low rider with smoked glass windows to roll in past Manny's truck and stop.

"Hey!" the man in the passenger seat yelled. Then he opened fire.

CHAPTER THIRTEEN

MANNY WAS CLOSE enough to his truck to dive toward it, hit the ground rolling, and come up behind it with his .45 drawn, but the shooter's car was already screaming out of the cul de sac. Manny got the plate number in an orgy of speed reading before the low rider disappeared. Then he looked around for any witnesses. The streets were quiet. The kids he'd seen were blocks away. He wasn't on duty and he wasn't carrying a police radio. He holstered his weapon without looking down, pulled out his cell phone, and called 911.

He walked, weary and shaking a little, back to his truck and started looking for spent cartridge cases, bullet holes, and other physical evidence. The TPD would be running this show so he didn't touch anything.

He bent down and eyeballed a nine-millimeter cartridge casing. The firing pin mark consisted of one line grooved in the primer, instead of a round depression. That line was the characteristic mark of a Glock firing pin. He'd been shot at with one of millions of Glock pistols, used by millions of people, on all sides of the law.

The shooter had used a quality weapon that was common as dirt. And the shooter was a lousy shot. Manny was reminded of that when he saw the nasty dent in his truck's front bumper. The chrome had been blown off around the dent but the bullet had bounced off the steel. The other two or three shots must have hit the lawn or the house. Manny swore and rose to his feet, wincing slightly from the bruises and bumps of the day. He hoped no bullets had hit the house. The light, fast nine-millimeter penetrated well, too well.

Disgusted, still trembling from the adrenaline, Aguilar went to the door he'd been approaching when all the noisy interruptions occurred. He knocked first, then pounded on the door, but no one was answering when the first two police cruisers sailed in from different directions and stopped, blocking the cul de sac from the street. Officers drew guns and called out to Manny, who held both hands over his head, one hand holding his badge and picture ID. He called back, identifying himself.

The officers moved in cautiously as two more patrol cars flew in from different directions, blocking the main street.

"Officer Bennett," Manny called to one of the pair approaching him, "it's me, Detective Aguilar, Sheriff's Department."

Officer Bennett, the dark haired, officious cop who had picked up Harper as a walking drunk and later identified him at the Forensic Center.

"I have the shooter's license number and vehicle description," Manny said. "Can you call it in right now?"

Manny and Bennett got the vehicle description called in and joined another officer who was banging on the door of the house. Deciding they'd get no answer from inside, they double-checked with police dispatch about who might live there. No Tony Cisneros. An Emily Johnson was the probable resident.

Nobody noticed, at first, when the large, white paratransit van pulled up and stopped just outside the ring of police cruisers that blocked the cul de sac where Emily Johnson lived.

"Danny, who do you live with?" the driver asked, looking back at one of his passengers. "Who helps take care of you?"

"Aah." Danny said, and laughed because he could not remember. The present was a happy place for Danny. He knew he was going somewhere, just sitting in his wheelchair, which was strapped to the floor of the big paratransit van.

The van driver worked his shift in low-grade terror of a traffic accident on the mean streets of Tucson. He was forever wondering whether the straps and hooks he routinely snapped into the fittings in the floor would hold the wheelchairs if anything happened. When he was not busy worrying, the driver wondered about his passengers. If they had mental handicaps, how did those handicaps affect them? What was, well, wrong with them? What were their lives like? Right now, the driver was trying to learn whether the kind lady who welcomed Danny home every day was a relative or a professional caretaker.

"It's his mother," Robert said. Robert was strapped in the wheelchair just in front of Danny. Robert spoke haltingly, as if he, too, could not remember facts or think quickly. He freelanced as a computer programmer. His disease only made him talk as if he could not think.

"Danny has memory problems," Robert said slowly. "He can't remember who takes care of him, but when he gets home and sees her, he'll remember."

The driver glanced back at Danny, who nodded and grinned. After awhile, Danny began to sing. All the words didn't come out in the right order, but his voice was sweet.

Officer Peralta was on the verge of telling the skinny guy in the paratransit van to just take off when the guy finally got through to him that he was dropping off a client who lived in the house.

"That house?" Peralta yelled, pointing at the weathered turquoise tract home with all the cops in front of it.

"Yes," the driver said. "Danny, he's the guy in the wheelchair, sir. He lives in that house."

"Somebody supposed to be home there?" Peralta said.

"Yeah, she's always home," the driver said, hoping he could communicate without being bullied any more than necessary.

"Hey," Peralta yelled at the group of officers. "Somebody's supposed to be home in there."

Then Peralta turned back to the driver and said, "And you ain't got a key?"

The driver shook his head.

"And you ain't got a key?" Peralta said to Robert.

Robert shook his head.

"And you ain't got a key?" Peralta said to Danny.

Danny just smiled.

When they'd asked the driver, all over again, what was going on, and he'd told them, and Robert, from his wheelchair, had told them, and Danny had smiled and nodded as best he could, the cops finally just called the situation in to dispatch and kicked the door down. They even had somebody cover the back, just in case Tony Cisneros, or some scumbag like him, was really in the house.

Manny came in through the front door, behind the police. The shades were drawn against the heat and light that can make a house uncomfortable in Arizona, even in winter. The walls were covered with framed bible quotations and photos of relatives. Oil paintings of Martin Luther King and Jesus Christ hung over the old television set. The sweet, moist smell of cinnamon rolls came from the kitchen.

Two officers were bending over a body on the floor. One of them was calling for paramedics and other one just looked up at Manny and shook his head. A small woman lay there, her dark red flannel robe still neatly tied around her waist. Falling down hadn't even knocked off her horn rimmed glasses. Her wig was still in place. She looked to be around retirement age but she was way beyond retired. The nine-millimeter bullet had slipped into the house, somehow, and killed Emily Johnson, who had been waiting, as she always did, for her son.

"Where you goin'?" one of the cops asked Manny, who was headed toward the kitchen.

"I am going to check on the cinnamon rolls," Manny said, a little too loudly, "because, as of right now, there is no longer anybody here to take them out of the oven."

Aguilar was tied up at the crime scene until almost sundown. When he did get a break from the TPD cops, who needed his purpose for being there, and his life story, so they could write their reports, he had tried to get hold of Rogers. No answer. The white paratransit van was still parked outside the ring of police cars when Aguilar left the scene.

He drove out of the Vistoso neighborhood and tried Randy's cell phone again. No answer. He left word at TPD, Downtown, that he wanted Rogers to call him. Then he just sat in his truck for a minute in front of a convenience market. He lifted his head and inhaled through his crooked nose while he counted to seven. He held his breath, clenched his teeth, and pushed his stomach out, hard. He let the air out of his lungs in a rush. He was dizzy for a second, then he was calm and clear. He turned on his radio, loud, kicking the band selector over to AM, to KQTL. For some reason, Spanish music made more sense. On impulse, he turned the radio off again and said a prayer for Emily Johnson. After that, he said another prayer for himself.

When he reached the hall Reggie had rented for Celina's *quinceanera*, Manny nodded to the moonlighting TPD cops Reggie had covering the door and went inside. He found Reina passing the time with some cousins of his. She knew he'd had a bad day as soon as she saw him. She also knew he looked like he was handling it okay. Manny hugged her and then he remembered something.

"Reina, I smell beans, carne, and tortillas. I'm going over there and get some."

In a minute he was back to the table, eating. He nodded at Reina to let her know everything was okay.

"I'm thirsty," she said. "Want anything?"

"A beer," Manny mumbled through a mouth full of carne. "Please."

"You're not having a drink?" one of Manny's half-drunk cousins asked Reina when she returned from the bar with a beer for Manny and a club soda for herself.

"I already drank," Reina said, and drained the glass of club soda.

"Now I associate alcohol with wanted men, unwanted pregnancies, and real bad car wrecks." She ran one finger down a hairline scar on the side of her jaw. "But hey," she said, looking Manny's half-drunk cousin in the eye, "that's just me."

Manny's cousin slumped back in his chair and gazed off, hoping to find somebody to talk to that was just as lean and sexual as Reina, but maybe a little less dangerous.

"Manny, how was your day?" Reina asked, when Manny finally came up for air after downing a plate of carne and refried beans, deftly using pieces of tortilla instead of a knife and fork.

"Somebody doesn't like me," Manny said, reaching for a paper napkin.

"Lots of people don't like you, Manny," Reina said. "You're a law enforcement geek. But me, I like you a lot. Tell me about it."

"I was just running down leads," Manny said to Reina, who was watching him and waiting for him to quit thinking and start talking, "Leads that don't amount to anything. Rogers gave me an address today. I went over there. It was another dead end."

"How dead?" Reina asked suspiciously.

"You don't want to know."

CHAPTER FOURTEEN

REINA TOOK MANNY to her place after the *quinceanera*. She lived in the Sam Hughes neighborhood, in central Tucson, in a California style bungalow built in the 1930s. The walls were white and the roof was done with mission tile. It looked very Raymond Chandler from the outside. Inside, Raymond Chandler met the Day of the Dead. The interior doorways were arched, the floors were hardwood, the rugs were expensive, and the fireplace was tiled in a dark blood red.

When they had first become lovers, two years before, Manny had taken in Reina's place, and Reina, like a sighted man trying to learn Braille. She was all there, in her long curved body, her mind, her spirit. But it hadn't been easy to feel his way through, he'd had little talent for it, and no choice, because he'd loved her, right away. Knowing her a little bit in high school, smoking the odd joint of marijuana was one thing. This, Manny often reflected, at the beginning of the relationship, was the whole enchilada. Learning all about Reina, this could take awhile.

He remembered the first time she had spoken to him about what she believed. That time, they had been at his house, at Manny's little place on Fifteenth Street, worlds away—in bed.

Since her 10th grade reading of Dante's Inferno, Reina had told him, she'd labeled herself a virtuous pagan.

"The virtuous pagans were people like Socrates, Virgil, Plato, Homer..." she began, after they had been busy having sex. They were still new lovers and it was only her second time in Manny's bedroom—a bedroom that spoke to her of brute utility in an uninspired *ménage a trois* with carelessness and marginal hygiene.

"They all had a special place in the uppermost level of hell and you would probably like it. Are these sheets clean?" She had pulled the top sheet back up on the bed, put her long nose to it, and sniffed.

Grayboy had watched her with sudden interest. He'd been sitting on an overflowing clothes hamper in the corner. He'd hoped she had found some sort of prey in the sheets and needed his help to tackle it. They hadn't been interesting before, only mildly alarming, struggling together on the mattress, making loud, human sounds of different pitches. They had finally stopped and Grayboy had been calmly inhaling the smell and hoping for some real action.

Manny remembered watching Reina, that night at his place, feeling a small fork of lightning come down and knock some dust off his prostate. He'd known he was going to have her again before they got out of that room.

"Virgil is Dante's guide, his master," Reina had said, dropping the sheet, apparently satisfied that it was passably clean. "Dante is forty-something, and he realizes he hasn't been paying attention to a large part of what life is about for a very long time. So, Virgil takes him to hell."

Manny was propped up on one elbow. He'd managed to keep a straight face, but it had not been easy because there was desire and there was this story that Reina insisted on telling him. Yeah, Manny thought, Virgil takes this guy to hell. He had mentally rolled his eyes and made sure that what he was thinking didn't show on his face.

"The first circle of hell is called the Citadel. It represents philosophy; human reason without the light of God. There are three main groups there: the heroes, the heroines, and the philosophers."

She had turned sideways then, facing Manny, propped up, like him, on one elbow. Her green eyes with their pinpoint pupils went sometimes to his, but sometimes she dropped her gaze. She was intense now, for some reason Manny couldn't exactly fathom, and she was shy. It is what she thinks, he'd realized, she never tells people what she thinks. He hadn't known whether to be glad or to get the hell away from her. He wasn't afraid, though. He'd heard a lot of stories, but he'd never heard one like this, from someone like this.

"And here is the quote," Reina went on, "at least part of it: 'And the Master, Virgil, said to me: You do not question what souls these are that suffer here before you? I wish you to know before you travel on that these were sinless. And still their merits fail… Their birth fell before the age of the Christian mysteries. For such defects are we lost, though spared the fire and suffering of Hell in one affliction only: that without hope we live on in desire.'"

When she had said that, two years before, in his little bedroom, a bell had tolled in his head and he'd been stilled, reflective, and tender. They had reached out together, the big brown man and the very white woman, and held each others' shoulders. He'd tilted his head, staring at her torso without really seeing it.

Reina's torso was long. Her stomach was flat and tight and covered with scars from stretch marks. There were other scars from a car accident.

"Yes," she said. "These scars."

"Scars are good," he'd told her, "I'll kiss your scars. Do you remember a history teacher told us something about the Aztec heaven? There's a special place for women who died in childbirth. They call them women warriors. I don't remember anything else about it." He had begun to trace her scars with his finger, one scar at a time. Grayboy then concluded they were both boring him deliberately and he'd slipped out of the house to spend the night hunting.

Reina's house had one full bath and what could really be called a water closet with no window. She'd painted it red and yellow. That little red and yellow water closet gave Manny the creeps every time he was in there and he didn't know why.

She was usually generous and relaxed about Manny and his ways, but he knew she had a thing about toilet seats being left up, so he had to watch that when he was in the water closet. In his own house, Manny left the toilet seat up so Grayboy could sit on the edge and drink out of the bowl. He had put out water for the cat, but the cat preferred the toilet bowl.

Aguilar wondered about the carved Mexican masks covering her walls and the small, unsettling art objects that were stashed everywhere. Reina built altars. On these she would place candles, sometimes bearing the image of the Virgin of Guadalupe, the dark woman in green.

"One time I called a priest about her," Reina once told Manny, "after I read, you know, the thing about Juan Diego, seeing her on a hill outside Mexico City in, what, 1531?"

"I don't know," Manny said, "sometime back there."

"He was a nice man, the priest, but he thought he smelled a lapsed Catholic. You know?" Reina asked.

Manny knew.

"He told me she was the first of a succession of Marian Apparitions that have happened since. She appeared near the equator, in the center of the world. The priest was real strict about one thing. He said she was the Virgin Mary appearing as an Indian, and not an Indian appearing as the Virgin Mary. Of course, if we know our pagan history, Manny, she is a manifestation of the Goddess."

"Okay," Manny had said, deciding to be proactive with the female energy he'd felt coming at him. "And she's waiting to be discovered?

Like a movie star?"

"She's not waiting for *nothin'*," Reina had replied. "She's making herself apparent."

Manny had never shown any disrespect to the Virgin. He'd been raised Catholic. The priest had bent over him long ago and told him that the Virgin of Guadalupe was not an Indian appearing as the Virgin, but the Virgin appearing as an Indian. Even as a boy, Manny figured this Juan Diego was having a dream. Later, when he was playing football in high school and smoking a little marijuana, along with drinking a fair amount of beer on the weekends, Aguilar decided Juan Diego was probably just stoned.

Reina would put skulls on the altars, too. Large skulls, made by artists and artisans, and small skulls made of sugar, which were given out at Mexican celebrations of the Day of the Dead. She hung tin images of skeletons dressed in the styles of people living life, standing in the attitudes of the living, couples dancing, or dining out. She explained to Manny that she didn't find the Day of the Dead a particularly dark celebration at all. She said she found it comforting, and even hilarious, depending on her mood.

When she was home, scented candles were almost always burning. Her lair smelled like vanilla, like rose petal, like something called ylang-ylang. Or it smelled like pear, cinnamon, lavender or pumpkin, depending. Depending on Reina.

And there were other things about the place, and about Reina in the place.

Manny kept seeing the living room walls change colors. They went from rose pink to a kind of beige. Then they'd go sage green and purple and the tints were not really like anything Manny had seen before. He'd looked for the colored lights at first, as he had in church as a boy, discovering the one that illuminated Jesus on the cross. After awhile, in Reina's house, he'd given up looking for the lights.

Once, when he went in the spare bedroom without turning on the light in there, he felt wind and he heard Reina's voice speaking in Spanish. Reina didn't speak Spanish.

"Reina," Manny said one night when they were lying together and she was about to go off to sleep, "what color did you paint the walls out there in the living room?"

"Ohh," Reina said sleepily. "The walls." She'd opened her large green eyes and stared across the room. "Busted," she said.

Manny was up on one elbow then, leaning forward so he could watch her face. What the hell, he thought, is she going to say now? What the hell does she mean "busted?" Does she sneak around and repaint the walls or what?

"I dreamed most of this place," Reina told him. "It started when I dreamed and I designed it so that I could remember my dreams. I dreamed some of the colors I painted. I've seen you look at the living room walls and I have a theory about why the colors change in there. I think my dreams like what I've done—but, you know, I think they find it a little strange...."

Don't do it, Manny thought to himself. Don't laugh. She's serious. Start laughing and you'll never make it out of this bedroom alive, let alone get laid anytime soon.

Reina kept talking. "I think this place moves in itself because it has been actualized by dreams, and that the dreams, and whatever moves inside them, are at work here, taking delight in this house, trying to understand why it is so familiar, even though it exists as something from their own sleep. Now that's just a guess, a bit of fancy. But it is the dreams, trying to understand my house; and me, designing to actualize my dreams, that causes these side effects, changes in colors and things, and causes you a little, well, consternation, Manny. Here in this house, my dreams and I go back and forth. We're more proximal here than in your normal household. More like family. Have I said too much? I hope not."

She hadn't looked at him. She'd continued to stare across the room, the room where there was always a little light from outside and the trees out there wrote Japanese characters on her wall with their shadows.

No, he'd thought, but you've said enough to make me think you're crazy. Enough to make him walk out of there before she came unglued some night and he woke up with a butcher knife in his chest. The trouble was, even as he said that to himself, he knew it'd never happen.

"Well," he said to her, "you said a mouthful."

"I know." She stared down at the bed, hair in her eyes.

Now she's sad, Manny thought. She might be thinking he would leave her. Or thinking that she should never talk to him this way again—never tell him her version of reality again because she'd be afraid he would leave her out of fear—or disgust—or both. But he wasn't buying into this stuff. He couldn't let her get away with it.

"What am I supposed to think?" he asked her.

"Maybe you're supposed to think I'm crazy," she said evenly.

"Wouldn't you think I was crazy if I told you that reality was different in my house and clocks walked around on legs, or—"

Reina had burst out laughing and tried to stop by stuffing her knuckles in her mouth. It hadn't worked.

"What, Reina?"

"Clocks on legs. Ohhh, that's—" she convulsed in laughter, then stopped. "I'm sorry, Manny. I am. You and I have experienced inter-subjectivity. We both see colors on the walls—we're both—"

"Having the same hallucination?"

"Yes, the same recurring hallucination. I've told you how mine got there as best I could. It means a lot to me that we have the same, well, the same hallucination. There's more to the mind and the universe than we know, that's all. There's a reason we see colors on the walls. Have you been harmed by them? Do you feel threatened?"

"Yeah, there are colors flying all over the walls and you think it's funny."

"What does your intuition say about it?"

"The colors are crazy—they shouldn't be there."

"What does your intuition say about me?" Reina said softly.

"You're okay…"

"If you want to take some time with this—"

"Don't talk down to me." His eyes looked like gun barrels. "And don't provoke me."

She hung her head and her voice was small but steady. "I didn't mean to. It took courage to ask you what you thought of me. I misspoke. I know you…know your own mind. I didn't mean to try to manage you, or condescend to you—"

"Reina, you think it didn't take courage for me to ask you about the goddammed walls? Do I have to hallucinate to love you? Jesus Christ. If you were crazy or dangerous I'd already know it and I'd already be gone. You're kind and loving and you're beautiful. Okay…if the goddammed walls change colors—if I'm living in your dream and this house is dreaming some damn dream of its own—it's—it's better than what I see out there every day. Yeah, I need some time to get used to it, but maybe I'm used to it already. So we might as well go to sleep so we can get the hell up and go to work tomorrow."

That had been the biggest fight they'd had that first year. By the second year he'd been in Reina's life, he'd gotten to like the walls.

Reina had two bedrooms in her house and not enough closet space, a problem compounded by a weakness for clothes. Perennially cheap, he was glad he wasn't paying the bills.

"I always like being here," Manny told her, when they came into her place that night after the *quinceanera*. "You have good taste."

"That's one thing I like about you, Manny," Reina said. "You appreciate good taste—as it's in somebody else's house."

"Are you going to start about my chair and the rest of the stuff in my place?" Manny asked.

"Manny, you know, that chair...Your cat won't even sit in that chair."

"That's because he knows it's my chair," Manny said.

"One thing I need to mention," Reina said, looking Manny in the eye. "I doubt that even someone as mentally challenged as a male human being would miss this, and I know a woman never would. You left the church today in a black suit and came back in a pair of black Dockers and a different shirt."

"Yeah," Manny said, "but I still got my Justin Roper boots and the same gun."

"Well, Manny," Reina said, "I've seen men do a lot of stupid things, and I hope you don't have a death wish when it comes to this relationship."

"Reina, dammit, I don't. I had to take down a nut today." He told her about the kid at the pay phone.

"Fine, Manny," Reina said. "There's one more thing. I want to be with you. I want you alive. You're putting yourself in danger. You haven't said much about this, but I know your leaving the church today has to do with this one case, with the Harper guy. Why don't you back off? You're scarin' me."

Manny mentally thanked a couple of saints that he'd kept his mouth shut to Reina about getting shot at that day. He told her he was not in any danger and that the Harper case was becoming low priority for law enforcement, and that it would probably be shelved as just another unsolved murder.

Even if he wanted to back off the case now, he couldn't. It was starting to look like people were coming after him and those people might not leave him alone. The thought came again. It was almost as if that shooter had missed him on purpose—fired a warning shot at him. Maybe the message was: Keep looking for Tony Cisneros and this Rico character and you'll get shot for real.

But there was another problem for Manuel Aguilar. He had to live with himself. If he stopped doing his job because there might be an assassin after him, he might as well have never been a cop. Manny did the only thing he could do. He made love to Reina and told her how much he loved her. He could carry this burden in silence and he could face the possibility of his own death and he could communicate to

Reina and to his family that he loved them very much. That was all, he realized, finally, that he could do.

Manny's last thought, before he went to sleep, lying sideways with one arm draped over Reina, was that it had been one king-hell bitch of a Saturday.

CHAPTER FIFTEEN

AT NINE O'CLOCK the next morning, Manny was sitting thigh to thigh with Reina on her couch. Their legs were propped up on the coffee table and they were reading the Sunday paper.

"Hey," Reina said suddenly, giving Manny a dig with her elbow. "What do you think of this furniture?"

"It's nice," Manny said, hoping to go back to the paper.

"Know how I got this furniture?"

"Know how good the Dallas Cowboys are doing this year?"

"You're going to hear about the furniture," Reina said.

"Why now?"

"Because," Reina said, "I have the time to tell you a long story and the story of this furniture is a *historia larga*."

"Okay," Manny said. "It's nice furniture. Tell me about it."

"Well, Manny, the coffee table that we have under our feet dates from the 1930's and my aunt, who lived and died in LA, had it imported from Denmark. All of this furniture is 1930's and '40's originals. My oldest brother, Terry—"

"The gay antique collector?"

"Well, yeah, Manny, he was both of those things and he was a very successful commercial artist. And I doubt he ever cared about the Dallas Cowboys. Shut up and let me tell this story."

Manny looked at her and waited.

"When he met Taylor, the man who would be his longtime companion, my brother gave the furniture to my oldest sister, who was in nursing school. Taylor, you see, had a huge antique collection and that made my brother's stuff kind of redundant around there."

Reina looked pointedly at Manny to see if he was listening. Manny met her gaze and nodded, hoping she'd relax and tell him the story so he could get back to the paper.

"So," Reina went on, "when I got divorced—"

"From Elvin Strayhorn, the coke dealer?"

"Yeah, Manny, from Elvin Strayhorn the coke dealer."

"Successful coke dealer, too," Manny said. "Right up until the time he got busted by the DEA."

"We live and learn, Manny," Reina said.

"Some of us learn quicker than others, Reina."

"Shut up, I'm on the right side of the law now, Manny, and Strayhorn was always going to get financed with his deals and go into straight business. His dad was a banker for Crissake, I thought—"

"I know, you thought he'd change." Manny struggled to keep from laughing.

"Yeah. I did. Thank you for that kind insight, even though you're just making a mean joke. And I know what else you're thinking and you're right, Manny. I liked the money, okay? Those were different times. You know damn well I started divorcing him before he got busted because he was no good and his drugs were no good. I look back on it and shiver, so enjoy your little cop victory here, okay?"

"So Strayhorn went to jail and then what?"

"And then I had two kids to take care of and no money to exercise my good taste. And, at that point, my sister gave me this furniture."

"We bounced off each other somewhere in there, too." Manny said.

"We were both too wild and hurt to make a go of it, weren't we?"

"Guess so."

"Well, don't you think so? I was just stressed. I had two kids, I had to make it. I wasn't long out of that relationship with Strayhorn. You were just out of the Army. You were wild and spooky from that, I guess. I was learning to stay away from alcohol and you seemed to like the stuff then more than you do now. What happened with you? You wouldn't talk about something—I mean, when you talked about the military there was always something you were leaving out. It seems that way to me. What was it?"

"I worked with codes," Manny said. "I spent a lot of time sitting around in rooms working with codes. Picking up coded information, sending out coded information. One time I heard something and I let the brass know. They had me send a reply back and some people got killed that shouldn't have been killed. It wouldn't be smart to say any more than that, even now. If I did, I wouldn't be a cop for long. And, given the kind of people I worked for, I might not be around for long. I like what I do now. I look for murderers and the people I bring to jail need to be there. The people I've caught were guilty. I've been sure of that in every murder case I've ever worked."

"Does a man good, huh?" Reina said, grinning.

"Yeah," Manny said, "it does. That and the sports page."

"Were you hoping I'd forgotten about the furniture?"

"I was hoping."

"Well, I haven't. When I moved back here from the coast I gave the furniture to Arturo."

"Who's Arturo?"

"My oldest brother's son. Terry was the oldest. He caught hell. My grandfather, that mean old Castilian, sent him to a private boarding school. Terry could joke about it later. He said the headmaster and the rest of these religious homophobes got word Terry was keeping company with certain types and coming back from the woods with grass stains on his knees. So they pull him in and give him this intensive counseling and convince him he's not gay. Then he gets married, has a son he loves very much, and gets divorced because he's gay. Not an unusual story."

"Okay," Manny said, trying to look like he cared.

"And don't try to look like you care," Reina said. "Well, anyway, years later my kids moved out of the house and I began to miss the furniture. I bought it back from Arturo and now here we sit, Manny."

"Up to our butts in furniture history," Manny said.

"Yeah, in a manner of speaking," Reina replied. "And you damn well better appreciate it."

"I do," Manny said.

"Well go ahead, read your paper," Reina said.

Manny checked the paper, hoping his name hadn't come up in the Vistoso neighborhood drive-by shooting. It had. Manny started getting mentally ready to tell Reina what really went on after he left her at the *quinceanera*. The death of Emily Johnson in the Vistoso neighborhood was news. Drive-by shootings still sold newspapers, even though they had been going on for years, particularly in urban areas of Southern California.

Reina glanced at Manny's section of the paper.

"Another drive-by?" she said, wondering why she'd perceived a very subtle tension in Manny when he'd rather ponderously read over the drive-by article.

"Yeah, at least it's not as bad as California," Manny said, repeating an old Arizona adage.

"What's wrong with California, Manny?" Reina said. "They got Mickey Mouse over there. We Hispanics like Mickey Mouse."

"Shut up, Reina," Manny said, "or I'll spank your big *guera* butt. You're only half Hispanic, anyway."

"Always with the promises," Reina said.

Manny shifted on the couch and grabbed for Reina's hips while she grinned and gritted her teeth, shoved the newspaper in his face, and tried to kick him.

The phone rang, spoiling what had been turning into a very good morning, and spoiling it even more when Rogers' voice came through the answering machine. He sounded scared and apologetic. Damn right, Manny thought, as he picked up the phone, you better be concerned about my welfare, you crazy bastard.

"Manny, you okay?" Rogers said.

"Yeah, considering. We need to talk about this. I'll call you back. We'll set up a meet."

When Manny hung up and turned to Reina. She gave him a sour look.

"Randy Rogers," she said, "the rock and roll narcotics cop. He lies on the witness stand and he assaults suspects whenever he can get away with it. Jeff's had a showdown or two in court with him."

"Jeff?" Manny asked, pretending ignorance.

"Yeah, Jeff Goldman, my employer, the criminal defense attorney—you goofball."

"You mean the dope lawyer with the pony tail," Manny said, happy to have an opportunity to bait his lover. "So what?"

"If you're cooking up a deal with Randy Rogers, I'm suspicious."

"You're suspicious anyway, Reina," Manny said.

"I pretty much have to be," Reina said, holding up the paper with the drive-by article. It hadn't been any challenge for her to glance at the open paper and see that Manuel Aguilar, a Pima County Sheriff Detective, was involved.

Manny confessed and apologized while managing to withhold his real reason for being in the Vistoso.

Reina kept the lecture short. "You wouldn't like it if somebody shot at me and you had to read about it in the newspapers. Think about it—Dammit." Then she let it drop.

They took a nap together. It had been another long week. Tomorrow would be another Monday.

The next morning Manny called in to the office. Daryl Trainor answered the phone and Manny told him he'd be an hour or so late. Then Manny headed for the Downtown Division to meet with Rogers.

"How are you, man?" Rogers asked.

"It seems like the guy knew I was coming. What can you tell me about it?"

"Hoss, I'll tell you what I know," Rogers said, "and I'm sorry as hell.

Oh, the plate numbers you got off the shooter's car? It was stolen. We found it abandoned. The evidence techs went over it. I don't know what they got. But, anyway, I checked on the last known address of Cisneros by looking at what he put down the last time we popped him. That's all we had. Nobody would have known but me—no civilians, anyway. Somebody in here could have seen I used the computer. That's all. I'm sorry as hell, man, but that's the way it is. I didn't get that information from another junkie. It was what we had in our computer."

"You didn't bust Cisneros at his house? I thought you did."

"No. We got him in a parking lot with a lousy half pound of pot. We got information from him for that Vistoso address. We thought he was a small time dealer. He said he stayed in the Vistoso. We didn't go down there and kick in his door and look under his bed. We took him down for the dope, booked him. He was sentenced, did a little jail time. Deportation would have been automatic after that. I gave you the address we had, man, and I told you it was just the last known."

"A woman got killed, Rogers. Emily Johnson. She'd lived at that address for years—and nobody at TPD checked it out. So, you were telling me you deported Cisneros?"

"Yeah, man, didn't you know that? He's a Mexican national. He's a border rat. He sneaks in and out of Arizona all the time."

"Who took him down, Randy? You?"

"No, a street cop took him down for the dope. Nickel-dime stuff."

"What about smuggling? You said you remembered DEA had him one time for smuggling."

"Yeah," Rogers said. "I couldn't get that kind of information from them. He's never taken a fall for it and they won't give us anything they don't want to give us if something is ongoing or they suspect somebody."

"How'd you know then?" Manny asked.

"Know what?"

"About smuggling, Tony Cisneros, DEA."

"Heard his name a few months ago, DEA was asking. Like I said, I called them back, they wouldn't say jack."

"So how do you account for this shooter, Randy?"

"I know it looks like somebody knew you were coming, Manny," Rogers said, and looked as serious as Manny had ever seen him look, "but I can't give you a good answer right now. Only thing I can think is some cowboy just took a crack at you. Hey, we got premise information on dozens of kids, that's kids under eighteen, in the Vistoso, that hate cops and have guns—not to mention the adults. Every other house down there has got an alpha-henry in it—an asshole. The street cops get a call, they look at their computer, and the premise flags start popping up. Sometimes we got premise information on the house we're going to and the houses on either side. It's a dangerous neighborhood."

Manny and Randy looked at each other. Manny looked as hard at Randy as he could. Randy looked as regretful and honest as he could. It was a stalemate. They'd known each other for years. Sometimes things happen, Manny thought, and it's just nobody's fault.

"Okay, Rogers," Manny said. "Okay."

"Hey, who loves ya, man?" Rogers said. Manny thought he could actually see sweat on Rogers' brow.

"Wait a minute," Manny said, holding up his hand. "Any known associates of Tony Cisneros? Where is Tony Cisneros now?"

"I'm glad you asked me that question. I'll dig out what I can. We can question him if we can find him. Swear to God, man, I put out the word. We'll bag him in a heartbeat if he shows up anywhere."

"Get me his jacket," Manny said.

"What?"

"Get me Cisneros's records. I need his mug shot. Get me anything you can get on him."

"Okay. I'll see if I can get anything and I'll shoot by your house tonight. I'll bring the beer."

"Yeah," Manny said, "and I'd appreciate it if you didn't use the word *shoot* around me for awhile. And be real sure not to use the words *shoot by my house*."

CHAPTER SIXTEEN

MANNY CAME INTO the homicide detective's section of the sheriff's department on the Benson Highway around ten o'clock the next morning.

"The lieutenant wants to see you," Daryl said, from behind his desk. Manny could see from the look in Daryl's eyes that something was up. He walked over to the lieutenant's office and stood outside, tapping on the half open door.

The lieutenant took Manny to Captain Juvera's office. Juvera wasted no time. "What were you doing in the Vistoso neighborhood on Saturday?"

"I got an anonymous tip on a case from last year about that shooter, Carbajal," Manny lied. "The informant gave a Vistoso address and said there was a male subject there. The informant knew the guy only by his first name. The informant said the guy might be willing to talk about Carbajal. I went down there, I got shot at. That's it."

"Aguilar," Juvera said, "in a very short time period you've been involved in three shootings. I'll say it again: three shootings. One took the lives of three bad guys. It was justified, but it was a high profile incident. It happened during daylight hours in the parking lot of a hospital full of people. Bullets were flying all over the place.

"In that incident, you said you were there on another matter. You noticed Granger, lying on a gurney, and we know what happened next. I am not making an accusation here, but this department needs to revisit our investigation of that shooting.

"Now it's Monday morning. Let's look at how your weekend went. On Saturday you were the apparent target during a shooting where a female bystander was killed—a church member and a caretaker who never hurt anybody in her life—and known in both her church and her community as such. Looks like you took Sunday off," Juvera paused and sat back, watching him, "because I haven't gotten any hysterical calls about what an asshole you were on Sunday."

Manny shifted in his chair and waited for more.

"But wait, there's more," Juvera said. He leaned forward and started up again. "You and Detective Trainor were recently reprimanded for returning fire received from a building, the occupants thereof being unknown at the time. That action was further complicated by the fact that you and Trainor could have retreated, but you opened fire instead. Detective Aguilar, the sheriff's department is dealing, right now, with a lot of negative perception—the perception being that you, the detective involved in all these incidents, must be doing something wrong and the department must be allowing you to do wrong.

"The city councilperson from Ward 5, for example, is expressing concern regarding your weekend incident—that's the latest kick in the ass for this department. He was on my phone at 8:01 this morning. You are a good detective, but you've created a big problem, and I will also tell you that information has come to us indicating you may have been acting on your own agenda in these shooting incidents. It may not be accurate or complete information. We will investigate and make a determination. Meanwhile, you are suspended. We will be in touch with you. Do you understand?"

"I understand," Manny said, "and how would you get information that I've been acting on my own agenda in three separate and unrelated incidents and why would you believe it if somebody told you that?"

"You're not doing yourself any good here, Manny," the lieutenant said.

"You people aren't doing so well, either—unless you count walking around without having a spine as a good thing."

Juvera leaned forward across his desk. "Lieutenant, escort Detective Aguilar out."

Manny blew out of the room and walked down the hall, radiating enough rage to send people scurrying to get out of his way.

That evening, just as the sun was going down, Manny saw Randy Rogers' blue corvette turn off the street and glide into his driveway.

Manny opened the side door of his house and Rogers walked in with a smile and a six-pack of longnecks. Rogers averted his eyes from Grayboy's stare. As he did so, he noticed a trail of feathers running through the house. Manny and his cats, Rogers thought. It's goofy.

Rogers had never seen a cat like Grayboy. Grayboy was not afraid of anybody who came into Manny's house. Instead, the cat sat on his haunches and stared people right in the eye. It was clear to Rogers that the cat didn't necessarily know what was going on with people. Grayboy just thought of himself as people, as near as Rogers could tell. Rogers always wanted to stomp his feet and hiss at Grayboy to see what he'd do, but he knew how Manny felt about his damn cats. Manny always had cats, even in high school. It always made Rogers laugh a little, seeing this big serious guy, who played football and never showed too much emotion, out in back of his parents' house, wearing a letterman's sweater and feeding his cats.

Rogers took a seat on the couch and propped up his boots on the half dead coffee table. He twisted the cap off of a beer and tossed it into an ashtray. Manny returned from the kitchen with a glass, sat down in his green club chair, poured a beer, and put the glass on the table. Rogers sensed movement and realized that Grayboy had jumped up on the far end of the couch. Grayboy stared past Rogers. Rogers followed the cat's gaze, which seemed to be fixed on Manny's still untouched beer glass.

"What's with your cat?" Rogers asked.

"He watches the bubbles," Manny said.

"Whaddaya mean?"

"He watches the bubbles in beer glasses. He watches the bubbles in soda and seltzer glasses, too."

Rogers rolled his eyes at the ceiling. "Bet the two of you have a lot of fun around here at night, huh? Just watchin' the bubbles. If I didn't know you had a day job and a redheaded girlfriend that was built for speed, I'd tell you to get yourself a life, man." Rogers grinned and tipped his bottle up while Manny smiled slightly.

"I don't think I have that day job anymore," Manny said. Keep the rage in, he said to himself, don't start whining and don't start punching walls. Stay in control of yourself and you get respect from other people.

Rogers sprayed a mouthful of beer across the room. "What?" Grayboy gave Rogers a disgusted look and went back to watching the bubbles in Manny's glass.

"They suspended me. I've been making a lot of waves."

"Yeah," Rogers said, "politics is what it is. Did they say when they'd let you know their decision?"

"No."

"What are you going to do—worst case scenario?"

"Get a PI license, if I have to," Manny said. "Have you got that folder on Cisneros?"

"Yeah. I copied what we had. I left it in the car. You still want it?"

"I do," Manny said, "because, when I'm not doing what PIs do, I'm going to be looking to clear my name. There's a reason three guys tried to kidnap Granger. And there is a reason Perez and Granger were afraid. And that guy, Corral, he's dead, too. All of them were associated with Harper."

"Perez?" Rogers said. "You don't believe that jive about the governor or whatever the hell it was, do you? Come on, Manny. Perez killed Harper. Perez overdosed in jail. That's it."

"I don't know what to believe. Right now, I want to know about Rico. I want to know about Cisneros."

"Yeah," Rogers said, "but what's to say Granger wasn't lying as he was dying. Or just saying whatever came into his head. You got this Harper, he's a drunk. And you've got Perez, who's a liar. But then you got Granger, who says he's scared and talks about dealers. I don't know why anybody would try to kidnap a punk like Granger, but Granger and Perez probably killed Harper and then Granger just got crosswise with the wrong people—maybe he didn't pay his drug bill. Maybe he stole dope from some big boys."

"Maybe," Manny said. "So what have you got in that folder?"

Reina called just after Rogers left. "Manuel, I love you," she said, after she heard he'd been suspended and that he expected to be fired, "but you got a head like a rock. You're honest, Manny. You're stubborn and you're honest. If you had to stay on the Harper case, then there must be something to it. I'd rather you got the hell off it, but that has to be up to you. I love you. I believe in you. You get a PI license and I'll get some kind of work for you with Jeff. There's work here."

"I would hesitate to work for your boss," Manny said. "I have nothing against dope lawyers. But I have as little to do with the war on drugs as possible—unless there's a murder involved."

"Jeff works for the victims, Manny, for the users, for the small time dealers. What did we both do when we were kids, Manny?"

"You were never a kid, Reina. You were eighteen when you were fifteen and your boss defends some bad people."

"Manny," Reina said, "what did we do?"

"We smoked pot," Manny said. "So what?"

"The point is that we all experimented with dope. I became addicted to alcohol, as bad a drug as any, maybe the worst, but that was okay with the law because alcohol is legal. Anyway, we all grew up and we don't do that anymore. I love you, Manny, I do. We both know the drug wars are a joke, and I know you wouldn't be happy doing a lot of things that PIs do, but you have everything to lose by being a stuffed shirt about doing investigations to defend ordinary people who are arrested in these idiotic drug wars."

"So I go to work for a dope lawyer named Jeffrey who wears a pony tail, is that it?"

He knew it was stupid pride. He knew he was raging because he didn't want to lose face by accepting charity from his brainy girlfriend and her boss. He felt like a fool as soon as the words came out, but he was a homicide investigator, not a little creep who snooped around, trying to defend kids who got caught with dope.

"Jeff has a murder case he's working on now," Reina said, "and the kid who supposedly did it is, we believe, innocent beyond a reasonable doubt. The system can fail people, Manny. It's not just defending dopers. That's just one kind of case we get. I know how smart you are. I know you never quit and I know you led the way in solving a lot of homicides. If you want, you can help us solve this one."

She's smart, that Reina, Manny thought. Always knows the right words. She's got heart. Manny had talked to his share of women who always knew the right words. This time, he knew he had somebody who cared about him, had her own life together, and meant what she said. He could fall back on his habitual, macho lawman's distrust and pride or he could believe the evidence. The evidence, he knew, pointed to Manny and Reina being a solid pair. The job she offered was at least a start.

The next morning, Manny had coffee and went through the house with a broom and a dustpan, cleaning up a trail of feathers. He was always in the mood to look for evidence and the evidence in this case suggested that Grayboy had gotten into an altercation with a mockingbird. The mockingbird probably started it by dive bombing the cat in the back yard. The cat must have jumped and knocked the bird down before it could climb out of range. Looking at the crime scene, Manny decided that the two of them had fought each other from the rear window in the kitchen to the front window of the living room, at which point the mockingbird had escaped to parts unknown.

Manny dumped the feathers in the wastebasket under the sink and had a look around the house for Grayboy. He found him in the bedroom, mangling a lizard. Manny pried the lizard out of the growling cat's jaws and carried it outside. Grayboy followed, now silent and intent. He jumped on the lizard again as soon as Manny pitched its body into the backyard.

Manny got in his truck and drove down to the Department of Public Safety offices on Valencia Road where he picked up an application for a private investigator's license.

An hour later he was back at his house, filling out the application and looking at the state statutes which outlined the responsibilities of a PI. Manny cursed softly about the application fee and the bond, which was several thousand dollars.

He swept his eyes over the laundry list of responsibilities for a PI. He must, on demand, divulge any information acquired as to a criminal offense to the proper authorities.

"Yeah, but I won't play by those rules," Manny said aloud. Grayboy, who was sitting on Manny's battered file cabinet, stared at him expectantly.

Private investigators were not supposed to impersonate a sworn law enforcement officer. Forget that, Manny thought. He would impersonate whoever he had to impersonate. Then there was the rule about not assaulting anyone, kidnapping anyone, or using force or violence. But Manny had less to lose now. He expected to be fired from a job he'd done for sixteen years and the people responsible for what had happened in the Harper case would not be allowed to walk away when he found them. They would either come in or he would carry them in, dead or alive. He sat back and thought about all of it.

He knew Harper's room was searched by somebody who hoped nobody would notice. Perez made accusations, and then he supposedly overdosed in Pima County jail. Paco Corral died of an apparent overdose. Then the goons came for Granger at the hospital. But Harper's killing may not have been connected with that. It was time to concentrate on Granger. There was nothing to do but keep looking.

Manny called the sheriff's department and asked them to send a summary of his experience, on department letterhead, to DPS for verification leading to approval for a PI license. He knew that being fired for not staying off a case was not grounds to deny him a PI license in Arizona. He hadn't done anything criminal.

The phone rang a few minutes later. Captain Juvera claimed it gave him no pleasure to say that the review board had concluded its investigation and recommended dismissal. Manny could come down sometime during the week and complete some necessary paperwork. He could appeal if he wished.

"Don't waste my time," Manny said. He slammed the phone down, spun around, and punched a hole in the living room wall.

Afterward, he bandaged his hand so he didn't bleed on the PI paperwork. But it was worth it, he decided. He felt better. He would fix the wall later, hopefully before Reina noticed.

He finished the application, wrote a check for the fee the DPS needed, and called a bonding company to start the bonding process. Then it was time to go to Jeff Goldman's office and get oriented for the new job.

CHAPTER SEVENTEEN

GOLDMAN DID BUSINESS from a nondescript white bungalow in the West University Neighborhood of central Tucson. Manny knew Jeff had practiced criminal law for a dozen years and that he'd graduated from the University of Arizona law school. When Reina brought him into Goldman's office the lawyer was leaning back in his chair with his feet on the desk, reading a file.

Goldman unfolded himself from his chair and rose to shake Manny's hand. Manny reflexively estimated Goldman's height. Six feet. The guy was lean. Either he's in shape or he doesn't eat much, Manny thought. Handsome, angular face, dark eyes. And there's the ponytail. Going gray—maybe defending the guilty gives you gray hair.

"Mr. Aguilar, pleased to meet you," Jeff said.

"Call him Manny," Reina said, and left the room to go back to work.

"Manny, we've got a kid from the south side we're defending on a murder charge. Reina told you?"

"Yes."

Jeff turned so quick his ponytail whipped sideways. He pulled a file from a small cabinet by his desk. Then he sat and opened the file, talking with his head down while he scanned the text.

"TPD tagged this kid, based on a description of the suspect's car. And, by the way, this is about a drive-by on South 12th Avenue, three days ago. Remember that from the papers?"

Manny nodded.

"The deal is our guy, Larry Armenta, was driving the car. He tells me he had a passenger, who's older, some idiot in his thirties who's hanging around with kids. Larry says the older guy pulled the trigger, just for kicks." Goldman looked down at the file and started reading silently to himself.

Manny waited.

"Is our boy Larry a good guy?" Jeff said, finally. "He's neither good nor bad. I've only interviewed his parents on the phone, but they say he dropped out of high school and was working on getting a job when this happened. He was living with his parents. When I talk to him, I see a normal kid—maybe not the sharpest tool in the shed, but who cares. Thing is, he just turned eighteen so he gets tried as an adult. The other guy, our shooter, supposedly bailed out of the car after it happened. Larry knew him as Tito. I do a lot of my own investigative work, but I don't want to look for this Tito myself. I don't have time. Do you want to do the investigation?"

Manny said he did.

"You want to talk to the kid, don't you?" Jeff asked and didn't wait for a response. "He's in county jail. I'll call them and tell them you're coming down. They love me a lot down there." Goldman grinned.

Manny nodded. Drug lawyer with a pony tail. They love him at county.

"Want to read the file first? You want to read the file first." Jeff handed the file across the desk. Goldman's funny—to a point, Manny thought.

"Oh, and pay," Jeff added. "Twenty dollars an hour to start and compensation for expenses—within reason."

"What?"

"Hey, it's your first job," Jeff said.

Manny picked up the file and started out the door.

"And Manny," Jeff said, grinning and holding up a finger. "Thank God for reasonable doubt."

Manny just looked at him and left the room. Reasonable doubt, the cornerstone for criminal defense lawyers. Spin a web of reasonable doubt and bad guys get back on the streets. Roll with it, Manny told himself. He'd already punched one wall today, punching a lawyer wouldn't help.

Reina winked as Manny passed her workstation. He read the file in Goldman's lobby and checked back with Jeff to make sure he'd be able to see Larry Armenta. Then he drove to the jail, a six story high rise on the west side of town near a sand channel that people still called the Santa Cruz River.

Larry Armenta was a bony kid who came off as sulky, probably because he was young and scared and, in the shuffle of life, Manny guessed, nobody had taken the trouble to convince him not to be a punk.

"How did you know Tito?" Manny asked, resting his elbows on the table in the interview room provided by the good folks at the county jail.

"Just around, you know," Larry said, looking down at his orange jailhouse flip-flops.

"Where'd you meet him?

Armenta kept looking at the flip-flops. "I met him at a friend's house."

"What friend?"

Larry looked up, angry now. "It don't matter, I told Jeff all this anyway."

"Why doesn't it matter?" Manny asked.

"I don't want my friend to get involved."

"Okay," Manny said. "You spend a long time in jail to protect your friend. You are eighteen years old. They're going to try you as an adult. You will go to state prison and you will get hurt, maybe killed. Was this was the first time you'd met Tito? What were you doing when this happened?"

"I took him to a liquor store, he bought some beers."

"And you rode around together and drank them?"

"Yeah."

"And then this shooting happened. If your friend knows more about Tito, I need to talk to your friend. We're not after your friend, we're after this guy you call Tito, and we can save your ass—or not. Why take a murder rap because you won't let us find out who the killer is? Why not tell us about your friend? If he didn't do it, he's got nothing to worry about."

"Hey," the kid said, "my friend don't know the guy neither."

"Why was Tito there?"

"Just hanging out. I told Jeff."

"I don't believe that, Larry. You've been in this jail, what? Two days? You don't get the picture. We find this Tito or you grow old in the state prison up in Florence. It's not a nice place. For one thing, they don't have air conditioning in the cells up there. Summers are a bitch. But that's going to be the least of your worries because prisoners get away with assaults and rapes up there and you're a good looking young guy. How do they say it? Oh yeah, I remember: It's gonna' *suck* to be you in Florence, Larry."

"I don't know nothing."

Manny leaned into the kid's face. "Listen to me. I am going to talk to your parents and your friends. I will find out who you are protecting and why. I've got the time to do it. The Tucson Police do not. Neither does your attorney. I do. I'm going to be all over your parents and all over your friends until somebody tells me something."

Larry started shaking. "Okay, if I tell you why I was with him you won't tell nobody?"

"That depends. Why were you with him?"

"I'm like, bi, okay? My parents don't know. I was trying to get some beers and I see Tito. We—he knows I'm like that. I know he's gay. We just know. He's older, he buys the beers. Then we're going to ride around some and then—you know. Don't tell my parents. There ain't no friends I'm protecting. My parents would kick me out if they knew. It's a sin. I can't even tell it in Confession. I got a girlfriend. Everybody thinks I'm straight." Armenta put his head in his hands and looked down at the jailhouse floor.

"I don't think your parents or your friends need to know that you're bi," Manny said. "We'll look for this Tito guy. We'll work to prove your innocence, now that you let us do it. I need to hear one thing one more time. Do you swear you do not know Tito? Can you tell me with complete honesty that you never saw him before?"

"No, I never saw him before. I swear."

"Would you recognize Tito if you saw his picture?"

"Yeah, but Jeff showed me some pictures and he ain't there."

"Where, in the mug shots?"

"Yeah, he ain't there."

Manny already knew that. Jeff had the arrest report from TPD and Manny had called their detectives before he talked to Larry. Armenta had looked at a lot of mug shots under the kindly direction of the Tucson Police. He claimed to recognize no one. No Tito. TPD could only believe that Larry Armenta was a liar and charge him with murder.

"Okay. Maybe we find out what Tito looks like first."

"I can tell you what he looks like," the kid said.

"Yes," Manny said patiently, "but we're going draw a picture. I'm going to get an artist down here. You tell him what Tito looks like and he'll draw us a picture. Got it? And one more thing, Larry. Your arrest report didn't say anything about alcohol, either in your blood or in the car. What happened to the beer?"

"We'd just got them beers when Tito shot…when he shot that guy. I shoved them beers out of the car and took off."

CHAPTER EIGHTEEN

"HELLO." HAMILTON'S VOICE sounded like it always did. The voice wanted whoever was calling to get to the point. The voice had done its part, it had answered the phone. The caller could state his business and then the voice could get back to its own business and the sooner the better.

"Bill Hamilton?"

"Who is this?"

"Bill, this is Manuel Aguilar."

"Deputy Dawg," the voice said. Manny said nothing.

"Deputy Man Well. Zorro," the voice went on. "The only thing standin' between us and them."

"I need an artist," Aguilar said.

"You got police artists."

"There will be pay involved here," Manny said.

"Manny, do you know what I'm doing right now?"

"No," Manny said, knowing he might as well listen to whatever Hamilton was going to say next.

"I'm drawing. And my back is screwed up from moving furniture, which I do for a living, so I'm taking pain pills, which don't even get me high, and I'm wondering why you and Rogers and all the other people I used to get high with went straight and turned into cops and firemen and bureaucrats."

"I want to hire you. I need you to listen to a kid's description and do a drawing."

"Why?" Bill asked.

"The guy I want you to draw killed somebody. I can't get a police artist because I'm a private investigator now. I got fired from the sheriff's department."

"For what?"

"For shooting too many people."

"You shot some people?"

"Yeah, it's been all over the news."

"I don't watch the news. Gives me bad dreams. I'm sorry you got fired, but I'll still like you even though you're not a cop anymore. What are you payin' me?"

"It pays two hundred dollars. So I'll pick you up and we'll go there."

"Where we going?"

"County jail."

"Jail. I already been in jail. I don't want to go to jail."

"It's nicer than it used to be," Manny said. "See you in a couple minutes."

CHAPTER NINETEEN

MANNY PULLED HIS truck to the curb on a side street in Tucson's Pie Allen neighborhood, named after a former Tucson mayor who sold pies to the US cavalry in the 1870s. The Bar Nine was just down the street. So was the junkie house.

Manny walked up Hamilton's cement steps and knocked. Roaring barks began inside and something big and heavy started banging around on the other side of the door. Then Manny heard Hamilton yelling, "Shut up, Sally. Shut up. Get back there." The barking and banging noises subsided.

Hamilton jerked the door open and Manny was looking up at a huge, bearded man, staring down at him through tortoise shell glasses.

"Get in here," Hamilton said, "so the dog can eat ya. She's hungry, ain't had a cop to eat in about a week. You still like cats? She'd eat you just for the way you smell if you smell like cats." The huge man laughed.

Manny stepped inside. The Rottweiler, Sally, was a friendly, quivering meatloaf of a dog that plowed under Manny's legs, looking for affection. Manny danced with her, more or less staggering across the living room and into Bill's studio.

"I been workin' on this for awhile," Bill said, pointing at a pen and ink drawing of palm fronds and Prussian soldiers in spiked helmets. Adolf Hitler and Jesus Christ were in there, too. Bill opened the drawer in his drawing table and picked up some pencils lying next to a blue steel Smith and Wesson. Then he reached for a sketchpad.

Whatever it is that Hamilton does he never quits, Manny thought. He sees something other people don't.

Two hours later, in the county jail, Larry Armenta and Hamilton were admiring their work.

"This is the ugliest Mexican I've ever seen, Larry," Bill Hamilton said loudly, looking at the finished sketch of Tito. "He's even uglier than Manny." The two collaborators looked at Manny and laughed.

Manny looked at the drawing. It showed a man with a cruel face and a shaved head. The guy looked familiar.

After he checked out of the jail and dropped off Hamilton, Manny sat in his truck and got out the folder Rogers had given him. He compared Tony Cisneros's mugshot with Hamilton's drawing. The guy in the mugshot had short hair. Manny covered the top of the head with his hand, comparing the faces. It was the same guy. Adrenaline started zipping through Manny's body.

Tony Cisneros, small time dope dealer, purported smuggler, named by a dying junkie, David Granger, and verified as to his criminal record by Randall Rogers. Tony Cisneros yet again, drive-by shooter, known to young Larry Armenta as "Tito." Did Cisneros lack judgment? Was he crazy enough to mix business with pleasure and do a hit on somebody while riding around with a kid he'd just met? That's what it looked like. And, so far, it was working out for Cisneros. Larry Armenta was as good as convicted for the drive-by killing.

Whoever had ordered Granger's kidnapping might well be happy, now that Granger was dead—and that must have been the point: grab the junkie, kill him so he won't talk. All anybody had to do was read the papers to know Granger died in that hospital parking lot. The bad guys would think Granger died without giving up information. What if they didn't?

Manny thought about it on his way home. If he got to Cisneros, then this Rico guy—if there was a Rico—might realize that Granger had named him as well. Rico would know Manny was hunting him. Rico wouldn't like that.

Manny circled the block and looked carefully at his house before pulling into the driveway. It was something law enforcement people sometimes do. Manny hadn't done it in years.

Eladio Durango, the sheriff's department specialist in charge of interface with the government of Mexico, took Manny's call the next morning at nine. Durango listened to Manny's pitch for help in locating one Tony Cisneros, possibly known as Tito, and then said that he, Durango, knew that Manny knew that the sheriff's department wasn't in the business of helping private investigators. Manny said he needed the favor anyway. Durango bowed out of the conversation, but not before Manny reminded him that debts were owed from long ago.

Manny was getting to like being a pain in the ass after years of department politics. He'd be back for Eladio. Manny put in a call to

Detective Daryl Trainor.

"Daryl, can you get out of the office for awhile? I need to know all I can about those three guys who killed Granger."

They met in a coffee shop on Speedway Boulevard and slipped into a booth. Light danced off Daryl's bald head as he reached down, snapped open his briefcase, and dropped three files on the table.

There was a thick jacket on Marion Casey, with a long list of aliases. There was a Charles D'Angelo, with aliases listed. Both were Americans. Then, there was Bernardo Hauptmann, a Mexican citizen, formerly a member of the Federales, the Mexican national police. Manny recognized D'Angelo as the man who'd called himself Petrocelli, but it was Hauptmann who most interested him.

"This Hauptmann, he's got the right qualifications to work for a Mexican drug cartel," Manny said. "What's the department doing about these guys?"

"Nothing that I know of," Daryl said, "and there's nothing more I could find on Hauptmann. D'Angelo lived here in Tucson for a few years, moved here from New York."

"What are you saying?"

"I checked on his connections here and back east," Daryl said. "He had some Mafia associates—and a criminal record going back for years. You saw his jacket. He's been up for assault, illegal weapons possession, drugs."

Manny let some Tucson Mafia history flash through his mind, just to see if any of it could spark any reason to think the Mafia might be involved in the Granger case. The Mafia liked to launder money in Arizona and the FBI had spent a lot of time going after an old man who lived in Tucson, a Mafia boss who was known all over the country. Arizona politicians would show up for his birthday parties. Little information about the Mafia surfaced in Arizona's newspapers these days. That didn't mean they were gone.

Manny had his own information, though, and that information came from a junkie who had lied or withheld information right up until the time he was dying and no longer had anything to lose. Granger hadn't been telling Mafia stories when he was prone in a parking lot with bullet holes in his chest. He'd named Mexicans who dealt drugs.

"Do they miss me at the sheriff's department?" Manny asked Daryl.

"Yeah, they do, Manny," Daryl said. "The lieutenant and the captain know you were a good detective. Rumor has it there's a lot of politics around this."

"What do you know about the politics?"

"Word is the DPS brass started asking questions about you right after the shooting incident at Saint Mary's. I don't know why. I heard their excuse was something about the magnitude of the situation, what with three men dead—and there being a Mexican national involved. They were talking to our higher ups. Seems like they wanted you to look ugly. Nobody knows why."

"DPS, the state police. Did the State Attorney General's Office send them?"

"I don't know." Daryl said, shrugging. "They could have been sent by the governor, too, but we don't know that either."

"I owe you a favor," Manny said. "Let me know if I can ever help you with a job. Drop by, drink a beer. Thanks for bringing out the jackets on the bad guys."

"I'll drop by one of these days. You still have that cat that watches beer glasses?"

"Yeah. He's ten years old."

"Nice cat," Trainor said.

Manny drove to the West University neighborhood and parked in front of Goldman's office. He'd get Reina to go to lunch and show Goldman the drawing—without telling him the shooter was Tony Cisneros. Working his own case on Goldman's time served both Goldman and Larry Armenta. They would all benefit when he found Cisneros and put him away. His only worry was whether or not he could connect Cisneros with Granger and the three dead goons who'd tried the kidnapping.

Reina looked up from her computer when he came through the door. He looked into her green eyes and he wanted to cry. It's just stress, he thought. Three gunfights in the last month, he'd got shot, he'd killed three people—they were dead, he couldn't bring them back, even if they were scumbags. He'd gotten fired from his job. But he still felt gratitude, pure and simple. She's the light, this woman, Manny thought. She's the lamp in the window.

"Okay, I think you know the plan," Jeff Goldman said, when Manny showed him Hamilton's sketch. "Get down to TPD, try to match this drawing with a mugshot. If you get a hit, tell TPD and let them start looking. Ask them to check the jails, try to check the prisons. This freak could be in custody for something else. No hit with the police? Then beat the streets. Use the mugshot, make flyers, go to South 12th Avenue, and show them around. Find witnesses, if you can, and place this guy in the area the day of the shooting. I'm going to lunch with Judge Soto. Keep me posted."

Manny and Reina walked up University Avenue and had lunch at Gentle Ben's. They sat by a window and Manny watched the sunlight fall into Reina's eyes.

"When do I get my first domestic?" he asked her.

"What?"

"When are you and Goldman giving me a husband or wife to follow so we can see if they're having an affair?"

"You're full of it," Reina said.

"By the way," Manny said, "it's official. I got the call from the sheriff's department. They fired me."

"Oh, Manny, I'm sorry."

"It'd be a lot worse if I didn't think it would all work out. And look, Reina, I'd be in a lot worse shape if you weren't around. Thanks." He'd told her how he felt—sort of. Best he could do.

After lunch, Manny ducked into a space in Jeff's bungalow that served as a small conference room and picked up the phone. Time to put the screws on Eladio Durango.

"Eladio," Manny said, when the law enforcement bureaucrat answered his phone. "You need to talk to me."

"No I don't, Manny. You're a civilian now."

"I bailed you out when you were a homicide detective," Manny replied. "I bailed you out more than once because you weren't very smart—and you know it. If you don't talk to me, I let your wife know you got yourself a mistress right after you got promoted. I'll do it, too—since I'm a nothing but a civilian. You know which hot little deputy I'm talking about. Hang up the phone if you think I'm joking."

Durango agreed to meet, naming a chain restaurant on Speedway Boulevard.

Twenty minutes later, Manny slid into a corner booth where he could watch the whole place. He checked the reflective glass surfaces around him, using them as mirrors to see behind and to the sides. The joint was a typical *mélange* of visual pabulum, a place you couldn't describe from memory one second after you'd pushed your way out the door.

Eladio Durango walked in, wearing a suit and tie. Manny watched the tall, elegant cop make his way down the aisle. A distracted, staring waitress crashed into the stainless steel salad bar. She was a plump woman with spirit and mischief in her eyes. She slid along the salad bar as Durango passed, grinning at him, embarrassed, but bold. She laughed at herself and checked out Durango's backside at the same time. Manny looked on without smiling. Durango slipped easily into the booth.

"I'm glad you have no problem with helping me," Manny said.

"I'm glad you have no problem threatening me, Aguilar."

"Like I told you on the phone, Eladio," Manny said. "I bailed you out a dozen times when you worked homicide."

They stared at each other. Two big men with dark eyes. Manny finally broke the silence. "Do the right thing. Help me clear a case. People will get killed if you can't help." Manny looked at Durango and waited.

"I looked up your guy Cisneros," Durango said. "He's from Sonora. He is tied in with the Guadalajara drug scene and the drug scene in Nogales, Sonora. And, yes," Eladio continued, pushing ahead so he wouldn't have to listen to Manny's inevitable question, "the DEA knows about him. They have his name coming up in connection with the cartel in Guadalajara. They would like to talk to him, of course, but they have no reason to, yet, and so they are waiting.

"They believe Cisneros guards drug shipments. They also believe he gets paid to beat people, maybe kill them. He used to be a boxer. He's had some fights, done some time on the circuit. And, yes, I have checked with Mexican authorities and he has no official criminal record there, but they know he's a bad guy. He has been caught twelve times here in Arizona and returned to Mexico. Mexican police couldn't tell me his present whereabouts but they believe he's where he usually is when he's not down in Guadalajara—and that would be in Nogales. Also, he has been picked up by the Border Patrol in California. He may have connections in Tijuana. And yes, police in Nogales have agreed to call me if he turns up there. And yes," Eladio held up his hand to stop Manny from talking, "I will call you when I hear from authorities in Nogales."

"Do you have the name of somebody in Nogales I can talk to?"

"Aguilar," Durango said, "I'm not going to let this blow up in anybody's face. You don't fool around when you deal between national governments."

"I know," Manny said, "and you know all I'm asking for is somebody I can talk to in Nogales."

"No, Aguilar," Durango said. "No. I will call you if they find anything. If you go down there, you go down there on your own. I'm not putting myself in a position where I am found to be the one who told you could go down to Mexico and start asking questions. I don't want to get fired, like you."

"The way you kiss ass, Eladio? You'd never get fired, you little housecat."

Durango lit up like a kitchen match. Both men were on their feet when the waitress stuck a coffeepot between them.

"More coffee, boys?" she said, looking from one to the other. "Fresh pot, and it's decaffeinated, too."

Manny left the waitress a good tip and headed for the south side. The drive paid off. The clerk at Kippy's Liquors, on South 12th Avenue and Missouri, remembered Tony "Tito" Cisneros very well—as the rude thug who'd come in a few days ago and managed to make a lasting impression for meanness in the short time it took to buy a twelve pack. What day was that? The clerk cogitated, said it was the day of the drive-by shooting. Did the store have surveillance video? Of course. It didn't take long to find Cisneros on the tape.

Manny made Tucson Police Operations Division, Downtown, his next stop. No longer a sheriff's detective, he had to present his PI credentials and explain himself. He pretended to search mug shots and came up with Cisneros in less than ten minutes. Manny reported Cisneros as a suspect in a murder and asked TPD to put a pickup order out—not that anybody knew where Cisneros was. He wasn't in jail. TPD was happy to establish that.

Now, Manny thought, Jeff Goldman has a case to take to court, even if it isn't a strong case, and Larry Armenta has a chance of getting off. He could leave it at that, but he wanted Cisneros and there was only one way he could hunt him without walking off the job: Do a sitdown with Jeff Goldman and tell him what he learned from Eladio Durango. Come clean, tell Goldman why he personally wanted Cisneros, and tell him about Harper and Granger. Then ask Goldman to let him investigate, bring Cisneros to court, prove Armenta's story. Manny headed back to Goldman's bungalow in West University.

"I am not completely happy with your personal agenda here," Goldman said, "and I think you can understand why. I'll support your efforts to locate Cisneros because it serves our client, Larry Armenta. Keep me advised. One other thing, if you're not mistaken about how all these shootings relate to each other, you're in danger. You need to tell Reina. She's already seen you hurt physically and professionally over all this. Good luck with that. I'd advise diplomacy."

Was that sensitivity and compassion coming from Goldman? Manny had to admit that it was. Telling Reina was hard. Manny did the best he could. So did Reina.

CHAPTER TWENTY

THE BORDER IS a blade stuck between the United States and Mexico. It starts near Tijuana and ends some 2,100 miles east, around Brownsville, Texas. The border is its own country. It has its own rules.

"What is the purpose of your visit?" the Mexican cop watched Manny with large, still eyes. The cop wore a military cap and the design of it had come from Germany, a country with which Mexico had a good historical relationship. Manny always thought about Nazis when he looked at these border cops.

Manny said he was going shopping. He said it politely in Spanish. The officer's eyes softened slightly at this display of respect, but he had two more questions, and he asked them in English.

"What do you have in your truck?"

Manny told him he had nothing.

"Any guns?"

"No," Manny said. "No guns."

The officer was satisfied because he had watched Manny carefully and with a faculty highly developed in his country—an intuition so practiced it sometimes appeared to be mind reading.

Manny had gone through his truck before coming south. He'd vacuumed the interior and checked under the seats and in the glove box for as much as one stray handgun cartridge. Anybody bringing guns or ammunition into Mexico found themselves in a Mexican jail. The handguns that were visible there hung on the belts of Mexican law enforcement officers, who wore a variety of uniforms. Cops were everywhere in Nogales, Sonora. Manny watched four of them roll past on bicycles as he headed for Avenida Obregon, the busiest street in town.

He found a parking space on a side road filled with potholes and covered with a nasty, eternal paste of dust. Pieces of discarded paper lay on top of the dust. No money budgeted for street sweeping machines here.

Large buildings lined Avenida Obregon, but none looked to be over five stories high. The black, netted shapes of satellite dishes nested on rooftops, angled up expectantly towards the sky, mouths open, gathering in a vast harvest of colored images from the rich life of those who lived on television. Where the buildings met the pavement, beggars and trinket vendors sat on the sidewalks, selling chewing gum and bracelets.

Manny took a seat in Leos, a large, glassed-in coffee shop, perfect for watching the street. He ordered black coffee and waited for Hector. There was no hurry. It was ten o'clock on a Sunday morning and he had the rest of the day in front of him. He'd left Reina's home at eight. They both wanted to stay in bed with each other and then read the Sunday paper all morning, but he had his plan and she had hers.

Manny unzipped his briefcase and looked over the flyers he'd made. Bill Hamilton's drawing of Cisneros stared at him from the page. Hamilton was right. Tony Cisneros, also known as Tito, was ugly. It's not so much his face as the way he wears it, Manny thought. This guy is vicious in his soul. The eyes and mouth conspired to produce a cruel, habitual sneer. Scars split his eyebrows. His nose was small, flat, crooked. Cisneros looked fearless—a sociopath. Negative reinforcement, like jail, for instance, would not deter this man. He was wired different. The text under the picture read: *Missing. Reward.* Certain circumstances were briefly described and contact information listed. Manny had given Cisneros a new name: *Roberto Flores.*

"Hey, Manny." Hector stood there, grinning. Manny knew him through family connections and he'd shared a table with the tall, skinny accountant at the wedding of a mutual friend.

Manny grinned back and gestured to a chair. "*Sientate, por favor.* You want coffee?" Manny got the attention of a waiter and, eventually, Hector got his coffee.

"Here's the guy I'm looking for." Manny spun a flyer around and Hector took a look.

"Why would you want to find a guy like that?" Hector said. "That guy should stay lost."

"I wish he'd stay lost, too, but I'm getting paid to look. Can we take a drive around later? Maybe you could show me the police station and the newspaper offices."

After a drive and a lunch with Hector, Manny headed to police headquarters and presented his identification and his flyer to the desk sergeant.

"Why do you want this man?" the sergeant asked.

"Flores has a history of mental illness," Manny said. "He has a loving family in the United States. Roberto was in the process of getting US citizenship when he suffered a mental breakdown and disappeared. His relatives will reward anyone who can offer a tip that will lead to him."

The desk officer took the flyer and gave Manuel Aguilar a look that said: Do you really expect me to believe this story about some asshole who ran away? Don't you think I know private investigators tell lies like this all the time?

On the way back down to Avenida Obregon Manny was able to work his way into a conversation with some bicycle cops. These men were young, still excited about a career doing baby sitting for the public, but seldom came across anything really interesting, like a drug dealing murderer who was tied to organized crime. They enjoyed talking to an American cop who spoke Spanish. They were happy to take Manny's flyer. Manny told them the runaway story as if it were just his job to do so. Then he did some wink and nod body language to let them know a game was afoot. They could be part of it—and get a reward.

He stopped in bars, dull places with largely blank walls, sometimes painted in dark colors, maybe a set of bull's horns hanging up, a few liquor advertisements. Nondescript, bitter day drinkers, wearing pompadours and sideburns, nursing their beers.

Bartenders were polite, but they didn't trust the big American. It was easy to make Manuel Aguilar as a cop. He'd spent too many years on the right side of the law, and not enough in the gray area in between. Randy Rogers, Manny thought, might have done better, even though he was an Anglo and spoke lousy Spanish. He finally put it on the line with the bartenders, telling them there was an extra hundred dollar bill in it for them if they could come up with something that led to the man on the flyer. He told them the runaway story the same way he'd told it to the street cops and let them believe what they wanted to believe.

In shops, he spoke politely to the owners, when he could find them, and to the salespeople. If they asked for a flyer, he gave them one.

Manny met Adelaida on the second floor of a furniture store. He'd been looking at a gang of massive colonial style armoires and trying to figure out, with his comparatively limited fashion sense, whether Reina could stand anything like that in her home. He didn't think she could.

Adelaida approached and asked if she could help. Randy Rogers, Manny thought, would have said that her tight black sweater fit her like a sock on duck's nose. Her little black skirt made a three word statement: Here Comes Trouble.

She has to be five-eleven in heels, Manny thought—and she's in heels. Heels make everything look like a million bucks—and it already looks like a million bucks. He did the math with the tiny fragment of his brain that hadn't dropped south of his belt buckle: two million bucks. Big eyes with wicked, heavy lids. Get your head out of your butt, Manny, he told himself, you're working a job here.

She touched him with her fingertips, in the middle of his forearm, when she asked if she could help him, and it was clear she intended the shock to go right down to his toes. It went half way, and that was the first time in two years that Manny had felt anything from a woman other than Reina.

He urged himself to forget about this shop girl. It was time to focus his intentions and ignore this chance to cheat on his girlfriend, an opportunity that was rolling down on him like a very large truck. This lady was just having herself a little fun, knocking some American guy out with her sexuality to stave off the boredom of minding the store.

"I was looking at the armoires," he said, "and trying to decide whether my girlfriend would like them. How are they priced?"

Manny had spoken in Spanish and she let him know, with her eyes, just how much she appreciated that, and she let him see an image in her mind of what he could do to her. Manny lifted his head, looked high into a corner, and took a long, deep breath. This was a game, but he was still hooked.

Adelaida gave him the prices and he tried to let her know she wasn't on top of his situation by the way he played it. She was unlikely to know anything about a bottom feeder like Cisneros, but that didn't mean she wouldn't recognize him if she saw him. The story, as Manny told it, demanded sympathy.

She began treating Manny with a display of compassion that would have taxed the composure of any male. He tried to keep himself from dissolving while Adelaida made herself increasingly concerned with poor Roberto Flores's plight. When Manny said Flores had gone mental, Adelaida's eyes grew wide with horror and she stepped close to Manny's side, head bent, looking at the poster, her long nails tickling Manny's forearm again, this time on the inside. She shifted and leaned close, now working his bicep on the inside with the tips of her nails, brushing her hair and the hard curve of her breast against him. Manny had the impression that somebody had sprayed liquid nitrogen over his entire body.

Mexican women, he thought, desperately, they're culturally different. He knew Mexican women could be both more flirtatious and yet more chaste than American women. He held on to that thought for a second. It didn't help. He wanted to go after Adelaida like a stallion with its ears laid back and chase her as far as he could. He thought again about

Reina. Thinking about Reina finally gave him back the core of his body. Lust, often called a deadly sin, and an emotion so ordinary that he wanted to deny it could hurt him, dropped off and snuck away like a coyote. Adelaida gave no indication she'd sensed Manny had broken her spell.

Pobrecitio, Adelaida said, when Manny got to the part of the story where Flores disappeared, just when it looked like he'd be able to stay with his family in the US. She looked up at him and turned herself to him, and he to her, in one motion. When she'd done that, she just looked at him, speechless, wanting him to do something to save her from the horror of a world where the emotionally unstable vanish without a trace.

Manny took a half step back and broke contact by grabbing a pen and scribbling his phone number on the flyer, holding both the pen and the flyer up high and watching her over the top of the paper. It was the basic cop technique of holding a writing tablet up high so you can see who you're writing about at the same time. She didn't back off or shrink in the least, but she didn't keep coming closer. He spun one of the flyers into her fingers, thanked her for her concern, commented on a wrought iron lamp, and left.

Manny got down to the street and made his way through a crowd commuting on foot and in cars, flowing back into Nogales, Mexico, after a day of working across the border in Nogales, Arizona. He felt like a jerk, letting a woman in a furniture store make him nuts. He let it go and laughed at himself.

His truck sat where he'd left it and he drove through Nogales and got in the line for the American side of the border. It was like swimming upstream. People selling trinkets worked the sea of waiting vehicles. He had to exchange only a word or two with the American customs officers. Then he was driving north toward Tucson on Interstate 19, glad to be going home.

Manny watched the Santa Rita Mountains off to the east of the highway, across the Santa Cruz River Valley. Geronimo and his band had used this route, slipping past the homes of their European ancestered enemies. They had gone to the Catalina Mountains and lit signal fires that were seen from Tucson. Men set out to chase them, but by then the Apaches were gone. Manny drove and watched the mountains. The valley was filling with houses. There was a golf course. The day went the color of amber—October light. The sun went down and the Santa Ritas bled pink.

Manuel Aguilar got home at twilight. His place looked wrong somehow, even from the street, when he drove by. He parked up the block and walked the alley behind his house. He had no gun. He would call the cops with his cell phone if it looked like anybody was in there.

Grayboy appeared from underneath a small pile of old lumber and logs used for backyard barbecues. The cat meowed as if Manny had been gone for a million years. Unusual behavior. Manny scanned the house and listened for a minute. When he heard and saw nothing, he went in.

CHAPTER TWENTY-ONE

HIS PLACE HAD been ransacked. He saw that the bad guys had broken a window in the kitchen and crawled in over the sink. They had used the classic method of jerking the drawers out of Manny's bedroom chest and turning them upside down in the middle of the floor. The thieves missed the handguns he owned, a good camera, and some personal documents, all kept in a gun safe under the closet floorboards. A radio, the videotape player, and some money he'd left on the dresser were missing. The TV set was still around and they'd ignored the beer in the refrigerator.

Manny swept the broken glass from the kitchen floor, opened a beer, and sat down to brood and relax for a while. Calling TPD and making a report would only draw attention to him—and cops didn't care about burglary in Tucson, anyway. Property crime was rampant.

He knew somebody might have been looking for something special in his house and had covered their intent by going through it like an ordinary burglar. That might have happened to Bernard Harper, post mortem, in his flop house. Manny thought about the possibility that he was being hunted. He got up, went back in the bedroom, unlocked his gun safe, and slipped his 1911 Colt inside his waistband, just behind the crest of his hip bone. Old timers called it the Mexican carry.

One boot hit something on the floor as he started out of the bedroom. Keys. A spare set for his house and truck. He bent to pick them up. They were caught in the drawstrings of a leather pouch, a souvenir from childhood. He'd untangle them later. He stuffed everything in his pocket, got a beer from the kitchen, took a seat in the living room, and called Reina.

It was a work night and she was kind enough to ask him to come over and stay with her, since his place was upside down, but that was too much effort on both their parts.

Manny was tired and all the bad guys would have to wait. It looked like he might as well pay for some wrought iron bars for his windows. Most of the rest of the neighborhood had them. He had pins to keep the windows from going all the way up, but that hadn't been enough. The kitchen window was still broken. He nailed a board across it.

He went to his bedroom, put the Colt back in the gun safe, and took out a snub nosed revolver with a hump where the hammer should have been—his backup gun, a Smith and Wesson, loaded with five rounds of expensive ammunition that didn't create a watermelon sized ball of muzzle flash when you shot at somebody in the dark. He stripped down to his shorts, put on a black T shirt, got a shoulder holster, put the Smith in it, and went to bed.

The shoulder holster fixed the gun in position for a draw and it moved when he moved. Nobody could take it from him while he slept. Manny didn't like the idea of somebody slipping up on him, picking up his own gun from the nightstand, and shooting him with it. He could fire the hammerless revolver from under the covers, and from inside a coat or a sleeping bag, without it catching on the fabric. Guns weren't Manny's favorite things, but they were a tool of his trade.

He went to sleep, thinking about Reina, thinking about her hips and her shoulders. When he dreamed, he saw the withered old woman, his grandmother, pacing back and forth in front of her shack in the desert. Just you wait, she seemed to be saying. *Wait for what* he was asking in the dream.

The next morning he got coffee and a shower and put his house back together, clearing the floor of his bedroom and straightening up the living room.

Reina answered when he called Jeff's office. The attorney wanted him over there for something. Manny slipped a high ride holster on his belt, put the 1911 Colt in it, threw on his ugly polyester jacket, and headed for the white bungalow on University Avenue.

Reina was out of her chair and they were hugging each other before either of them could think about it. Lean, restless Jeff Goldman shot out of his office, a file folder in his hand, and stopped to stare out the window until his employees could peel themselves off of each other and pay attention.

"Manny," Jeff said. "Skip tracing."

"I can do that," Manny said, as he and Reina pulled apart. Reina was across the room with her long, straight nose back in her computer screen in a second, eyes now focused on an abstract she was knocking out at a fearsome rate.

"That guy. I hate that guy," Jeff said, as if Manny knew what he was talking about.

"Skip tracing," Manny said, hoping to clear Jeff's mind.

"Fenton," Jeff said. "Fenton and Yaloski."

"Bail bondsmen," Manny said.

"Greedy bastards," Jeff said. "You couldn't find worse scum than Tim Fenton if you looked under every pile of dog waste in Tucson. They bonded a guy I'm defending and he skipped. They need a PI because they're such cheats nobody will work for them. They'll never pay if they can get you to do the work first. I told them you could go after this guy, provided I don't need you for something else, if they could come up with a retainer. They actually did come up with some cash. Anyway, here's the guy, and here's the paperwork." Jeff handed Manny a folder.

"Now," Jeff said, "what about the shooter for Larry Armenta?"

"I don't have him, yet. I'll keep looking in town and I gave some flyers out in Nogales over the weekend."

Jeff nodded. Reina keyboarded. Manny went on talking.

"So this is Mickey Soames," Manny said, turning his attention to the photograph of the man in Jeff's file. "Burglar, car thief, drunk, doper, bail jumper."

"And innocent until proven guilty," Jeff said. "You watch television, Manny. Who are the culture heroes these days? The cops, right? I've seen them abuse civil rights, make racist remarks, call Hispanics *cafe mochas*, and beat people for no reason at all—on a television program—and I think you know how some of them behave in court and on the streets of Tucson. If you don't, I can tell you. And the public is stupid enough—and racist enough—to buy into that. Now go get Mickey Soames."

Jeff stomped back into his office. Manny had to stop himself from laughing. But Goldman's right, Manny thought, and he himself was now just another civilian in a society that was having a love affair with law enforcement.

Reina stopped typing, just for a second, put her hands around her mouth, megaphone style, and whispered in Manny's direction.

"Jeff's just a little on the rag today," she lisped and nodded her head like a little girl. Then she started whipping her fingers over the keyboard again.

"I heard that," Jeff yelled from the other room. "Manny, go get Mickey Soames. Reina, get in here and help me with this jury selection, you're supposed to be a paralegal."

Reina stopped typing, sat up straight, and did a momentary slow burn. "Then why am I doing all my own secretarial work?" she called softly, in the direction of Jeff's office.

"Go get Mickey Soames," Jeff yelled. "Reina, get in here."

Manny grinned and went out the door. The illustrious Mickey Soames needed tracing, and the tracing would begin where he could use the telephone in peace—and from a telephone number that would fool caller ID. Manny decided to get two things done at once.

Five minutes later, he was shaking hands with the Kelly brothers. They gossiped about fellow classmates from Tucson High for awhile and then Manny told them he needed wrought iron bars for his windows. Sean set up a time to come by and take measurements.

"Need to use your phone before I go," Manny said.

"Yeah?" Colin said, sensing that Manny had a hidden agenda. "You're two blocks from your own house and you've got a cell phone."

"That's right," Manny said, "but I need to call somebody who has caller ID."

"Go ahead," Colin said, pointing at the phone. "Glad I have an honest trade. Too bad how you turned out."

Manny nodded and started dialing.

"This is Bob Ramos, from Kelly Brothers. I'm calling about a place we rented for our drivers. Michael Soames's name should be on the account. Michael got cable TV over there for us, since he was onsite. We've rented another place for our drivers and we need to pay our bill and close our account."

"You said Michael Soames, sir?"

"Yes, could be Mickey Soames."

"And the address?"

"That's the problem. Somebody dropped the ball in my office. Nobody here can find a copy of the lease. It's embarrassing, but that's the situation."

"We have a Mickey Soames at 325 East Kelso Street, sir."

"And what's the current amount due on the bill?"

"The account is in arrears, sir. Thirty-one dollars and fourteen cents is past due from last month. The current billing cycle hasn't closed."

"Thank you," Manny said. "We'll be taking care of that."

"He's just one of them kids with hair sticking out from under his cap," Mr. Brydsong was saying. "Drives this car, look like a rocket. Sound like one, too."

"Would that be a Pontiac Firebird?" Manny asked. The two men were standing in Byrdsong's yard on Kelso Street, one of Tucson's near north side streets, where, Manny knew, bad things sometimes happened to good people. Byrdsong had been gardening and he was dressed in blue bib overalls.

"I don't know," Byrdsong said. He took off his cap and scratched his head. "I stopped payin' attention to cars when they start lookin' like airplanes and rocket ships and whatnot. None of them good as a truck anyway."

Manny showed Byrdsong a photograph of a young blond man in a baseball cap. Soames had wide eyes and an expectant, slightly dazed look. He was holding a can of beer and leaning against a red Pontiac Firebird.

"Yeah, that's him," Byrdsong said.

"And he drove away from that house this morning?" Manny pointed at the small, white house next door.

"Yeah, about noon. I don't think he works. Hear that damn car all around the block."

Manny thanked Byrdsong and drove fifty feet up a side street with a view of Soames's rented house. Manny waited, detaching himself from his body and sitting very still, drifting into a kind of hypnosis he'd learned from years of doing stakeouts.

His grandmother appeared at the edges of his mind, pacing back and forth in front of her house and looking at him. He reached down and touched the outside of his pants pocket. The small medicine bag she had given him was still there, the bag that had been tangled up with the keys on his bedroom floor. For some reason he carried it now, in spite of not believing in such things.

He didn't remember what she'd told him, thirty years before, when she'd reached her old brown claws down and put it in his pocket. She'd mutter in Spanish and in some Native American speech she called sacred language. He'd more or less endured any contact with his weird Indian grandmother, and with some of his fellow Catholics, who sometimes bought charms from the priests which were guaranteed to heal sore backs, fix their eyesight, or protect them from drive-by shootings. He preferred football, science and history, rather than religion. He kept the bag the way someone else might keep a marble, to remind him that things used to be simple.

Soames's red car rumbled up to the little house on Kelso about three hours later. Manny started his truck and pulled in at an angle, just far enough in front of the Firebird to block it. Then he slid out the passenger side of the truck and pointed his Colt at the middle of Mickey's face just as the lad was lifting himself out of the Pontiac. Soames had his keys in his right hand and a six-pack of beer in his left hand. His eyes flew open wide and he jerked sideways, trying to run.

Manny kicked the door of the Firebird and pinned Soames against the door frame.

"Ow," Soames yelled, and dropped both his keys and the six-pack.

"Police," Manny said. "Turn around. Now. Put your hands on top of the car."

Manny drew his leg back in and let Soames turn his sore body around. Manny handcuffed Soames's hands behind his back, palms out, and then frisked him.

"You know why I arrested you?"

"No," Soames said.

"Yes you do and I'll tell you anyway," Manny said. "You are under arrest for jumping bail. Are you going to give me any trouble on the way to county jail?"

"Guess not," Soames said, sulking.

Manny put Soames in the truck and made use of a small luxury he'd wanted when he'd ordered the truck from his brother Reggie: electric door locks.

With Soames secured, Manny drove to the Pima County jail. He walked Soames in, presented identification, and took him to the pretrial services area. A detention officer took charge of Soames, guiding him into the search room. Manny exchanged paperwork with the intake support specialists and left as they were introducing Soames to Touch Print, a computer program that would record his fingerprints.

"That was fast," Jeff said when Manny got back to the office. "These guys jump bail, don't know how to cover their tracks and don't even leave town. Business as usual."

Manny spent the night at Reina's. She told him that, given a few more years of practice, he might develop into a guy who could give a decent massage. He told her he'd never seen a woman who would get off her butt and return the favor. She told him that, morose, uncommunicative and preoccupied as he was, he was lucky he'd ever seen a woman at all.

Candles were burning. He noticed more objects on Reina's altar. Sugar skulls were laid out on a white tablecloth. October was coming to an end. November would follow and with it the Day of the Dead.

CHAPTER TWENTY-TWO

MANNY STOPPED BY his house the next morning to meet the Kelly brothers. Sean and Colin had already unloaded their truck. Black wrought iron grills of varying sizes were propped against the outside walls around Manny's house, ready to go on the windows.

Manny greeted the men and let them in. Grayboy appeared, scuttling in through the narrow opening Manny had left at the bottom of the kitchen window when he'd nailed it shut. The cat wanted food and Manny fed him.

Sean and Colin had started drilling holes in the window frames when Manny noticed that he had a message on his cell phone. He shut the bedroom door to cut the noise and punched in his password.

Adelaida had spoken politely, delicately, in Spanish. Mentioning a girlfriend had only made her hungrier. A wire, wrapped up in that soft voice, said she could beat any competition any other woman threw at her. There was a party in Nogales, could he come? Perhaps he'd meet someone who could help him find the poor man he'd described to her. So many people would be there, some in the upper echelons of the police, some who were in business and local government. She left a number.

Manny called her back. She was probably telling the truth and he had gotten a lot of bad men by playing along until it was time to make a move.

Adelaida was delighted to hear from him. She asked if he could meet her at the store, they could drive out to the rancho for the party.

Manny hung up the phone, then picked it up again. Going to Mexico, at least to the border, wasn't his idea of a good time. He would let Rogers know, or Daryl Trainor, and ask them to be ready to back him up if he called them or went missing. But being uneasy made his mind shy sideways, like a spooked horse—and it landed on Blackie Cate. Hamilton might still know the man. Manny called Hamilton.

"No, I ain't seen that guy for years," Bill Hamilton said cautiously.

"Do you know where to find him?" Manny asked.

"You know I don't like phones," Hamilton said. "If you want to know somethin', come over here."

A half hour later, Manny found himself sitting in Hamilton's studio. Hamilton leaned over a drawing and delicately pulled his Rapidograph pen across the page, making a thin, very black line.

"Yeah," Hamilton said, straightening up, leaning back, tilting his head, looking at the line and everything around it. "Cate's supposed to be dead. I heard he did something bad, or had something to do with something real bad, him and them other bikers, having themselves a biker war. So the word is, he's got himself dropped out of the computers somehow, got himself deceased." Hamilton pulled at his beard and watched Manny.

"So you saw him?"

"What the do you want him for, Manny? You want to arrest his ass? When it comes to cops and robbers, I don't give a damn, but I'm more on the robber side than I am on the cop side, just by my lifestyle. I smoke dope and drink beer on my own porch and that's supposed to be a hanging crime. You and your cop friends be jumping all over me. And, old buddy, nobody I know, including me, would drop a dime on Blackie Cate for a damn thing, on account of we all want to live long and prosper. Blackie will hurt you if you short him, cheat him, or rat on him. And he might just hurt you anyway. He can get things done if he don't just do them himself. See what I'm sayin'?" Hamilton looked hard at Manny.

"I'm looking for some people," Manny said. "I don't know who they are and I don't have sources who can tell me. I think they killed a guy who drank around the corner, at the Bar Nine. I thought of Cate because he knows something about most of the crime in town. He knows the strip clubs and the houses of prostitution. He knows the people who own these places. He knows some big guys in the drug trade. He knows about people who kill and people who have people killed—just like you said."

"He lives where he always lived," Hamilton said, "and don't tell him it was me that told you. If he mentions my name, tell him you ain't seen me in awhile. No, wait, I'll find his phone number. I can't have you going over there and me being here and Cate not knowing and all that." Hamilton slipped an address book out from under a sketchpad. He found a number and dialed it.

"Hey," Hamilton said into the phone. "Yeah, my dog's okay. How's your dogs? Good. Listen, you remember Manny? Sure, from the old flyin' days...Well, he ain't a cop no more... Got fired....Yeah, I think it's funny, too…" Hamilton looked at Manny and laughed. "So he says he wants to see you…I don't know… He says he wants to buy himself a motorcycle…Okay, I'll tell him…Bye."

Hamilton hung up the phone. "Blackie says to tell you motorcycles are expensive."

"Yeah, I know they are," Manny said. "Larry Armenta says hello. Your artwork paid off. We identified a guy. Larry's got a chance in court, now."

"Yeah? Tell Larry not to let the bulls keep him down."

Manny waited until late the next morning. Then he got in his truck and drove, trying to remember where Cate lived. When Manny found the place he pulled into the alley, parked behind what he assumed was Cate's current pickup truck, and stood at the chain link fence and waited while two Dobermans barked and bared their teeth, ten inches away, on the other side.

It was impossible to figure out how large the house was by looking at it from the back. All anybody could make out was that there was a wall with a door, a draped window, and a roof that slanted down to it from somewhere. After awhile a woman came out and walked toward him across the yard.

"Can I help you?" she said, making no move to unlock the gate. Manny knew he was dealing with a female biker who would bring a con and a stall down on him while Blackie Cate, waiting inside, would do whatever he thought he needed to do.

"I'm an old friend of Blackie Cate's. A buddy of mine called him yesterday. Blackie's expecting me."

"I don't know." The woman smiled and shook her head, shifting her body girlishly. "I rent this place through an agency." She had the look of a bad dog and one of her front teeth was discolored.

"If you see Blackie," Manny said, "tell him this is just about old times. It's not about anything else." Manny turned back toward his truck.

"Hey," the voice was soft, but it carried. Cate was just visible now, behind the screen. The woman concentrated on unlocking the gate. She let Manny in and he stood still and the Dobermans barked and raged around him. They knew a cop when they smelled one and they didn't like it. The woman yelled at them and they went away.

Manny walked across the yard with his head up, keeping eye contact with the little man behind the screen door. There was a grin on Cate's face.

"Hamilton told me you was coming over," Cate said. He pushed the screen door out to Manny, then turned and walked back into the house.

He was pulling beer out of the refrigerator by the time Manny got in the door. He handed one to Manny without making eye contact and sat down in a chair that reminded Manny of his own chair at home. Blackie cast his eyes upward to the television set mounted high in the corner of the room, just a few feet away from where he sat. He surfed from a porn channel to a football game, commented that the Cowboys were doing well this year, and launched into a short monologue about their journey through the football season. The woman came into the house and passed by, heading for the bedroom.

The two men watched the game in silence for a long ten minutes until it was over and the Cowboys had won. Blackie nodded his head in satisfaction, looking at Manny as if he'd seen him yesterday and not ten or fifteen years before. Then he hit the remote, flipping back to the porn, and muted the set as images of naked women, slathering each others' breasts with oil, played on the screen.

Blackie's girlfriend came back into the room and started doing dishes in the tiny kitchen, four feet from where they sat.

"Manny, that's Judy," Blackie said, gesturing politely between the two. Manny looked at Judy and nodded and she smiled at him over her shoulder and went back to washing breakfast dishes.

Blackie reached over to a table cluttered with papers, tools, and drug paraphernalia. He gracefully lifted a tray from the table and swung it onto his lap. He snapped one thin sheet out of a pack of rolling papers and deftly rolled a pinwheel joint. He picked up the lighter lying next to the tray, fired up the joint, and blew the smoke across the room.

"Don't smoke?" he asked Manny, casually offering him the joint, which was about as thick as a paperclip. When Manny flicked his head no, Blackie continued to suck on the tiny cigarette, exuberantly blowing smoke into the soft light that fell into the room from a dirty window over the cluttered table. Judy finished the dishes and disappeared into the bedroom again.

Cate was getting down to the end of the joint now. He twisted sideways in his chair and came up with the key ring he wore snapped into a keeper on the outside of his belt. There was a tiny crescent wrench on the key ring and Blackie slipped the edge of the roach between the jaws of the wrench and continued to smoke, lightly tapping off ashes on the edge of an old saucer. The keys clanked.

When the joint went out Blackie carefully emptied it into an ashtray, laboriously snapped his keys onto his belt again, and settled back in his chair. He took a Camel Straight directly out of the pack in his shirt pocket without looking down—a convict's gesture. Blue smoke made a marbled shaft in the air. Blackie exhaled more smoke, making a point of ignoring eye contact with Manny. It was Manny's cue to start talking. Manny knew that anybody who came into Cate's house wanting something had to play cat and mouse. Most people wanted drugs. Manny wanted information. Either way, Blackie always got to be the cat.

"I'm looking into the deaths of several people," Manny said.

"Would any of them be the dudes you shot down at the hospital?" Blackie snorted, laughing at his own joke, just glancing at Manny before staring off into space again and chuckling some more.

"One of them was a guy named Granger," Manny said.

"Yeah, and I know about the others."

"How do you know?"

Blackie laughed. "Just what I read in the papers."

Manny decided to do his own stall, just for the hell of it.

"Use your bathroom?"

"Sure," Blackie said. "It's right in there."

Manny walked to the end of the room and turned left. Blackie slept in a loft he'd built. When he glanced up Manny could see black nylon holsters nailed to the beams above the bed. Pistols were snapped into the holsters, ready to drop into a hand with a flick of the thumb. Judy was propped up on her elbow in the loft, reading. She glanced up and gave him a fake smile.

A dresser stood against the wall with two sets of dope scales sitting on it, one for weighing grams and one that went up to 2.2 pounds, a kilo. A riot shotgun leaned against the dresser. Sitting next it was a bathroom scale for weighing larger amounts of pot.

Manny went into the toilet, shut the door, and looked around him. There were colored images of nude women everywhere, on pages ripped from magazines and pinned to the toilet walls. Naked and nasty, Manny thought. What a life this guy lives. But Manny knew there was more to Blackie than that. Cate was an OB, an old biker. He had survived over the long haul, like the good Army trucker he'd been in Vietnam, where he'd been shot at more than once. In his off duty hours, Cate had turned Vietnamese women out for prostitution and dealt heroin to other soldiers.

Blackie didn't roll over on his friends when he got busted. Manny recalled that from the old days, too. Blackie had been arrested with a cousin of Manny's.

"Help yourself out," the cops had said to Blackie Cate, after they separated the two drug culprits. "Your buddy is over in that other car telling us all about it right now."

"Then let *him* tell ya," Cate had said. He'd gone to jail for a year.

Manny sauntered back out to Blackie's cluttered table.

"Seen your cousin?" Blackie asked, his eyes on the television.

"No, I don't see him," Manny said. "He's pretty much gone on cocaine, last time I heard."

"Couldn't hold his mud, huh?" Blackie laughed.

Somehow, Blackie wasn't so addicted to dope that it ate up every second of his life. Manny knew Blackie could use it, deal it, and make the numbers come out right at the end of the day. Addicts were scared of Blackie because he could do something they couldn't do: he could hold his mud.

CHAPTER TWENTY-THREE

CATE PULLED A vial of cocaine from his jeans. A tiny spoon fitted inside the vial's cap. The spoon came out full of white powder and Blackie deftly transferred it to his nose without spilling a speck of the drug and sucked the contents up one nostril. He sighed with pleasure and did the other nostril. He screwed the cap back on the vial and grinned at Manny. He seemed to like doing coke in front of a cop—an ex-cop, anyway. That was close enough for Blackie.

"So you're looking into some deaths," Blackie laughed. "I'm looking into some deaths, too."

"I don't know who's killing who with the bikers these days," Manny said pleasantly, "so I can't help you there."

"Out of touch, huh?" Blackie said. "Why don't you get into those computers? Tell me some stuff the cops know."

"I can't do that," Manny said, "but I can pay you for information."

"Want me to snitch somebody off?" Blackie laughed some more.

"I want to know about anybody who wanted a guy named David Granger dead. He had some junkie buddies—"

"I don't deal with junkies."

"I didn't say you did. Granger had some buddies. They're dead, too. Their names were Perez and Corral."

Blackie turned his palms up and rolled his eyes at the ceiling.

"Then there is Barney Harper, another dead guy."

"White guy?"

"White guy."

"Now you're talkin'." Blackie laughed some more.

"If you hear anything about who killed any of those guys—"

"Who do you think killed them?" Blackie asked, staring at the television.

"I don't know, maybe Mexicans, maybe somebody else. Whoever it was operates around here, at least some of the time. They wanted this guy Granger out of the way bad enough to come and try to get him at the hospital."

"Whyn't you ask the bulls?" Blackie said.

"Corrections officers? Why ask those guys?"

"Ain't nothin' lower," Blackie said cheerfully. "And they let him go, right?"

"We did ask them. The kidnappers had papers and passable identification."

"Yeah, somebody with connections," Blackie said. "Sounds like cops to me."

"I have no way of knowing that. But I believe Granger had connections of his own—to Mexican drug dealers."

"And you want me to give up drug dealers? I'd screw up my own connections."

"No, I want you to help me solve a murder, maybe a couple of murders."

"I'll ask around," Blackie said carelessly. "What's it worth to you?"

"What do you want?"

"It'll cost you at least a thousand, depending on what I find."

"I don't have a thousand."

"You're an ex-cop. Ask the cops. They got all that drug money from the RICO Act and what they don't turn in, they steal for themselves. All you cops are rich."

"I'm not a cop anymore, remember? I'll pay for it myself," Manny lied. He would get Jeff to pay for it if he could. If he couldn't, he would pay for the information himself.

"If I find anything it's going to cost," Blackie said.

"I need good information. If I can use it, I can pay you for it."

Manny crossed the border in the late afternoon and it took awhile to get through the crowd of workers returning to Mexico. He drove straight to the furniture store and found a parking space.

Adelaida came out just after five. She stepped in close and wrapped her arm around his, pressing the side of her body against him.

"How are you?" she said. "Come to my house. I'll change clothes and then we'll go."

Yeah, like we've been weekend lovers for years, Manny thought, and either there was a carrot growing in his shorts or he was glad to see her, too.

They walked to her late model Ford while she kept the lock on his arm, falling in step with him. Playful. Here's a girl who's ready for a Saturday night. Manny figured she would probably be mad when he left and didn't come back.

She lived in a one-story building, modest on the outside, richly furnished on the inside. He recognized kilims, a hand woven rug he wouldn't have known about if it hadn't been for Reina.

Adelaida excused herself and went to the bedroom to change, but not before snapping on a huge television and getting Manny a beer. She made sure he saw her, once or twice, moving past the half-open bedroom door in a black slip.

It took her only twenty minutes to make herself even more striking than she already was and Manny was never quite ready for how well a woman could look. He watched her come out in a midnight blue sheath dress, her hair piled high, her make up perfect and subtle. The diamonds around her neck looked real. Money was coming to this woman from somewhere and he didn't like what that probably meant. Play the hand, a voice said to him, play the hand. In his mind he saw a card fall out of shadow and across a shaft of light. The ace of spades.

The rancho was forty minutes from town and it was dark when they got there. The main house was large, two-story, and brightly lit. The entrance was gated and the men waiting there looked bored, but ready. It clicked in Manny's head that they were some kind of off duty cops. New four wheel drive trucks sat in the front yard, along with some expensive cars. The chrome gleamed in the headlights. Several more men leaned against the vehicles and watched the parking lot.

She took his arm again as they walked inside. Many of the men were older and many of the women were younger and dressed expensively, like Adelaida.

"That's our host," she said, pointing with a small nod of her head at a tall, hawk-faced man who didn't look like he'd done any ranching of late. Manny felt her dragging him toward the guy.

"Mr. Mendoza, this is Mr. Aguilar," Adelaida said, making a seamless formal introduction.

Mendoza's grip felt strong when he shook Manny's hand. "Welcome. Enjoy your evening," he said, before turning back to his other guests.

"He's a big businessman," Adelaida said. " He likes to pretend he's a rancher—just like you American guys with your, how do you say, your trophy ranches. Let's get a drink."

She guided Manny to the bar. He got a beer and the two of them drank and watched the party. Manny could see a walled back yard through the big glass windows on the other side of the room. Men and women sat around a lighted pool. Steam rose from it, evaporating in the cool November air. Nobody swam.

They finished their drinks, got more, and then Adelaida took his arm again and led him outside. They found chairs and she made a lot of talk, some of it about the shop, the furniture. Some of it about the fences and the heightened security at the border. He answered her questions about his work, telling her only what she already knew.

After awhile she went away and came back with a stout, serious looking man in dull clothing.

"Manuel, this is Major Durand, of the Nogales police. Major, this Manuel Aguilar."

The three of them sat and made small talk for awhile. Manny was telling the guy about the plight of the mentally ill who disappear, probably to Nogales, when he began to feel dizzy. He sat down hard on a chair, poolside. He looked up and didn't recognize the sky.

CHAPTER TWENTY-FOUR

MANNY HAD CALLED Reina, told her he was going to Nogales, Mexico to follow up leads on Tony Cisneros. He'd be back late that night. He would call when he woke up Sunday morning. He'd let Daryl Trainor know, too. Both of them would be looking for him if he didn't make contact on Sunday morning.

Against her better judgment, Reina hadn't pressed him for a specific explanation of what the hell he'd be doing in Nogales on a Saturday night. What kind of fool did he think she was? That question crawled across her mind that evening as she slipped around her house, her long body carrying her quick hands, her green eyes missing nothing.

She turned the kitchen into a spotless white specimen, camera ready. Bring on *Sunset* magazine. The tile shone, original tile, from the 1930s. She aced what little was out of place in the living room and checked the bathroom. Having gone to the office and done some extra work on Saturday, she'd taken a long bath after, by candlelight. She'd missed Manny then and there was edginess, anger, in her fox's eyes when she'd risen from the bath. She didn't like physically and emotionally needing some, well, bastard, just then. She sniffed in disgust, like a horsy old aunt. And this was happening on her favorite holiday, too. Tomorrow would be the Day of the Dead.

She'd had a good week, confounding Jeff when she showed up to work on Halloween dressed in black robes and wearing her peaked witches' hat.

"Reina," Jeff said, "did I mention this is a law office?"

"It's the High Holidays, Jeff," she'd replied, and stared at him like the twisted girl she was until he had to roll his eyes and tacitly assent to going along with the joke.

"You're good help, Reina," Jeff said, "but you're *strange* help."

Reina began cleaning her bathroom at warp speed, smiling slightly at the memory of Jeff's reaction.

She could call her daughter, she thought, in San Diego—or her friend, Hope Wells—but it's Saturday night, nobody would want to talk. A roommate might make her place a little more fun to live in. She had that extra bedroom....

What was she doing without a cat, she asked herself. Her tortoise-shell, Tiger Lily, had disappeared months before.

Hmm, she thought, but how many women would pay money for this kind of solitude, tonight, in this kind of house?

As for men, she couldn't be sure they even understood houses. They haunted them like ghosts—just a cave to hang their haunches.

Reina mentally fingered through a rolodex of rejected men. She'd known one or two guys who could decorate and keep a house. But then there was Milt, who hired decorators with poor taste to pick out sculpture, wall art, and furniture. And then there was Bruce, who hung up animal skins.

She was smart, she was experienced, and it all went out the freaking window when she was in love. There were two things that always pissed her off, she decided: pretentious men and tasteless home decoration. She smiled, propped up on two feather pillows now, wearing a negligee the color of late summer.

Durand waited until Manny's head dropped and then whistled once in the direction of the back wall. Looking over it, he could see the Sonoran desert hills in moonlight, black shadows of arroyos between them. Out there at night, nothing was sure. Anything could disappear— like this American *payaso*.

Durand watched Adelaida turn her back and go into the house. Durand could see her from inside, embracing the host; the tall, dark man with cavernous features and hawk's eyes.

Durand heard the door of a truck open and slam shut. Then another door and another. He opened the side gate into the yard and four men in jeans and dark shirts slouched through it. The leader stepped up to where Manny sat. The leader blocked the view from inside the house with his body. Not necessary, Durand thought, everybody turned away when they saw the American's head was on his chest.

The leader reached down, grabbed a handful of Manny's hair, pulled his head up, and spat in his face. Manny stared dazed, not noticing the spit, only pondering, through layers of the kind of glass that drugs put over the brain, what Tony Cisneros was doing here, in his dreams.

"Did 'chu want to see me?" Tony said, in his best hoodlum English. "Well, 'chur seeing me now, cocksocker."

Tony stepped away and jerked his head towards the gate. Two of the men hauled Manny out. Durand shut the gate and turned away, staring out again at the moonlit hills. Goodbye, *payaso*, he thought.

They threw Manny into a Chevy Suburban and shoved him into the middle of the seat. Then they jumped in on either side. Somebody drove while Tony Cisneros looked over his shoulder, rested his arm on the front seat, cursed Manny, and told him he was going to cut his nuts off.

Manny just stared, wondering what it was all about. This was a dream where the phantom Tony Cisneros was angry. Manny thought it was almost funny. A slight grin came on Manny's face and Cisneros hit his own head on the ceiling of the Suburban, lunging across the seat to crack Manny in the jaw. Cisneros could hit, and that was to Manny's advantage, because the pain brought him out of the stupor enough to know this was real and he'd be better served if he acted as if he still thought it was a dream.

Cisneros yelled and held onto his head. Then he leaned across the seat carefully, without lunging this time, and laid a wicked jab into Manny's cheekbone while the guys on either side pinned his arms. It didn't have the power of the right cross that Cisneros had put in before, but it was nasty.

"That all you got, bitch?" Manny slurred, leering at nothing in particular, mostly because he could see nothing in particular.

"You, you shit bag," Cisneros said. "We got something for you, you shit bag cop."

The guys on either side of Manny grinned and made eye contact. Tony could be real funny when he got mad.

Reina was sitting up in bed now. She had been reading, or thought she had. Maybe she'd been dozing. A sound bite had snapped loose in the room. Noise from another dimension. Since she was a girl, Reina had experienced auditory intrusions when she was nearing sleep. Music would break in and play in her head. Voices from her day would repeat. Reina liked such visitations and only feared them enough to give them respect. It had never shown her it wouldn't stop if she wanted it to. Psychedelics had been a good time when she was a kid, but they hadn't come with this sound show she got every evening, in her right mind. Hypnogogic hallucinations—just part of the deal, Reina thought to herself. Usually they were nice, or at least neutral. This one wasn't. The tires had roared on dirt and rock. Dust had flown. It was night. That was all. That was enough. She was an orphan, now. In her forties. Her father was dead. She had thought her mother might stick around longer.

But no, she checked out before dad. Most of the time, Reina felt anything but small and alone. Most of the time.

One old framed poster hung on the wall in Reina's bedroom, centered above the severe, vertical lines of her black wrought iron headboard: Robert Mapplethorpe's photo for the cover of Patti Smith's album, *Horses*.

Reina's bedroom floor was bare, polished oak. At one end of the room was a door, painted white, even the doorknob. Almost nothing besides the white walls, the rectangle of the bed, and the woman on it, staring, holding one hand curved over her mouth. For the Japanese, she had once told Manny, white is the color of mourning.

When the driver braked the Suburban, Manny pitched forward and hit the seat in front of him. The men hauled him into a desert coated with downy silver light and dragged him to a clearing in the brush. Cisneros came in, crouching, hitting with the strength of a trained boxer. Things in Manny's face broke. Hearing them break was pretty easy. Feeling them break was easy, too. He was more in the other world, now, than this one. This world, however, was where he was dying.

Finally, Cisneros straddled him and drew a blue steel nine-millimeter. He shoved the muzzle into Manny's teeth.

"Open your mouth," Tony said. "Open it wide."

Manny opened his mouth and felt the cold snout of the weapon against his tongue, against his teeth, then against his upper palate. He could taste the oil and the steel beneath it. Cisneros over lubricates his weapons, Manny thought. He almost started laughing again.

"Listen. Listen," Cisneros hissed, leaning in Manny's face. Cisneros cocked the gun. Manny heard the hammer clicking but he couldn't count the clicks. Funny, and he'd just heard them, too. He waited for Cisneros to pull the trigger, knowing he would never hear the gun go off.

"Now, fight me," Cisneros said. "Fight me."

Manny didn't fight him. Cisneros left the pistol stuck between Manny's teeth.

"Bet you thought we were going to shoot you, didn't you?" Cisneros said. "Didn't you?"

Cisneros slowly pulled the pistol out of Manny's mouth and angled the muzzle slightly up, so that it pointed between Manny's eyes.

"We got a better plan for you," Cisneros said.

Other men had followed the Suburban in a Chevy 4X4. One of them was carrying a metal box toward them now. It gleamed soft in the moonlight and there was a sound coming from it, a sound that had dimension to it. A sound that had power. Trademark sound of one of nature's lesser gods—the rattlesnake. Manny knew, from the sounds, that these idiots had more than one in there, but it was no use trying to do anything. He was flat on his back, staring straight up now. He couldn't see as well as he would have liked, but he could see. Cisneros was a boxer and a torturer. He'd only closed one of Manny's eyes because he wanted his victim to see.

The recognition grew in Manny that the sky had contorted. All the stars were off, none of them recognizable, and they were set disturbingly, as if by human intention. Green seeped through the blue and black spaces between them. The stars themselves were amber colored, and larger, even than Mars.

This sky was not benign, Manny knew, not a pretty heaven. He was in a different world now, not knowing if this canopy had been inside him, waiting to take over, or if it had replaced the sky, taken the sky itself over from the outside. Or maybe he'd just traveled, without remembering, or had been taken, here.

There was a vague awareness of moving, being dragged. Navigation would not be possible by those stars. Even if he lived through whatever they were doing to him, he'd die in another world.

He heard his brother Luis being dragged nearby. He sensed that Luis was feeling foolish because he, too, could not recognize a single star. Manny knew only enemies dragged the dead. Friends carried the dead when they could. He wondered about the people doing all this dragging. He wondered how they could have missed the sky.

There was no ceiling fan in Reina's bedroom, nothing to break the detached chalk white. In my bedroom there are no extravagances, Reina was thinking, as she sat on the bed. She could sit with this grief. She could live through anything.

They threw Manny down in the pit and dumped the two rattlesnakes on top of him. The pit hadn't been dug deep and the sides weren't vertical—an old mining prospect, left in the rocky ground. The snakes started up the sides and the men kicked dirt on them, cursing because their comic book plan wasn't working. One of the men threw a rock and hit Manny in the groin. When he doubled up, one snake recoiled and then struck him, just above the knee.

Manny felt the sharp sting and lay still while the snakes wound themselves in circles around him, still trying to climb the sides of the pit.

"They got him," one of the men said. "One of them got him."

He heard himself say, "The snakes. It's for the snakes."

His grandmother appeared up above, a shape, shimmering like a mirage in the shadows near the edge of the pit. She stood with her back half to him, wearing a dark dress. Her jaw was set and she pumped the forefinger of one brown claw toward the middle of his body.

Then he could smell her. Age, sweat, herbs, dirt. Rank, musty. Grandmother. Black eyes, obsidian sparks burning in the leather creases of her face. She turned and leaned in, bent from the waist and still pumping that finger. Her breath stank and she hissed. Those missing teeth, sunken cheeks. Spit flying.

"For the snakes," she rasped.

The snakes were making their way up the sides of the pit and the men above were backing off, still cursing.

Tony and his pals kept moving back, toward the trucks, where they finally stood and watched the rattlers crawl out of the pit and slither away. From where the men stood, they could no longer see Manny clearly.

"I saw him get bit a couple of times," one of the men said.

"Think that's enough? We better shoot him," the other one said.

"No, stupid, we ain't going to shoot him," Tony Cisneros said. "He'll be dead pretty quick. And nobody who finds him is going to know we got his ass. It'll look like he got to fooling around, got drunk somewheres and got the crap beat out of him. Then he wanders off and gets snake bit. Shit happens."

Everybody laughed.

"Nobody can prove nothing," Cisneros went on. "And if somebody sent him down here, they will know we killed him and that will teach them a lesson not to screw with us. We got the snakes to do everything."

Everybody laughed some more. Then they lit cigarettes. Somebody lit a joint. Somebody else fumbled for a bottle, found it, and passed it around.

Manny began to move his hand, still watching the angry ghost who kept silently working her mouth and pointing. She's pissed off, he thought, getting his hand into his pants pocket, feeling it close around the medicine bag. The pouch was out of his pocket now. She wants me to eat the stuff in the pouch. Why not. Makes as much sense as anything else. He fumbled until he got the leather bag open. His hand floated up by itself and pressed against his bloody mouth. Powdery plug of something bitter. Nonsense phrases popped in his flickering mind. He chewed the plug and swallowed it. Green skies with amber stars. Crazy ghost of grandmother, still looking angry. He was lucky he hadn't choked on that crap. Hey, grandma, got anything to wash this stuff down? She was gone. Stars gone. All gone.

Twenty minutes later they hauled Manny out of the pit by his ankles and poured the last of the tequila on him. Then they threw him in a truck.

CHAPTER TWENTY-FIVE

GUSTAVO ORTIZ'S MOTHER moved him up Calle Reforma at a steady pace, even though he was in no hurry. There was too much to see. The motorcycle police had the street blocked off so the traffic could only go one way—toward the graveyard. Every fourth vehicle was a truck with a gaggle of kids about Gustavo's age sitting in the back. He would stare at them and they would stare back. Nothing better to do, the traffic was hardly moving anyway.

It was after ten in the morning. Gustavo's mother felt ashamed, getting out this late to visit her husband—to visit his grave, anyway. Her husband, less than forty years old, and dead from cancer. His parents would already be there.

The Americans located manufacturing plants just south of the border, to avoid the inconvenience of obeying US pollution statutes. The Mexicans themselves had no real regulations about pollutants. Pockets of cancer were popping up all over Nogales, on both sides of the border.

There was no sidewalk along Calle Reforma, so they picked their way along until they got to the open air market, located on both sides of the street, just in front of the graveyard, which ran up the raw desert hills on either side of the street.

Gustavo could see a little ahead and he felt the excitement, knowing they'd be in the middle of the market soon, but he was not tall and he kept his attention close to him.

He noticed right away when an alert, lean man with narrow tiger's eyes turned a purple flower sideways and it became something else, something powerful and sleek. The blossoms were furry purple clumps. Beneath them was an expanse of brown that widened up to the blossoms. The shape of a mountain lion's paw.

"What is it?" he asked the man.

"*Manopanteras*," the man said. Panther paws.

Gustavo glanced at the vendor's other flowers, the yellow ones. Then his mother pulled him away, into the crowd.

People sold *coronas*, wreaths of cloth and wire, for the graves. The outside edges were triangular spikes of bright satin ribbon, folded back across itself from two sides, forming a point. The *coronas* had mounds of paper roses in the middle, often in white or in pastels. The spiked edges of the wreaths, in reds and yellows, spoke to Gustavo of the sun, of a burning that never burned out. The paper roses looked as if they were exploding out of a spiked sun.

He felt the shiver on his neck again. He had felt it only once before, at his father's burial. Something picking him up by the hairs on his neck.

At his father's burial it had been as if his father was showing him a picture and saying: One piece of advice: Don't look here. Feel the sky pull you up by the back of your neck and look out there, over those hills, at that horizon. The earth is soft but it is not enough. Part of you is sky. Stand up. You can have your death when you die, not before. Until then, stand up and stay in places where you can see for some distance.

The graveyard climbed the brown hills on either side of Calle Reforma. In front of its two parts was the open-air market with its maze of stalls, tents and signs: *Taqueria California. Flotes. Huaraches.*

They went by a sidewalk restaurant under a ramada covered with blue plastic. Red-orange tables and chairs sat underneath it. The words *Coca Cola* were stamped in white on the backs of the chairs.

The boy's mother led him into the graveyard from the north side of the street, just behind a man who carried a huge load of cotton candy on one long pole. The servings of cotton candy hung together, somehow, like the top of a bushy pink tree.

Gustavo kept looking at the people thronged in the graveyard, in the bright sunlight. Younger people in T-shirts, baseball caps and jeans. Men dressed in snap button cowboy shirts, white straw hats, boots and jeans.

Gustavo saw the Tohono O'odham symbol of a figure standing at the entrance to a circular maze. It was burned into the flat leather face of a man's belt buckle. When the man turned his back, Gustavo saw the name *John Bravo* tooled into the leather of the belt itself.

They arrived at the grave. Gustavo's grandparents were there and they had put down their flowers and waited, drinking sodas. They gave Gustavo a broom and he began to sweep shriveled flowers from the cement slab. When he had done that, his mother held a trash bag and he dumped the old flowers into it with his hands. Then they all began to wash the slab with water, and to wash the cement cross above it that bore the name of Gustavo's father.

"No," a woman said sharply and Gustavo turned to see her putting out her hand to stop a photographer, an Anglo, from photographing her and the grave she attended. The photographer kept walking, up the hill toward where the wealthier people were buried. Some of their graves looked like plaster and marble houses to Gustavo. You could go inside and walk back and forth. He could see a few flowers there, and he could see the names and the image of Jesus Christ on the walls. But the odd thing was, no one attended those graves, it seemed, even on this day, November second, The Day of the Dead.

He got permission to wander when they were done washing the grave and laying their yellow flowers on it. There was little danger of being left behind. This was also a wake. People would stay here. Women sat now, by graves, holding umbrellas against the sun. People were everywhere. He was standing half way up the hill and he could look across at the opposite hill and see the same images he saw here.

He decided he would go down through the graves to the market. Perhaps he would go, also, to the other side. He passed a man holding a fine-tipped paintbrush out in front of him. The man was skillful. He was touching up the white letters of a name on a thin black cross.

Gustavo had no money to buy a soda from the men who kept them in tubs of melting ice. He was thirsty and he stopped and drank at the spigot at the bottom of the hill, where people filled gallon plastic jugs to carry back to the graves. A pile of refuse lay nearby. They had given him the bag of old flowers. He left it on the pile.

Turning toward the sound of *mariachis*, he saw them a little way up the hill, playing at a gravesite. A woman with a bushy head of graying hair sat on the narrow cement wall by the grave. She was alone. She smoked a cigarette, blowing the smoke out tensely, sometimes shaking her head as if she were someplace else. Yet she was very self-conscious and looked around sharply from time to time.

Gustavo could see into people but he could not decide on what he saw. He felt these things and wished he could think about them so that they would make sense. She was there and wanted to draw attention to herself. That might have been important to her. Perhaps she thought about the little deaths in her own life, as well as the death of the person she had paid the band to serenade. He looked to the opposite hill and saw *mariachis* there too, playing for other people beside another grave.

The boy went down to the market. A pile of grasshopper-green corn sat on a plastic tarp the color of red wine. A man stood and sliced sugar cane. The chunks spat from the blade, one after the other, two or three in the air at the same time. Gustavo watched with pleasure. Behind the worker, looking like thick stalks of bamboo, tall as a man, the green poles of uncut cane leaned against the chain link fence around the graveyard and waited for the knife. The sections would be cut again, this time in half. People bought them and sucked out the sweet pulp.

Gustavo was on the south side of Calle Reforma now, looking at more wares for sale. He saw a tall Anglo and his two sons in their jeans and baseball caps buying shovels from a vendor who had the tools stacked on the ground. It was clear from the way they moved that they were intent on their own purposes and wanted nothing to do with the Day of the Dead. They kept their heads down and walked off, carrying their new shovels, looking a little like grave diggers.

He stopped when he saw a fresh mound of rich, dark earth, piled high. Red and yellow flowers lay on top. Someone had poured water over the whole mound and the water had run down it in rivulets that narrowed and came to points on the flat, dry ground. Gustavo saw this as a wet starburst. This wetness passed through the areola of colored stones around the base. White Styrofoam cups lay in the dust. A woman hoisted a purple umbrella. Another painter loaded his brush and touched a cross with it. A faded name began its way back to life.

Wreaths in reds, whites, pinks, bright blues and lavenders hung on crosses and grave markers at different heights. Gustavo liked the picture: *coronas* so bright they made the background disappear, seeming to suspend themselves in midair like pinwheels.

Gustavo turned, standing where he was in the bottom of the south section of the graveyard, and saw a man covered with balloons. There was the yellow Smiley Face. Mickey and Minnie. Tigger in orange.

He looked down on the rectangular grave of a child, edged by a border of cobalt blue cement. On the cover of this grave, in its center, someone had placed an infant who stared at him from a shaded white carrier.

The sun was bright and warm, but somehow not harsh and white. He saw the Anglo with the camera. This time, he had it up to his eye and was weaving up and down, fighting with it, trying to get a shot in the direction of the sun without the colored sprites of halation entering the lens. Halation, the noisy, unwanted signature of pure light.

Gustavo could see the photographer was trying for the cotton candy vendor, who was still carrying his tree of pink bundles, each one partly sheathed in plastic, like bouquets. And the light was so full and near as the sun slipped west that it concentrated on the top of the candy tree, fell upwards, danced whitely, and slipped off into pure blue sky while long, rich shadows of people and crosses threw themselves over the ground, violent as lovers in full embrace. This was the sun's work, in November, in Mexico.

Staring as he wandered into the street, he almost walked into the white truck. It was big, a two and a half-ton Chevrolet. Square headlights stared out from behind its elaborate wrought iron grill. Somebody had painted the grill chalk white.

The truck was parked facing the sun and Gustavo felt as if the truck was bearing down on him, driven by no one. A velour curtain, of a certain color of scarlet, hung, rich folds intact, behind the windshield. It was drawn all the way around the inside of the cab.

The scarlet curtain could have been a blouse for a black haired woman. Could have been a matador's cape. Could have hung in a puppet theatre, or lined a casket. The truck had high sides around the bed, the front frame of which came up in the center in three points, like a kite. The triangular top had a gray tarp pulled down over it so that the truck looked a little like a Spanish sailing ship, unstoppable.

On the front bumper was a white license plate with very green numbers. Under them, the letters MEX MEX. Did it mean the truck came from Mexicali? Gustavo wondered. But, anyway, he thought, it means Mexico. Mexico, for sure.

It was time to turn back. He was a little tired now. He waited for his chance, because there was still plenty of traffic past the graveyard, and crossed to the north side. He went straight up to his father's grave, felt the pain of memory, kept his head up, and found his mother and his grandparents still sitting and talking about the most ordinary things, hardly noticing, as if he had not been gone at all.

They had saved a soda for him. He sat down with them and drank it. Then he decided to go up to that high place where there were no people. He liked the black iron fences around many plots, which he saw as he walked. The tops of the vertical bars formed individual crosses, small ones. Wrought iron in the shape of black hearts decorated the verticals between cross sections of metal.

In the clutter of the larger graves, the ones so big you could walk inside, he picked out a particular roofed monument and stepped into its deep shadows.

Looking down, he saw a man lying there. Gustavo ran.

CHAPTER TWENTY-SIX

WHEN THE ADULTS found Manny he was barely alive. One leg swollen, bitten. Face swollen, beaten. It was a noisy mess getting him out of the graveyard. Excited babble. Flashing lights.

"If this guy wasn't wearing a coat the hypothermia would of killed him, let alone all these other wounds," one of the medics said to a police officer. The officer looked away without answering. This guy is dying from that snakebite, the officer thought, coat or no coat.

Manny wasn't conscious enough to talk until the next day and when he did start talking he mumbled in English, but it was nothing anybody needed to hear.

"Feed my cat. Feed my cat," he kept saying.

"Forget your cat, hombre, tell us who you are."

Confused, forgetting he'd told Reina he would contact her, he told Nogales authorities to call his brother Reggie so Reina wouldn't see him, at least until he could get to the hospital in Tucson. Then he told them to call Jeff's office because he began to realize how long he'd been gone. His employer, his lover, and his cat. They would all miss him. He finally remembered his truck. The Nogales police found it for him, parked in front of the furniture store. By that time, Detective Daryl Trainor had arrived in Nogales, looking for Manny, and had arranged for transport back to Tucson.

Manny ended up in a bed in Saint Mary's Hospital, a couple of floors down from the secured ward where they'd held Granger until he'd been killed in a crossfire in the back parking lot.

"You," Reina said, by way of greeting him. "You look terrible."

Manny's grin wasn't much of a grin. Everything he liked to call his face was swollen.

"Did you miss me?" he managed to mumble, taking her hand.

"I was furious," Reina went on, "but I got over it. What happened?"

Manny didn't answer for awhile. Then he told her about Tony Cisneros.

"What were you thinking?" Reina said. "In fact, were you thinking at all? Help me out here, Manny, I'm pretty upset. I love you to pieces but I need you in one piece, dammit." She hit the bed with her fist and started crying.

"I love you, Reina," Manny said.

Reina stopped crying. "Your cat is at my house," she said, "and he's been there long enough so he likes it. You could come to my house and get well if you like."

"He's been ther' 'wo daze 'nd he wikes it?" Manny mumbled.

"You know, Manny, what with the beat up mouth, the painkillers and all, your speech is sounding a little quaint. I like it, actually. It's kind of charming."

"Reina, I'm not in the mood right now," Manny said, as distinctly as he could, still thinking about how he could nail Tony Cisneros and why his cat was such a punk. Of course, he was taking Reina's word for it. The cat probably wanted out of there, like any sane tomcat that'd been eating the good, cheap dried food Manny fed him, supplemented by mice and lizards from the wood pile out back. Not to mention the fights with the other cats. Manny figured Grayboy had to be missing those.

They let Manny out five days later and Reina drove him to her place. It'll be a couple weeks before he could do anything, he thought to himself. November was shot and he was only a week into it.

"The doc told me he'd never seen anybody recover from a rattlesnake bite that fast," Reina told him as they drove to her bungalow. She gave him a sidelong glance. Manny looked away, staring out the window.

Manny found Grayboy eating salmon in the kitchen.

"That's what, three or four dollars a can?"

"Three. I get the salmon at Trader Joe's and it's the best," Reina said.

"You've turned my cat into a *maricón*."

"Get over it."

Manny woke the next morning when it was getting light. Reina was in the room, dressed, lovely, and in command. Nobody he'd loved before could be as quick as she was, as responsive. She was on the bed in her black business suit and kissing him, telling him she'd see him after work and that the cat was fed. He felt embarrassed and weak and in love with her. He didn't show it, he thought, except for the part about loving her.

Reina had left her cordless phone on the nightstand and when it rang Manny managed to get it turned on and stuffed against his ear.

"Hey," Bill Hamilton said, "how you doing, Aguilar? I called the office where you said you worked."

"Not doing too bad," Manny said. "What's up?"

"You sound like hell, man. You got a cold or something?"

"No."

"Remember that guy you went to see?"

"The guy with the Dobermans."

"He says that you don't want to stay on this one. Stay away from whatever you was looking for. He says there ain't enough money in the world to make that any less of a fact. And he don't want to see you no more. Just passing it along."

"Yeah, thanks," Manny said. "I'll remember that." He hung up the phone.

He was lying on his ass and the world was passing him by. His head ached. His leg was swollen. The docs said he better rest and keep in touch for some time to come. Anger and sadness liked to jump on him when he was down. He imagined putting both of those feelings in a big clay jar, standing in the cool shadow of a wall, left there a thousand years ago, and forgotten.

Grayboy jumped up on the bed and meowed in Manny's face. Grayboy's breath stank of salmon. Manny stroked the cat's head and talked to him in Spanish. Then he fell back to sleep.

Reina was in the room again, leaning over him, when Manny woke up. He stared, too dazed to return her nuzzle.

"I'm showering now," she said, and spun around, heading out of the bedroom. "And by the way, how'd you get to that ranch, out there in the butt crack of nowhere, before they drugged you and took you off, honey?"

"What's butt crack of nowhere all about?" Manny said. "Where'd you get that?"

"My granddaughter," Reina said. "She talks like that all the time." Reina disappeared into the bath.

"You have a granddaughter?"

"Thanks for keeping up, Manny. You're a sensitive guy."

Manny lay back and waited for the shower to start. He could see Grayboy sitting in the hallway, staring into the bathroom, waiting for his evening salmon. A bra sailed out the bathroom door and landed on the cat. Grayboy looked delighted and immediately began hauling it across his body with his teeth.

"Me and Mr. Grayboy, we got a thing going on," Reina called from the bathroom. "I know what cats like—especially tom cats."

Manny was starting to wonder about that cat. You could buy his loyalty for a can of salmon. And if Manny didn't get out of here pretty soon, he'd be lying around sucking on a pacifier like a little kid.

"How'd you get out to that ranch, Manny?" Reina asked again from inside the bathroom.

"Some nice lady gave me a ride," Manny said.

"You pathetic bastard," Reina said pleasantly. "You're going to tell me all about it when I get out of this shower."

Reina sat in the dark with Manny beside her in the white bedroom. Some light came from the neighbor's backyard, filtered through the thin curtains. Tree shadows stamped the walls with faint Japanese script.

He'd once believed Reina could see in the dark. Her eyes flashed like a cat's in the headlights of his truck, once, as he pulled into her driveway. No human he'd ever seen, especially no adult human, was supposed to be able to reflect light in that way, from their eyes.

He would watch her sometimes after that, after he saw her eyes glow, just wondering what she was, really. It would cross his mind that she might not be human in the usual way. It's my grandmother and her shape shifter bullshit sneaking up on me, he would think. It's a hangover from too much television when I was a kid. The rear, curved surface of her eyes is very reflective, that's all there is to it.

Reina never seemed to mind when he watched her. He did it as covertly as he could.

"So you got taken for a ride," she said, after hearing his story. "How did I know that? Let me say that I, for one, am glad you're still in one piece, and you better be glad, too, because you're valuable, at least to me. You can catch bad men and there'll still be plenty left. And, working for Jeff, you'll find no end to them. Let's curl up and be happy."

She was in his arms, then, taking it easy because he still hurt. He stroked her face with his big nose and kissed her until she slipped her back into his side. He thought she would sleep.

"There's something you haven't told me," she said.

"What would that be?"

"I know you're not telling me something," Reina said.

"There is no story with this woman in Nogales," Manny said. "She set me up."

"It's not that. Something happened to you that you don't want to talk about. Something happened to your spirit. You look like you've had a visitation, Manny. You came pretty close to death. You were pretty much unconscious for a couple of days. Do you remember any of that?"

"Not much," Manny said.

"Did you see anything?"

"What do you mean?"

"Visions or visitations. Did anyone come to you? I used to try to come to people but it's not entirely possible for me. Who came to you, Manny? Who saved you?"

"What do you mean you used to try to come to people?"

"I used to try to bring my consciousness to other people so they could see me or feel me and sense that I cared about them. I still try to do that. I put the white light of protection around you every time you leave."

"Okay," Manny said, "but I don't think people can do that. I think it was the doctor who saved me—and some kid who found me. And the Mexican police and paramedics. They all saved me."

"No," Reina said.

"Reina," Manny said, "that's all that happened."

"Who came?"

"Aah," Manny said.

"Who was there for you?"

"Aie," Manny said.

"Your grandmother?" Reina asked. "Yep, your grandmother."

"I was out of my head. That's first, Reina. That is number one."

"Were you? What happened with your grandmother?"

"Reina, one time I arrested a little dope dealer. He was also a burglar. Guy by the name of Shy Jackson. I'm talking to him and he is talking to me about having some gypsy woman solve his problems with some spirit who's bothering him. And I am pretending to listen because I know that when people start to get spiritual they are about to cooperate with me. The woman gets an egg. She says some words over the egg. Then she breaks it open. This little man comes sneaking out of there. Then things are much better for Shy Jackson—until he gets arrested. Why didn't the woman or the little guy in the egg tell Shy Jackson that dealing crack and stealing from people could complicate his life, Reina? I could tell you more stories, too, but you don't need to hear them from me. All you have to do is read the newspapers or watch television."

"What happened with your grandmother?" Reina asked.

"Okay," Manny said, "it was like she was there. I could even smell her. That used to bother me about her when I was little because she smelled. . . ." Manny had to laugh and then he had to hold his ribs because he'd recently had them kicked in.

When he was done laughing Reina said, "Go on."

Manny told her the story about the snakes and the bitter plug of herb he swallowed.

"You know I watch you," Reina said. "I know you watch me."

Damn right I watch you, Manny thought. Anytime you're in love with somebody and one night you notice their eyes glow in the headlights like a cat's, you watch them.

"You don't know what I am, Manny. I don't know what I am either. I know I'm a woman. You make me respond and it's not just the sex. It's your decency, too, for one thing. You were given a gift—a visitation. Mexican people are wonderful. They accept magic and visions. Native Americans, too. It doesn't ruin their lives—it enriches their lives. All people used to do that—everybody. Asian people do it today, educated Asian people. We're missing a lot. We shut out a way of knowing the world."

"That's okay with me," Manny said, "but I picked up a leather bag in my bedroom. I put it in my pocket for no reason. Later, I had some kind of vision of my grandmother. I chewed what was in the bag. If the docs say it helped the snake bite, that's good. I was hallucinating. I can't put any belief into it, Reina."

"She gave you intuition, Manny. Even magic. Just accept it. Accept it like the way you think about physical pain. Pain is just something you notice and don't have to push away. Allow these images and visions to be in your life, like a tall clay jar along a wall that's just stood there for a thousand years."

"Why do you talk about a jar?"

"I don't know," Reina said. Her eyes were wide. She shook her head. "It just came to me. That's how you deal with anger, or pain. I watch you. You are strong in that way. And quiet. It's romantic—I mean do you freaking mind, here, Manny, I can't talk to you all the time about you, for cryin' out loud."

"We were talking about a jar," Manny said.

"Yeah. So?"

Manny gave up on figuring out how she knew that he'd thought about a tall, clay jar. And if he told her she read his mind, he'd lose the argument for sure.

"I have gut feelings," he said, "but I can't always act on them. I have cases to make here, Reina, crimes, and I don't solve them with magic, I solve them with facts. If I imagine too much I start making up the facts, and I miss details."

"I help make cases, too, Manny."

"Yes, but . . . "

"Yes but what, Manny?"

Reina looked at him hard. Her look said she was a paralegal, a professional, with years of experience, and that she could write and think in the language of the law, a bloodless drum roll of logic and technicalities meant to be based on evidence—on facts.

"How can I trust visions and dreams, Reina?" Manny said. He was doing the best he could now, with her, he thought. He was admitting to fear and doubt. What the hell more could she want?

"You can trust visions and dreams because they are like the gut feelings detectives get. You're a detective, and you're trying to tell me you operate on facts and evidence alone. Spare me the bullshit, Manny, it pisses me off. These dreams or visions are more intrusive than a plain, solid gut feeling. Evaluate them in the same way. Does it feel right or is it just fluff that's generated by your synapses snapping? Does it come from some need you won't recognize? Just do it. Use what you feel in your gut about the dream or vision. If your gut tells you it was an authentic experience, accept it, even act on it. I think it saved your life in Mexico, Manny. And I know a visitation by a person you know to be dead, or by a stranger, or by some entity that is not even human, is a pretty terrible experience—one you don't want to believe and one you don't want repeated. So, you have to come up with an explanation to cope with it all. Now, maybe it wasn't your grandmother's spirit who visited you in Mexico, and maybe it was. But it saved your life, Manuel—and you still don't give it any credit. Don't be such an ass, you're smarter than that."

"Maybe," Manny said. "I will do that. Maybe. I know you do some, uh, rituals, or whatever, around the house here...."

They both started to grin.

"But you have your feet on the ground," Manny went on. "I guess it works for you."

"It's all about respecting the unconscious mind, Manny," Reina said. "It focuses the energy of intention. But I couldn't live if I didn't believe in something beyond the great tricks our minds do. So I believe in something and I'll call it The Goddess if I want. Maybe I'll do some rituals, too. So relax about how I am, and what I tell you, and how I act, sometimes. And I'll bet you've got foxhole religion. I'll bet you've prayed your ass off in the last year over something."

Manny thought about sitting in his pickup truck and praying the day Emily Johnson was killed by somebody who was trying to kill him.

"What of it?" he said. "I'll pray if I want to."

They lay sideways in the bed, watching each other warily.

"Welcome the dreams and visions and check them with your gut, dammit," Reina said, giving him an acerbic look.

"Yeah, and I'll shove an eagle feather up my butt and see if it tickles," Manny said. And he reached for her.

Later, lying quietly, ribs, leg, and face hurting, Manny stared into the faint light in Reina's room. His eyes looked larger and darker than usual, Reina thought, glancing at him before she curled into him and started off to sleep.

What is it about Cisneros, he thought. Who is he connected with? What are they protecting? I can't touch Cisneros through any agency, but I'll try. I'll go back to the DEA or the Mexican cops—and waste my time. I can solve this another way, maybe, if I just do what investigators do: go backwards.

He thought about every creep and every ordinary citizen who'd been connected with Cisneros. He thought about giving them another look, even the dead ones. An image of Carole Harper appeared. The next person he saw after Carole Harper was the little green-eyed man, Granger.

He would go backward to Granger—and Mexico, he thought. He would look for Adelaida. But Granger came first. He would go to Mexico when he was in better shape. December, he thought. He would go in December.

Manny drifted off to sleep, seeing Harper's head on a platter in the morgue. The mouth opened. Harper spoke soundlessly. Manny read his lips and caught it the second time around: "Save yourself."

CHAPTER TWENTY-SEVEN

MANNY SAID GOODBYE to Reina when she went off to work the next morning, then limped into the bathroom and took a shower. When he finished he picked up Reina's blow drier and cleared a spot on the mirror. His face was only a little misshapen, but it wasn't pretty. He felt soft and weak.

He gave up on looking in the mirror and turned to where Grayboy sat in the hall, watching and waiting. The cat's eyes looked large and happy. As soon as Manny noticed him Grayboy started to meow and stood up, starting toward the kitchen and then coming back again to meow some more.

Manny sidled into the kitchen, a towel wrapped around his waist. An unopened can of salmon sat on the counter with a can opener next to it. There was a pink sticky note on the counter with the word CAT in Reina's handwriting. Manny shook his head ruefully and started opening the can of salmon. When he was done he bent over, stiffly, and tapped the salmon out of the can and into Grayboy's bowl.

"When we get home," Manny told Grayboy, "we are going to eat like men."

Grayboy ignored him and chewed the salmon ferociously. Manny eased into Reina's bedroom to put on jeans and a snap button western shirt she'd found for him while shopping on her lunch break at the Goodwill on Fourth Avenue. His roper boots were still in the plastic bag from the hospital.

He climbed stiffly into his truck and drove to his house. Everything was in place. He took a notebook and a couple of pens and headed downtown.

Manny parked on a side street and cut across Jacome Plaza, passing the massive stack of triangular shapes comprising Tucson's main library. He fixed his eyes on the pink courthouse dome as he crossed Church Avenue. For some reason, the desert landscaping between the courtyard and the sidewalk caught his eye. Butterflies were hovering around an acacia. It's November, he thought. Are there a bunch of butterflies that come out in November?

Butterflies didn't matter. He had work to do inside this courthouse and he'd probably never get it done today. Then he saw his grandmother, squatting behind the acacia, taking a pee. He had to stop to stay on his feet and set his teeth to keep from crying out.

"You slept in your mind all these years," she cackled. Then she disappeared. He had to stop himself from running over to the bushes to check for urine and tracks. Nobody else had heard or seen her, he realized, looking around. Lots of people coming in and out, nobody looking at him like he was crazy. Manny looked at the acacia again. No grandmother, no butterflies. He walked over and stared down. No puddle of urine, no tracks. He'd told Reina he would try to accept this…this sick stuff, he thought, and what happens? He breathed deeply, in and out, swearing under his breath, and waited until his heart stopped pounding.

When he was able to walk again he made his way to the second floor. A clerk behind a glass barrier told him that no one named David Granger had owned a motor vehicle in the past few years.

Next door, in the court building, he emptied his pockets into a dish. He'd left his handguns at Reina's, knowing he'd be searched at the courthouse. He got through the metal detector without setting it off and headed to the criminal records section.

"The grand jurors of the County of Pima, in the name of the State of Arizona, and by its authority accuse David Granger...." Manny read several references to David Granger which began in just that way. Granger was a drug offender and a burglar with multiple convictions. Manny was surprised that Granger had never been sentenced to a little jolt in the state pen. He'd only spent a few months at a time in the county jail. This would be easier, Manny thought, if Granger's drug buddies weren't all dead.

He decided to take a wild shot at the marriage license section and the birth records section. Heroin addicts did marry, it was worth finding out if Granger had ever tried it. After that, Manny planned on finding Granger's parole officer, since Granger's particular PO was probably still around, working in the same complex.

Manny went down the hall, noticing the usual denizens of the court building. Defendants and their attorneys, cops and citizens. Johnny Oaks, who Manny knew for his work as a PI, didn't stand out somehow, Manny thought, as he nodded to him, even though Oaks was the biggest person in the hallway. Manny watched Oaks move into the birth records section. Manny went for the marriage license section.

Ten minutes later, Manny had a marriage license record. David Granger had married a Dawn Damiano fifteen years before. Manny went next door to the birth certificate section.

"Rhiannon Damiano Granger," the birth certificate read. Born five months after the wedding. Now she'd be a teenager, sixteen years old. Time to go back to the criminal section.

Dawn Damiano had been charged with felony possession and sales of heroin but proceedings had been closed because the respondent, Damiano, was deceased. Manny thought, for one nanosecond, about how well David Granger would function in the role of a single parent.

He called Randy Rogers and asked for a records check on Rhiannon Granger. Randy told him that Celia Christopherson, Rhiannon's aunt, had reported her as a runaway. The kid had been missing for several months. Manny dialed Celia's number and told her he was a Tucson policeman, checking on Rhiannon.

"She ran away and I don't care if the little bitch ever comes back," Christopherson said. "I don't know a dammed thing about her." Click.

Christopherson sounded drunk. Manny checked for a gut feeling about Celia and decided he didn't have a gut feeling just then—no visions, no hallucinations, nothing. Celia sounded drunk and that was it. Reina would be disappointed.

He made for the birth records section again, finding who he was looking for almost immediately: Johnny Oaks, the big guy wearing the cowboy hat.

"Who are you working for?" Johnny asked, after Manny did a little explaining. Johnny's voice carried well. It was a crisp, educated voice, but it was soft and there was a shadow in it, some sound from another tongue.

"Jeff Goldman," Manny said.

"That guy can squeeze a nickel until the buffalo's riding the Indian," Oaks said.

Manny grinned and watched while the big man shifted across the floor of the courthouse like sand, opened a door, and dissolved in sunlight.

"Oaks." Jeff Goldman said. "I thought you were the detective, Manny, why do you want Oaks?"

"He's a specialist," Manny said.

"Yeah, my ass he's a specialist. I know he gets runaways but who needs him?"

"We do," Reina said, looking up from her keyboard. "If this kid's been missing for a whole year and her aunt doesn't give a rat's rear end about her."

"What are you doing, Reina?" Jeff said. "I thought you were getting his freaking honor, Judge Soto, off *my* rear end. Do that, would you?"

"Yeah, I'll just drop down on my keyboard here and give Judge Soto some letterhead—make the nice man's toes curl up."

"Good God, Reina. You're indecent. Okay, hire Oaks." Jeff said, turning to Manny. "What is it with him? He's, he's—an Indian, right?"

"There it is: the I-word," Reina sang out while she keyboarded furiously. "Johnny's a Cherokee. What's your real problem, Jeff?"

"Aside from the expense? Super heroes," Jeff said. "It's starting to look like television wrestling around here. This Oaks guy looks like the world's largest cowboy. He's got the big hat. He wears this big, black frigging gun—"

"Well," Reina said, "I think it's that masters degree in juvenile justice and all that time working at juvenile detention centers that got him started in the business of finding runaways. He knows how to handle troubled kids and he's on speaking terms with a lot of them. He can get information."

"Oh screw it," Jeff said. "Just go ahead. And you, Reina, you buy lunch."

"You are the cheapest, most shameless, most flinty-assed person, Jeff," Reina said admiringly. "Manny here is cheap, wretchedly cheap, but you are the *man*."

Jeff bought lunch on University Avenue and they watched the students and strollers, talked baseball, and relaxed for an hour and a half.

After lunch, Manny went back to his place and drove by it instead of stopping. His vigilance level was up again. Manny's brother, Reggie, had checked the place while he was recovering at Reina's. Reggie had brought Manny his .45 and his snubnosed backup gun. Manny went by Reina's and picked up the big Colt, slipping it inside the waistband of his jeans. He put on a leather vest to hide the weapon, then went home, leaving Grayboy behind, looking lonely, since neither Reina nor Manny were staying around these days.

His house smelled of desertion and Manny took no joy in being there. He'd managed to work with the toilet seats and keep things picked up enough around Reina's house so that, he suddenly realized, he liked it over there more than he liked his own house.

He called Johnny Oaks's cell phone.

"Goldman's gonna' pay you. Have you got anything yet?" Manny said.

"I've already started," Oaks said. "This kid is going be hard to find. She's got no juvenile record, other than that she's a status offender because she's a runaway. She left her aunt once before and the aunt reported it. Nothing I could find, so far, about tagging, drugging, stealing, minor possession.... I'll interview the aunt and I'll talk to the people at her old school in the Vistoso neighborhood—Cienega Middle School. If you want to save Jeff some money—and you might not—you can take Cienega and I'll talk to the aunt."

"You would be doing me a favor," Manny said, "talking to the aunt."

"Live one?"

"I don't think she liked this girl, Rhiannon. And she sounded like she'd been drinking when I talked to her."

Manny parked his truck in the lot, almost swimming through a river of loud kids whose vocabulary choices caused him no amusement, and found his way to the office at Cienega Middle School.

He nodded to the School Resource Officer, a Tucson Police officer in plain clothes, who was talking to the clerk at the counter. The clerk got Manny into the principal's office.

The principal, Mr. Wade, dressed like Manny. Wade favored cowboy boots and jeans and, from the look of it, he pumped a fair amount of iron.

Manny identified himself, told Wade that Rhiannon was a runaway, and then sat back in the chair Wade motioned him into.

"I don't remember much about Rhiannon," Wade said. "She was spirited, but she wasn't a problem. She was a pretty good student. I'll get a yearbook."

The kid Manny saw in the photograph had short hair, nice teeth, large eyes, and a smile that struck him as being kind of sad. There was something else about her that Manny couldn't place. The kid sure didn't look like Granger—which was a good thing, Manny decided.

Wade showed Manny a school file on Rhiannon. She'd signed something. Manny noticed she was left handed.

"Could I have a copy of the page she signed?"

Wade made him a copy.

"Do you have a teacher who knew her?"

Wade named a Mrs. Pearl who was out sick and told Manny he'd call if she could talk to him later on.

"How about friends?"

"She had some. I'd have to look at the yearbook. Mrs. Pearl might know. Rhiannon was here for the 7th and 8th grades. She's been gone for three years now. Let's see..." Wade had a look at the yearbook and came up with a couple of smiling faces: Sheree Small and Tabatha Reisner. Manny got a couple copies of the yearbook pages.

He left Wade's office as the last bell rang and the kids crashed out into the hallways, cursing, laughing, and bouncing off the lockers.

Manny drove to Jeff's adobe. The attorney was in his office, working. Reina looked up and waited to hear what Manny needed. She called a clerk she knew who worked in juvenile justice and checked on Sheree Small and Tabatha Reisner. Neither teenager was making waves anywhere.

"There's something about Rhiannon, other than the sadness, that's different," Reina decided, looking at the photograph.

"What?"

"I think of her as male, somehow."

"You think this because you see something in this school photograph of somebody who was thirteen years old when it was taken?"

"I know it sounds tacky," Reina said. "It's just a thought. It could help."

Manny quickly decided to let that strange pronouncement sit like a labeled, unwrapped package in a little warehouse of possibilities.

Then he drove back to his house, sat down in his green chair, and called Oaks.

CHAPTER TWENTY-EIGHT

"HOW WAS MRS. Christopherson?"

"She acts like she doesn't care about Rhiannon," Oaks said, "but I think she's hiding something. She said Rhiannon ran away twice. After that she lost patience with the kid. Do you have some names from Cienega?"

Manny gave him Sheree Small and told him he'd try to talk to Reisner.

"I know some other students from Cienega," Johnny said, "and I'll pass these names around."

Manny picked up a phone book and looked through the listings for Reisners. There would be fewer of them than the Smalls. Every Reisner had a street address listed. That was good, Manny thought. They weren't hiding. Of course, people who don't hide often don't know anything about people who do.

It was almost five. He checked the refrigerator. Empty. Reina or Reggie had actually cleaned the dammed thing. Not that there was much to clean. He didn't keep much except beer, mustard, and salsa. Manny got a glass of water, watched the news, and started calling Reisners at six, when everybody who worked a day job would probably be home.

He asked for Tabatha, saying he was a clerk from a local department store, and that an item with her name on it had been found there. When he got to the house where Tabatha lived he hung up while whoever answered was calling Tabatha to the phone. Then he drove there, calling Reina before he left the house to let her know he'd be home later.

Tabatha was willing to talk to a PI who explained that relatives other than Rhiannon's aunt were concerned about her and hoped to provide support for her.

"She hasn't called me in a long time," Tabatha said. "It's been months."

"How well did you know her Aunt Celia?"

"I stayed at Rhiannon's a couple of times. Celia was nice. She used to make us bunny pancakes." Tabatha laughed.

"What are bunny pancakes?"

"You mix pancake batter, you pour three circles, one big, one medium size, and a little circle for the tail. Then you make the ears."

"You got me beat," Manny said. "I was heating tortillas on gas burners when I was thirteen."

"Sounds good," Tabatha said.

Manny nodded. "They were good."

Manny called Oaks on his way back to Reina's. Johnny had nothing on Sheree Small.

"This Celia Christopherson sounds like a good parent," Manny told Oaks. "I think you got the right feeling about her hiding something."

Reina was tired that night from hammering out legal language. The two of them started to fall asleep together while Grayboy lay and watched them from the foot of the bed.

"How do you feel about being devious, big fella?" Reina asked suddenly, shifting her body so she could watch him with her green eyes.

"What do you mean?"

"Well, as a detective, you could usually tell people who you were. You didn't have to trick them. Nowadays, in order to trace a skip you have to tell lies. For instance, if you haven't already conned the Social Security Administration to get a number, you'll have to sooner or later. How's that feel?"

"It doesn't matter," Manny said. "I had to lie when I was a sheriff's detective—and the biggest lies I had to tell were the ones I told myself about department politics not being a problem for me."

"I know you, Manny, and you don't like lying half the time, just to get the job done. Anything on that girl, Rhiannon?"

"No," Manny said sleepily, "but I learned how to make bunny pancakes." He told her about Tabatha Reisner.

"See how this job is better than being a sheriff's detective?" Reina said. "Let that part of you get bigger and have some fun with it."

"Spare me," Manny growled.

They curled up again and slept. Grayboy dozed, bored with the way humans could waste a good, dark night.

Reina, Manny thought, was looking fabulous at 7:30 the next morning, going out the door to work.

She suddenly stopped in the doorway and jerked her head for him to come. Johnny Oaks was sitting curbside in a Cadillac El Dorado convertible. The engine was running.

Manny held up one finger and disappeared to get his cell phone and his weapon. When he got in the Cadillac he saw Oaks was packing his trademark N frame Smith and Wesson revolver, blue steel, six-inch barrel, chambered in .45 Colt. The wheel gun was big as a coal shovel and Oaks had it strapped down with a leather thong. He appeared unselfconscious about his trappings and this morning he was even more serious than usual.

Reina knew Oaks slightly, Manny recalled, as he buckled his seatbelt and pulled his slab sided Colt automatic closer into the hollow behind his hip, and she had never joked about Johnny's style. Sometimes she had a word, maybe two, for people who looked like they were on their way to a rodeo. But never a remark about Johnny Oaks.

"I shook down a kid," Johnny said, "who owes me for keeping him out of jail. That got me to another kid and the other kid knew about Rhiannon Granger, only she calls herself Ronnie Santee now. She lives in a house with a couple other young people and works in an auto glass shop. We'll catch up to her in the shop. I talked to the owner and he understands."

When they came to the auto glass shop on Tucson's south side Oaks cut the engine and glided into a parking space that couldn't be seen from the open bays where workers were busy with the cars. They slipped into the office and the boss pointed with his chin at an old four-door Chevy in the nearest bay. A slender kid in dark clothing was getting in on the driver's side.

Manny came up one side of the car and Johnny Oaks came up the other. They blocked both front doors with their big bodies and leaned in from both sides, looking hard at the slender girl with a wool cap pulled down low on her face. They held up badges and picture IDs in leather cases.

Rhiannon could almost pass for a man, Manny thought, wondering once more at Reina's psychic ability. The teenage female's T shirt was baggy and so were her jeans. She wore polished combat boots on her feet and tattoos on her forearms. Rhiannon threw both locks down on the doors as the men reached for the outside handles. She planted her narrow back against the seat cushions of the car and kicked the windshield out on the first try. The girl dove forward through the opening and lunged across the hood, moving without vocalizing, and with the intelligent desperation of a feral cat.

The two big men got to her, but not before she could turn, where they trapped her against the wall of the old garage, and put hits and kicks on both of them until they got her wound up in her own arms and legs. Just when they thought they'd got her, she unwound herself and hit them three or four times with fists and feet, taking nicks out of their eyebrows, stinging their shins, and trying for their groins. They finally double teamed her and pushed her belly-down on the hood of the car, hard enough to knock the wind out of her. Oaks cuffed her and everybody took a few ragged breaths.

"Rhiannon," Johnny said quietly, "you lost. You lost this fight. We're doing our job here, that's all. You're a runaway. We have to clear some things up. You come with us. You respect us. We respect you. If not, you go to detention and we have you charged with assault and battery and you will go to jail for that. For right now, all we do is go outside, sit in a car, and talk this thing out. Stand up."

The two men pulled Rhiannon Granger upright and walked her gently out to the Cadillac while the other young workers and the boss stood around and looked on. The young guys in the shop started laughing. She kicked their asses, the young guys kept saying. They sobbed with laughter. They held on to each other to keep from laughing until they fell down. And they fell down anyway. The boss grinned ruefully and shook his head. Manny and Johnny got Rhiannon seated between them in the front seat of the Caddy and began talking to her.

"Do you want to go back to your aunt?"

Silence. Johnny started the Caddy.

"Where you going?' Rhiannon asked. Her voice was like the breath itself. It was full and husky and alive. Bigger than she was, bigger than everything, somehow, and the two men didn't care because they had a job to do and Manny had reason to believe he might not be around too long if he didn't get some answers.

"Talk to us," Manny said. "Why did you run away?"

"I can take care of myself," Rhiannon said.

"You know we talked to your aunt," Johnny said, and shut down the Cadillac, "and she said that after you left the second time she didn't care. She said you would call her once in awhile and you only stopped calling after your dad died."

"What about that?" Manny added.

Rhiannon tried fighting again but by then they'd cuffed her ankles, too, and strapped her in the seat. They let her get tired while they kept talking quietly.

"We are not the people who were after your father," Manny said. "Whoever was after your father needs to go to jail. We want to put them in jail. What do you know about it?"

"I don't know jack about my old man," Rhiannon said.

"You know something," Johnny said quietly. "Anything that you can remember would help us."

"Ever hear of Tony Cisneros?" Manny asked. "No? Ever hear of Larry Armenta? Or your father's friends? Perez? Corral? Harper?"

They spent a half an hour, talking, with no results.

"I have a suggestion," Manny said, finally. "Let's go to lunch."

Johnny and Rhiannon looked at him like he'd lost his mind. Manny dialed Jeff's office on his cell phone.

"Reina," he said, "we'll be at the office in a few minutes. We're bringing a friend to lunch."

There was silence on the way to Jeff's office. When Manny and Johnny brought Rhiannon in Reina told them to take the cuffs off and go sit down somewhere. Then she went in the bathroom with Rhiannon. After awhile they came out together and Rhiannon's hair was in place and she looked calm.

"You know what?" Reina said. "You guys are a mess. Why don't you go get cleaned up and go to lunch and Rhiannon and I will go to lunch on our own. We'll see you back here this afternoon."

Johnny and Manny watched the two women walk out the door, looked at each other, shrugged, and headed down to South Tucson for some Mexican food. They drew some stares when they walked into Guillermo's on South Fourth Avenue, but nobody really seemed to care. Oaks and Aguilar tore through two huge plates of food. Then they nursed a couple beers and talked shop until they figured Reina and Rhiannon would be back at the office. When they got back to Jeff's little white adobe they found Reina quietly tapping away at her workstation. They waited for a minute.

"Where's Rhiannon?" Manny finally asked.

"She's at my place, with the doors locked, and I told her to get some sleep," Reina said.

"What did she tell you?"

"She's a great kid and she needs our help," Reina said, "and she helped us. Johnny, thanks for finding her. I'll murder Jeff if he doesn't cut you a check and a bonus for this. But right now, I've got to talk to your pal here—alone."

Oaks and Aguilar gave each other a tired look and a goodbye nod.

"She knows all about her old man," Reina said, after Oaks had gone. "And she knows about Tony Cisneros. She says he was after her dad. Granger sent her into hiding because he ran afoul of Tony Cisneros.

This all seems to be about an audiotape and your dead guy from the dump, Harper. Granger told Rhiannon that Harper was at his house the night he disappeared. Harper was drunk and said he was going to blackmail a rich guy. Harper bragged that he had a tape recording proving something about the guy. He said he had stuff stashed away that would put the rich guy in jail.

"Harper walked out of Granger's place that night, saying he was going to meet the man on the corner, by the Bar Nine, and that he'd be back. He gave Granger and Granger's junkie roommates some money, and said something about how they'd already helped him out and didn't know it. He said he'd be back that night and he'd be rolling in dough. Harper never came back and the junkies started getting nervous. Rhiannon believes what her father told her. Does this fit in for you, Manny? I hope so, because I've got a feeling Rhiannon's telling the truth."

"Granger named Tony Cisneros as somebody who might explain why he was kidnapped," Manny said. "Granger never mentioned Rhiannon. Rhiannon's in danger if she's telling the truth. She told you all this?"

"Yes, her old man was so scared he talked it all out with her. And the bad guys phoned up Granger, whoever they are, and threatened him. They wanted to know what he knew. They said they knew about Rhiannon and they'd kill her if Granger didn't cooperate. Then his junkie buddies started disappearing—two men. She didn't know their names. "When you and the other detective came by to interview him, Granger must have thought you were working for whoever got Harper. He was already terrified, so he tried to shoot whoever was knocking on his door. He'd already talked with Rhiannon and told her he was on his way into hiding himself."

"I heard a story like this before," Manny said, "from a junkie named Perez. Randy Rogers arrested Perez for heroin. Perez started talking about Harper so we thought Perez killed him. Granger and another junkie named Corral lived with Perez. Perez and Corral are both dead. It sounded wrong then...."

"I know," Reina said, "but we don't have anything, unless...."

"Unless there really was a tape."

"Yes."

"It could be in that house," Manny said. "When Harper was killed I searched his room. Somebody went over Harper's room, a careful search, not making it obvious. They were looking for something like that, probably something Harper had."

"Whoever is behind this," Reina said, "is still looking for the tape, or at least for anybody who knows Granger's story. That means you and Rhiannon. Rhiannon is in danger. You could be in danger."

"I need to get to Granger's house," Manny said, "but first I need to get to Rhiannon. She's at your place. Now you're in danger, Reina. I need to get over there. I want to hear this again—from Rhiannon. Will she talk in front of me?"

"I think she will now," Reina said.

"Good," Manny said. "Where's Jeff?"

"He's in court."

"You should stay here until I can make sure Rhiannon is okay and your house is safe," Manny said. "I'll see if I can get Johnny over so you've got some security."

"I'm coming with you if you go to my house. But how critical is this, Manny? Rhiannon's been missing for a long time. She hid, successfully, until we found her. Aren't you being paranoid? Why would the bad guys know about this now?"

"They probably don't know, but you need to be very careful. Whoever got Granger out of that secured hospital had some influence. And, for that matter, this guy, Perez, Granger's friend, died in jail, possibly murdered. The bad guys have inside sources, Reina."

CHAPTER TWENTY-NINE

MANNY AND REINA drove to her house and circled it, cruising through the alley, and then parking two houses away on the street. They had passed through Reina's black wrought iron gate and were almost to the door when they heard a car pull up. Manny glimpsed Randy Rogers' blue corvette as it slid by the gate, stopping out of sight on the other side of Reina's wall. Rogers appeared, grinning when he saw Manny.

"You two look kind of tense," he said.

"What's up?" Manny said.

"Hadn't heard from you since you asked about that runaway. I found some stuff that could help. What's going on?"

"Nothing that matters," Manny lied. "We're just stopping by home on our way out again."

Manny didn't want a Tucson police officer involved just then, not until he'd had a chance to talk to Rhiannon Granger himself—and look for the tape that should, by all rights, lead to Harper's killer.

Reina opened the door with her key and disappeared inside. Manny knew she'd take Rhiannon in the back bedroom and keep her quiet.

"I got something on that kid," Rogers said, "your runaway. Have you got just a minute?" Rogers looked serious.

"Sure," Manny said. "Come on in."

Manny checked the fridge, feeling a little guilty for being short with Rogers.

"Beer?" Manny said, turning from the fridge with one in each hand.

Randy sat down at the coffee table and put his beer on it. Grayboy took a seat on the couch next to Randy and started watching the bubbles in his beer glass.

"I did find that the kid had a prior arrest...." Rogers began. Manny was still standing. Rogers waited for him to sit. When Manny didn't sit down, Rogers put his bottle on the coffee table and stood up slowly. His hand moved very fast and then Manny was looking at an automatic pistol with a sound suppressor screwed onto the muzzle.

"Not a sound, hoss," Rogers said. "I know the kid's here. I want the kid, I want the tape."

"What? Why are you doing this?"

"Because it's the last thing I need to do," Rogers whispered. "I got a little jet waiting for me. I can buy a new Corvette where I'm going. Have it shipped over special. I need the kid. I need the tape."

"Is this about money? Old ladies in Vistoso die so you can get money?" Manny felt calm now. If he had to die, he might as well die asking questions. And he knew he'd die anyway, because, in a second, he would try to jump Rogers and Rogers would shoot him, but it might buy Reina and the kid some time to get out of there.

Rogers smiled. "Didn't ya ever want to fool *everybody*, Manny? Have a little fun? I got their money, I got the highest pussy they could buy—it's my turn, jack. Now give me the tape and the kid or I'll kill you."

Manny heard a clunk and Rogers spun around. Grayboy had finally given in to the fascination of the bubbles in a beer glass. He'd jumped on Randy's beer bottle and the beer was steaming across the coffee table. Manny drew and began firing.

Rogers fell across the table, tipping it over on his way down to the floor. Manny watched it happen in slow motion. Then Randall Rogers was lying face down on a red and black rug, exit wounds ripped in his back.

Manny called to Reina, hardly able to hear his own voice after the gunfire. She and Rhiannon crept out, holding on to each other. Reina bent over to right the downed coffee table and Manny took her hand, pulled her up gently.

"Reina, look at me," he said. "Give me a thumbs up."

She looked at him like was talking to her through a piece of plumbing. Then she responded like a sleepwalker, coming out of it once she'd held that thumb up for a moment.

"Rhiannon," Manny said, "are you good?" He held his thumb up. She held up hers. "Don't look down there," he told them both. "Look up here."

Manny dropped to his knees and put his hand on Rogers' neck. When he looked up at Reina and shook his head, she walked Rhiannon over to a chair and sat her down. Then she reached for a phone.

"Jeff? No, I'm not all right…I know I sound *funny*," Her speech went to warp speed. "You remember Randy Rogers? Yeah, that narcotics cop who lied on the witness stand every chance he got. He just came over here and tried to shoot Manny. Manny shot him and he's dead. We'll be calling the cops now. Please come over. Yes, Jeff, "please" is in my vocabulary after all. And so is thank you very much. See you soon."

"What are you going to tell the police, Manny?" Reina asked as soon as she hung up the phone.

"I'm going to tell them the part of the story that has to do with Rogers," Manny said. "And then I'm going after that tape."

"What about me?" Rhiannon said. "What am I supposed do in all this?"

"Tell the police what you saw and what you heard," Manny said.

"I didn't hear anything but shooting," Rhiannon said. "Then I came out here and he was dead. What did he want? Was he after me?"

"We're going to make sure you're safe," Manny said.

"I have to go to the bathroom now," Rhiannon said.

Two detectives named Hauser and O'Brien sat down with Manuel Aguilar and started asking questions. Hauser was a big man with dark hair and light colored eyes. So was O'Brien. Tweedledee and Tweedledum, Reina thought, looking at them, the Retro Twins. Beefy bulls, straight from the 1950s. Judging from the mismatch on their pants and jackets, they're both colorblind, too—and those ties are, of course, horrific.

After the "What happened?" part of the questioning, everybody moved smoothly into the "Why?" part. Goldman sat quietly by, watching and listening. Manny told them Rogers was a crooked cop who came over to silence Rhiannon, who had only hearsay to offer about a blackmail attempt by Harper—who had been murdered as a result of the attempt.

"And you're saying Rogers knew you were investigating because you confided in him?" Hauser asked.

"And you say that when Rogers realized you were after someone that had to do with his criminal associates, he played you for awhile. When you found the witness he was looking for, he tried to kill you. Is that right?" O'Brien asked.

Finally, the talking was over and the forensics people were coming in and out of the door. Hauser stood up. O'Brien remained seated next to Manny.

"Mr. Aguilar," Hauser said, "you are under arrest. We will charge you with murder."

"This is wrong," Jeff Goldman said to their backs as they led Manny toward the door. "There were two guns drawn here. This is self defense. I need a moment with my client."

Hauser and O'Brien let Jeff take Manny over in a corner.

"I will try to get you out right away," Jeff said. "It's wrong that you would even go to jail under these circumstances. There were two guns drawn, Rogers came to this house on his own. It's a joke. These cops could be sued for making this decision to arrest—I'm convinced of it. If we can't get this turned around right away, you know that you have no criminal history, you have close ties to the community, and you are bondable. A good report from pretrial services can be prepared in 24 to 48 hours. "We've told them about Cisneros; you've told them about Harper. We have no direct proof, yet, that Rogers is involved and came here to kill a witness, but he had a gun with a sound suppressor and he tried to kill you. "I will have that pretrial services report pushed through. And I'll talk them into protective custody tonight, if I can. We will prepare to meet bond, if one should be set. My guess is that you're going to be out of jail about one second after a judge hears about this. If you don't get out tonight I'll be down to see you later."

Manny sat in the back of the squad car and thought about the audiotape. He had nothing he could use that might lead to the people Rogers worked for. He felt like he was climbing a rope in the dark. He hadn't told the police about the tape. Other Tucson cops might be like Randy Rogers. So far, only Reina knew about the tape. Reina and Rhiannon—and the bad guys, who seemed to have influence everywhere, including the jail where Manny was heading. Now, Manny knew, it was Reina who would be going to the junkie house to look for the tape—if there was a tape at all.

Ricky Martin was glad he wasn't smoking dope when he got the knock on his door. Omigod, the dope, he thought. It's still on the table, with the bong pipe and a bizillion empty beer cans.

Ricky liked to call it the college experience. He was a freshman at the University of Arizona, getting solid C's and D's, and he knew mom and dad, making big bucks out in Los Angeles, were happy with that.

He snatched up the bong pipe, the baggie and the ashtray, carrying everything into the kitchen. Then Ricky opened the door a crack and found himself looking at the pearl snap buttons on the shirt of what had to be the world's biggest cowboy—and the gun, the big black gun, thankfully still in its holster. Ricky decided it had to be old movie channels from the night before. Escaped cowboys, Ricky thought, from the television. Yeah, that's it: Hopalong Catastrophe. But the thought went away as soon as it came and Ricky steeled himself for more reality, which, he'd noticed, just kept coming at him, in spite of all his friends and the dope, beer, channel surfing and skipping classes.

The big man was speaking and identifying himself with a badge and a picture ID. And the big guy was making a point of saying he wasn't the cops. Ricky was feeling faint, but he was stout lad, and determined to survive and take an insider job in the family furniture rental business.

At the same time, Ricky was noticing the woman, who looked, to his manipulative eye, like nobody you'd want to play with. Dark red hair, green eyes with heavy lids, razor sharp pupils—eyes that had this really wicked don't mess with me Ricky I heard it all before look in them. She was clearly hipper than his mother, even though they had to be about the same age. And there was the scar on her jaw. She was kind of attractive, true, but nobody you'd want chasing you down the street, Ricky thought, what with that scar and all.

It was about a client of theirs who'd lived in the house. Well, the client's mother had lived in the house, and she was eccentric and had probably hidden some papers around, or maybe even a video or audiotape, with some necessary information on it about her will. The client was fighting with his relatives over the estate.

Did Ricky ever come across anything like that in the house? Could Ricky stand to make a hundred bucks to let them look around? And did he understand they weren't the cops and they weren't investigating his lifestyle? Reina told him these things while she held up a hundred-dollar bill. Ricky got it: He gets one hundred dollars and he doesn't get ratted out or arrested by these large, scary looking old people.

"I'll do the bedrooms," Oaks said, believing Reina would be disgusted enough by the kitchen and the bathroom without running her hands under the mattresses of young male substance abusers.

Reina put on a pair of rubber gloves and went into the bathroom, starting high and working down. She checked the shower stall first, tapping and prying at suspicious looking tiles. The shower curtain rod was near death and she left it propped in a corner of the stall after she'd examined it with a flashlight. She checked the toilet tank and the space behind it.

Some idiot had punched out the mirror over the sink and only the screws were left in the unpainted wall. She tapped on the wall with the butt of the flashlight just to be sure, then knelt on the filthy floor and pulled open the small wooden door in the wash stand under the sink.

The stand dated back to the 1920s. Many people had painted it, over and over, since then. The original wood was probably lovely and that was the real travesty for Reina. It was moldy under there. All her senses were in her fingertips and she hoped she wouldn't find a Brown Recluse or a Black Widow. Or a scorpion.

She ran her flashlight over the detritus in the bottom of the cabinet. The flashlight was always turning on by itself in her purse and running down the batteries. She was glad it was working today. She scrunched down more, looking up, following the beam of light around the plumbing and the rotted slats. There was no way to check the crosspiece just inside, over the door, except by touch. She hoped she wouldn't find a needle some junkie had stashed on a lip of wood that hadn't seen daylight since everybody wore hats. Her fingers, gloved, and swathed in some tissue paper she'd found, touched an object that fell some twenty-six inches from its perch, bounced off the rim of a rusty MJB coffee can, and landed at her knees. Black plastic. A tape.

CHAPTER THIRTY

FIVE MINUTES LATER, Reina and Johnny were playing the tape in Johnny's Cadillac. Reina thought she'd never listened so hard to a tape that seemed to have so much silence and so many muffled sounds.

"This is agonizing, Johnny."

Oaks nodded.

When it was over at last, they looked at each other and smiled cautiously.

"If this is really Harper," Reina said, "it's going to make Manny's day."

It was almost five o'clock and the winter sun was dropping fast.

"Well, I've got a cat to feed," Reina said, "and I need to call Rhiannon. Leaving her with her aunt worked out, didn't it?"

"Yeah," Oaks said, "the aunt had Manny and me both fooled. I think I better stay around your house until tomorrow. We'll probably have Manny out of jail by then."

"Well, sure, I guess so," Reina said, "but do you really think more bad guys will try to follow Rogers' act?"

"No telling," Johnny said, "and, well, you've...."

"Had a guy killed in my house?" Reina said. "Yeah, but I know how to deal with that."

"You one of those people that purifies houses?" Johnny said.

"Something like that. But not on an empty stomach. What kind of takeout do you want to eat?"

"Chinese," Johnny said, wondering a little at Reina's apparent lack of anxiety about the after effects of violent death. "A beer wouldn't hurt either."

"Manny's got beer. Drop me off at Jeff's office. I'll pick up my car. You mind running for Chinese food while I get the cat food and I'll meet you at the house?"

"No," Johnny said. "But take your time getting home. You shouldn't walk in there alone."

"I'll be careful," Reina said.

Reina had always been fast and it didn't surprise her that Johnny's Cadillac was nowhere to be seen when she pulled up in front of her house. The place looked deserted. No strange cars on the street. Her lair had been a zoo a few hours before and now it was quiet. Good. She popped her car door shut and charged inside, clutching a stuffed grocery bag and calling for Grayboy. She was reaching for a can of salmon when they grabbed her. She recognized one of them from his picture: Tony Cisneros. They hit her in the face. Then they began talking.

"Where's the tape?" Tony said.

"You're too late. We found it and we turned it over to the attorney general's office."

"You lie, bitch," Tony said. "We been on you since you and that big *pendejo* left the house where you found the tape. We watched you sit there and listen to it. You didn't go nowhere but here and the grocery store. And we'll get Manny Aguilar, too, you stupid bitch. He's a dead man, he's going to die tonight, right there in that jail. Give us the tape or we'll kill you right now."

Reina was already very sure they were going to kill her anyway but she had some news for them.

"You're wrong about me not going anywhere but the grocery store."

Tony and the other guy glanced at each other and fear glittered in their black eyes.

"Sun Station on Speedway," Reina said, "the Post Office. I pulled through the drive-in mail drop there, remember? I put that tape in an envelope and dropped it in a mail slot. It's addressed to a personal friend who works at the State Attorney General's office. By the way, we made a copy of that tape after we listened to it in the car. And I hope for your sake you sent somebody to follow the, uh, "big *pendejo*" because he's due here right now."

A key scratched in the front door lock and the two men looked at each other. Reina took the opportunity to fling a five pound bag of cat food at their faces and duck. Cisneros fired wildly before both men ran, flying through the back patio door together, bouncing off the doorframe and disappearing into the night.

"I'm okay," Reina yelled as Johnny Oaks charged into the room with his revolver drawn.

Johnny ran out the patio door after the men but they were gone. Tires screeched at the end of the alley. Reina ran after him into the back yard.

"We need to get to that jail," Reina yelled. "Cisneros said he'd kill Manny."

They sprinted for Johnny's Cadillac and Reina punched Jeff's number on the cell phone.

"Jeff, are you all right?"

"Why wouldn't I be?"

"Oh, I don't know, a couple of Mexican bad guys were waiting for me when I got home is all...yeah, I'm all right...but they said they were going to kill Manny in jail—tonight. I'm on my way there with Johnny right now. We're just going to start screaming and banging on the door. We'll do anything we can. Get on the phone. Help us."

She started dialing TPD but stopped dialing in disgust. She realized she was in a panic, that she shouldn't blindly trust the Tucson police. Jeff would be on his way to the jail, calling whoever he knew who could help. Then she thought about Rhiannon and called Jeff again.

"Jeff, Rhiannon's still in danger. We need somebody to go get her, to protect her...Calm down? I'll calm down, as soon as I know we didn't get that little girl killed after all this."

"How'd they get to your house? How'd they know about the tape?" Johnny asked her as he gunned the Cadillac down the street.

"You know," Reina said.

"Yeah, had to be Rogers," Johnny said. "But Mexicans? Who sent them?"

"The same guy that killed Harper," Reina said. "The guy Harper talked about on the tape."

"Maybe," Johnny Oaks said.

They fell silent and let the Cadillac roll. The top was down and a black wind fluttered over their faces.

Manny found himself emptying his pockets a few feet away from another prisoner.

"Hey," the stoner yelled. "Hey, remember me? You got me arrested just because I got pissed off at somebody on the phone. Now you're in the slam. Serves you right, you stinking cop. Ha, ha, ha, ha."

A couple of corrections officers dragged the kid off and Manny reflected briefly on how you met the nicest people in jail.

They put Manny in a large bay with a row of bunks running down either side of a long room. He was doing as little talking as possible with the other prisoners when a lone corrections officer motioned to him from the other side of the bars.

"Come here. You're being moved to another cell."

Red flag, Manny thought. Randy Rogers set up Perez in this jail.

Manny had seen it in his eyes when Randy tried to take Rhiannon. Randy got the junkies killed, one at a time, and then let Manny find the girl for him. Manny took a breath and got ready for whatever was coming.

The CO put him in an empty cell in a small bay of mostly empty cells. The place was dead quiet.

The jailer left and came back three minutes later with another prisoner. The guy was smiling when the CO let him into the cell. Hispanic kid, probably eighteen years old, harmless looking. A face you wouldn't remember. The young man took a step toward Manny, offering a handshake. Manny saw the man's white T-shirt and regulation orange pants. It was the tennis shoes with laces that gave it away—that, and his left hand, hanging at his side, with the fingers slightly curled.

Manny put up his guard. The young man just stood there smiling, looking surprised. The jailer disappeared like a wisp of smoke and the kid flew forward, slashing with the knife he'd been holding backwards in his left hand. Manny took the blade on the bone edge of his forearm so he could get close enough to the assassin to crush him against a wall and bang the kid's head on it until he fell down.

Manny got the knife, pulled off his own shirt, and tied it tight around his wounded arm. Then he sat on top of the dazed kid and held the knife up. Manny felt the hot rage scald him, spreading out from the base of his neck and along the sides of his face.

"Who told you to kill me?"

When the gangster didn't answer Manny put the knife against his groin.

"I'll cut your balls off," Manny said. "I got nothing to lose. For all I know, the COs will kill me when they come back. Who told you to kill me?"

The assassin tried to hiss an insult. Manny hit the kid two times, as hard as he could, breaking the kid's nose and cheekbone. Then he shoved the knife through the kid's genitals.

"Tito!" the kid screamed.

"Tony Cisneros?" Manny twisted the knife and the kid screamed again.

"Yeah, Tony. Please."

"Who's Tony's boss?"

When the little assassin hesitated Manny twisted the knife again. The kid screeched, "Rico, that's all I know."

"Where does Rico live?"

"Mexico. Please."

"What does he do?"

"Drugs. He's the boss, he's the boss."

"Why did they tell you to kill me?"

"I don't know."

Manny was twisting the knife once more when a gaggle of corrections officers showed up, along with a shift leader. Manny remained seated on the kid's chest, held up the bloody knife, and said, "If you come in, I kill him. A CO put this kid in my cell to kill me. I was a sheriff's detective. My name is Manuel Aguilar. I want my attorney, Jeff Goldman—or Detective Daryl Trainor. Trainor is the only one of you people I trust."

The COs stood frozen, hearing the craziness ring in Manny's voice like a broken bell.

Captain Juvera walked in and it took a few long seconds for everybody while Manny considered whether or not Juvera was just another corrupt cop. Manny was also wondering what the captain of the Criminal Investigations Division, headquartered way over on the Benson Highway, was doing at the jail this time of night.

"Your attorney is here," Juvera said. "Goldman's here. I'll bring him in if you want to see him." Juvera was talking soft, like somebody's mother. Manny could see the fear in Juvera's eyes.

"Bring him in," Manny said. His voice was cracking. He swallowed and licked his lips.

Jeff Goldman appeared.

"You get these guys to explain how I got taken out of a bay full of prisoners so this kid could knife me," Manny said. "Find the CO who put me here. The guy's nametag read Brown. I can describe him."

"It's safe, Manny," Jeff said. "Let him go."

Manny got off the gangbanger, who couldn't get up, and the COs let Manny stand without handcuffing him.

"Get a stretcher in here," Juvera said, "and get that prisoner an ambulance. Manny, let's walk and talk on our way to the dispensary. You need medical attention, too."

"You've got to identify that CO," Manny said. His eyes were wild.

"They've got him already. We had an informer in your bay. He got the word out when the CO took you."

"You'll be out of here tonight, Manny." Jeff Goldman said. He turned to Juvera. "And he never should have been here in the first place."

"I didn't arrest Manuel Aguilar, Counselor, the Tucson Police did," Juvera said. "I just got here as quick as I could when you called me."

"And I thank you for it," Jeff said. "And now that we've discovered that my investigator, Mr. Aguilar here, has survived his stay in Pima County jail, we'd like to be leaving as soon as possible."

Juvera left Manny with Goldman in the dispensary and went to a conference room where the jailhouse brass and one civilian, a bone-lean woman, was waiting for him with her chin on her knuckles. She wore wire rimmed spectacles that distorted her dark eyes, making them seem huge. Carrie Mack, the Pima County Sheriff's Department attorney, who was working late and not loving it, Juvera thought.

"So now we have a CO who's going up on charges because he's lying about moving this Manuel Aguilar by mistake," Carrie Mack said. "And we have Pedro Salas, who's probably denying he's a jailhouse assassin, even as they sew up the little bastard's balls. We've got Manuel Aguilar, and Aguilar's pissed off attorney—and, apparently, the attorney is pissed off with some justification, given the circumstances around the shooting TPD arrested him for—and I'd like to know what the hell TPD was thinking. Be that as it may, do you know what I'm thinking?"

Carrie's wire-rimmed, over-large eyes raked Juvera for a second and then she brought a cigarette to her lips, lit it, coughed, blew out the smoke, and stared at him again as she shook out the match. "I think we stepped on our pricks. Now let's go see Manny Aguilar, eat crow, deal with that smartass hippie lawyer, Goldman, and try to find out what the hell this is all about."

"What's going on here, Manuel?" Captain Juvera said softly, when they were all finally seated together in the conference room. "What's your story?"

"I can only tell you what you already know," Manny said. "Two people tried to kill me in the last four hours and I should not be in jail."

"We're providing protective custody for tonight, Mr. Aguilar," Carrie Mack said, leaning her chin on her knuckles. "We're putting you up at Saint Mary's hospital. You will have armed guards on your room there. We would appreciate hearing your side of this incident."

"You people can do your talking to my attorney," Manny said.

"Aguilar," Juvera said. "What the hell are you involved in that somebody would try to kill you?"

Goldman gave Carrie Mack and Captain Juvera a look that said a lawsuit against their department was as good as pending and they'd do well to tread lightly with his client.

"What can I tell you that I haven't told you already?" Manny asked them.

"You could give us the background, the big picture," Carrie Mack said.

"You're wasting your time," Manny said. "If you know the big picture, you can tell me what it is. You're the people with the assassins and the crooked cops."

When Jeff Goldman finally left the jail, he found Reina outside in the yard, smoking cigarettes with a couple of women who were taking a break from doing intake on prisoners.

"Since when do you smoke, Reina?" he said.

"You know, Jeff," Reina said, "before I started hanging out with you and Manny I thought I'd never smoke again. How's my man?"

They walked to where Johnny Oaks sat waiting in his Cadillac.

"He's a got a cut on his forearm. He'll be in protective custody for tonight at Saint Mary's. The sheriff's department is embarrassed, and rightly so. They'll have armed guards outside his room. I got him a hearing set for 10 o'clock tomorrow morning. He'll be released. We'll have to put up a bond."

"What if the armed guards kill him, Jeff? Did you think of that?"

"Nobody will touch him. This is way too high profile now. They've got a corrections officer in jail, a wannabe killer in the hospital, and all the department brass are going to be awake the rest of the night, trying to cover their butts and figure it all out."

"Who's the judge for the hearing?"

"Soto. He'll be okay. Soto has enough sense to know Manny shouldn't have gone to jail."

"I hope so. Thanks, Jeff," Reina said.

"The judge will set Manny's court date tomorrow. We can get those charges thrown out when Manny makes his appearance. I'm betting on it. TPD will be sorry they arrested him."

Jeff started away toward his car. "Take care of that shiner, Reina," he said, over his shoulder. "Put a steak on it or something. See you tomorrow at work and we'll listen to that tape."

Oaks cranked the engine on the Caddy. "Do you think it's safe to go back your house tonight?"

"The way Cisneros and his buddy blew out my back door, I'm betting they won't be back," Reina said.

"They wanted that tape. They'll keep trying," Oaks said. "How's your eye? Should we stop by an ER?"

"I'm okay," Reina said.

They found Grayboy sitting in the hallway, looking hopeful. His new mistress kept irregular hours and was not prompt with salmon, but she was a good woman just the same. Moreover, she'd brought Oaks, who smelled more or less like Manny. Grayboy looked them in the eye as they passed. Reina fed him and called Rhiannon Granger, warning her that the bad guys had been around, looking for the tape.

"Is your aunt okay with all of this?" Reina asked.

"She's happy I'm not dead. When is this going to be over?"

"Soon, honey," Reina said. "Soon, I hope," Reina said, after she'd hung up the phone.

Reina woke up first the next morning and slipped into the kitchen to brew some coffee. When she got it going she tapped on the door of the guest bedroom. Oaks appeared a moment later. His body brushed the walls on both sides of the hallway as he headed for the bathroom. After breakfast Reina left for Jeff's office, but not before she called again to check on Rhiannon.

Reina and Jeff Goldman arrived at Jeff's office at the same time. They got Jeff's car and headed for the courthouse.

Manuel Aguilar looked pale when the guards brought him in for his ten o'clock hearing. Judge Soto cut him loose in time for lunch with Reina and Jeff at Gentle Ben's. Then it was back to Goldman's office.

"So you had the tape all the time?" Jeff snapped the audio cassette into a recorder on Reina's desk.

"Hell yeah," Reina said. "I just dropped by Sun Station to mail a card to my granddaughter."

"You have a granddaughter?"

"Could we listen to the frickin' tape now, Jeff?"

CHAPTER THIRTY-ONE

BERNARD HARPER DID not feel well when he woke up that morning. Hung over from the night before, he moved to the kitchen and put on a pot of coffee. Afraid to shower before he was fully awake, he sat on his couch to wait for the strong, black stream to run out of the white coffeemaker and into the glass pot. As soon as he'd sat he was up again, peering out the window through the blinds. It was still foggy in Saratoga Springs, at least in his modest neighborhood. He fixed on a memory of last night's weather report. It was supposed to be a beautiful fall day.

He drank his coffee, needing a shot of vodka as soon as he was through with it. He had orange juice, tomato juice. He decided on tomato juice, poured a triple shot of vodka in a water glass, poured the juice on top, and squeezed a lime he'd cut the night before on top of everything. It took him one second to finish the glass. These days, when he lifted the glass to his nose, the smell of the vodka calmed him before he even felt it on his lips.

Harper looked at real estate listings after he'd shuffled out to the porch and scooped up the morning paper. He had no time left, then, and he showered, put on a jacket and tie, and got behind the wheel of his old Lincoln. He worried about how he could get a newer car to show clients around properties. Well, he thought, if he was going to pay for another car, and maybe more, it was going to be today.

He drove north through town, following the business route of Highway Nine. He made the call from a convenience mart.

"Mr. Weeks, this is Barney Harper. I appreciate your meeting me on this Dollanger business. Just wanted to let you know I'm on my way."

Ten minutes later, Harper pulled into a diner off Highway Nine, not five miles from Saratoga Springs. He spent the next hour sucking mints to hide the smell of vodka on his breath and talking to a forceful, abrupt old man named Weeks. Harper pretended to listen while Weeks laid out strategies for community action and described his experiences resisting the land buy-up teams Patrick Dollanger had sent out.

"He'll use fronts to get the land," Weeks said. "Seems like he's got everybody working for him. I wouldn't be talking to you if Audrey from the homeowner's association hadn't referred you."

"She's a nice person," Harper said, thankful that Dollanger had so many associates so well placed.

"Can I show you my property?" Harper asked. "We're not a mile from it. The woods are beautiful. Be a shame to see them subdivided for condos. Property belonged to my father." Harper let emotion into his voice. Emotion was hard to let in, because he was still feeling calm, refreshed and numb from the vodka. But he managed. Harper slipped one hand in his jacket pocket and put a finger over the depressed record button of his tape recorder.

He was only half sure why he was recording. He was afraid, that's all he knew for certain, aside from knowing he was a liar and a con who worked for a liar and a con. He couldn't sort out why he'd tape record something that would incriminate him in a court of law, except that, maybe, it would prove something, somehow. The deal with Weeks felt terrible, but he denied how it felt. Five thousand dollars was a good fee to deceive Weeks and drive him out in the woods.

"Take him out and show him the property you acquired for me last week," Dollanger had told Harper. "Get out, walk around, make it look convincing. Let the old guy kick some dirt clods with his boots." Then Dollanger told Harper when to set the meeting time and where to take Weeks. It was too detailed. Too fixed. Harper didn't care. He couldn't afford to care. He was alone, his ex-wife had finally stopped bothering about money since Carole was grown, but he was in debt and nearly broke, always.

D'Angelo could see Harper's Lincoln moving slowly down the graded dirt road. Trees in fall colors pressed in from either side. Their reflections, in the gray light of a high overcast, poured their shapes over the windshield of the black car. D'Angelo stepped behind a tree as the Lincoln turned off the road into a small space of cleared land, grown over now with green.

When Harper and Weeks were standing together, hands in pockets, talking, D'Angelo moved quietly out of the tree line behind them. He kept Harper's black Lincoln between them as he approached. D'Angelo drew his handgun as he edged around Harper's car.

"Hey," he said. The two men turned. Weeks's black eyes popped in his craggy old face. D'Angelo liked that. D'Angelo liked the look on Harper's face, too. The shaky real estate agent looked ridiculous with his thin gray hair plastered to one side of his head.

"Get out of here," D'Angelo said to Harper, who did a stumbling jog around the Lincoln, jumped inside, and backed up, stalled, backed up again, and finally got on the road. Harper never looked back and he could hear no gunfire. He trembled all the way to Highway Nine.

He remembered the tape recorder in his jacket pocket while waiting at a stoplight. He jammed his hand, which seemed huge because it shook so much, into the pocket. Harper spoke into the recorder, croaking out his name, the time of day, the date, the location. He said he worked for Patrick Dollanger. He said, "I just got a guy killed." Then he shut off the tape, whimpered and shook for awhile, then pulled onto the highway.

Harper stopped for a pint of vodka as soon as he could, sat in the liquor store parking lot, drank it, and went in for another. Later on, a tapping woke him up. It was very late. He'd been asleep. He'd left the keys in the ignition. The police took him in. It was his second DUI. When they let him out of jail, they gave him his tape recorder back, along with his wallet, pocket change and keys.

"What do you think?" Reina said.

Jeff had his feet on his desk. "About what?"

"Well, yeah, I guess, *about what*," Reina said. "What are we doing listening to Harper's tape anyway? We can turn it over the cops and be done with it."

Jeff and Manny found convenient corners to stare into so they wouldn't have to look at Reina just then. When Jeff started talking he was serious, even somber.

"This tape has limited value. I know you hoped it would be worth more," Jeff said. "It might generate an investigation if Arizona authorities sent it to New York State authorities, but it's not valuable for going after Harper's killers. The court would need proof it's Harper's voice. If it is Harper, he's clearly made an admission against interest. He recorded what he says is a prelude to a murder and admitted his part in it. But this New York business is remote from Harper's murder here in Tucson. Harper didn't even name the killer or the person killed. I heard nothing that sounded like shots fired on that tape, I heard only voices. They could never charge anyone on the evidence of this tape alone and admission of this tape into evidence would be the subject of a fierce pretrial battle. We have other resources we can use to argue the case for Harper's murder, but we don't have proof."

"Is Rhiannon Granger any help here?" Manny asked.

"We have hearsay from Rhiannon Granger. She claims that her father told her that Harper was blackmailing the land developer with a tape. I don't think a defense attorney would try to use Rhiannon."

Jeff paused, then looked at Reina. "Reina, you can testify to being assaulted by Cisneros. You can also testify that Cisneros said he wanted the tape, and that he claimed Manny would be killed in jail. But the law has no sure way to tie Dollanger to any of this and, again, there is nothing about Harper's death here. We can speculate that Harper could have been murdered in Tucson because he threatened blackmail with this tape, but we can't hope to prove anything with it. There's other information, but it's scattered."

"What about my sheriff's department case notes of my contact with Perez?" Manny asked.

"We know the sheriff's department has a report from you about your interview with the heroin addict, Perez. You can testify that Perez was talking about Harper and real estate developers and was asking for protective custody. But the tie between any Mexican gang and Dollanger, a legitimate businessman as far as we know, would have to be proven. Any reasonable person would guess that such a tie would be unlikely. You can testify that Cisneros left you for dead in Nogales and it has been documented by Mexican authorities that you were discovered and treated in Nogales. There's some continuity with Cisneros. He does reappear in all of this, but he remains at large and he can hide in Mexico."

"What about Dollanger, Jeff?" Reina asked. "We both know Arizona is a wide open state for developers."

Jeff nodded. "On the surface, Dollanger is a legitimate businessman. Scratch the surface and you find habitual quasi-legal activity. Anybody who looks at Arizona land developers in general, Dollanger aside, can trot out a laundry list of shady dealings. There are documented cases of conflicts of interest involving state and local government employees who benefited from their relationships with land developers. If we follow the money behind politicians who support land development in the Sonoran Desert here in Southern Arizona we find money coming from developers. Developers push for and get favorable rezoning, rent credit concessions, huge federal tax breaks for keeping a couple of cows on land they plan to develop anyway, permission to build in flood plains, and more. They've profited hugely from trades and sales involving state lands and the tax paying public has come up short."

"And we must consider the character of the Arizona State Legislature." Reina was grinning like a leopard over a fresh kill. Here we go, Manny thought, Goldman's on a roll and Reina's cheerleading.

Goldman settled back in his chair and tented his fingers. "The Arizona State Legislature is generally helpful to developers because development spurs the economy—and because their votes are frequently for sale and they tend to be crackpots who focus on crackpot legislation, such as legalizing gila monster ranching, rather than on managing our state resources. State land sales are supposed to benefit education, yet the Arizona public education system is consistently one of the bottom three in the whole country. Finally, land development, at least in the view of the anti-growth camp, results in over stressing, in gradually destroying, a unique ecosystem."

Manny sat silently. He wanted perpetrators, not politics.

"And none of this is complete without a mention of the Arizona Canal," Reina said, throwing a smirk at Manny. "Right, Jeff?"

"When our water-bearing Arizona politicians siphoned off the Colorado River, creating a 336 mile diversion canal, the biggest, the most expensive aqueduct system ever built in the United States, it was a done deal. Arizona would now be a new home for many millions of people and their golf courses, their air conditioning units, and their swimming pools. We use all the water the Central Arizona Project provides and it's not enough. In Southern Arizona, we're busy destroying the San Pedro River, the only river we've got left. We're sucking it dry. As for these developers, we can speculate on bribery, arson, frauds of various kinds, maybe even murders of the kind Harper's tape purports to document, but that is speculation only. If you've been listening, you've heard these developers do so well with sleaze that it's hardly worth the risk to do high crime. I would say Dollanger's got nothing to do with this and that it would be nearly impossible to prove it if he did."

Jeff took his feet off his desk, sat up, and continued, addressing Reina directly.

"Manny can testify that Randall Rogers claimed he came to Reina's home to kill Rhiannon, but you've told me that neither you nor Rhiannon could hear the conversation. You heard only gunshots and came out to find Rogers dead. Manny shouldn't have gone to jail, but that's of no use to us now, unless a witness comes forward to say there was some unusual pressure from someone to put him there. We have a lot of events. We do not have a lot of connections between them."

"So we turn the tape over to the courts and get ready to testify when they call us, right?" Reina said.

"Right, if they call us," Jeff said. "As I've said, the tape could be sent to New York State authorities. Even there, I doubt anything would come of it."

"Who do you think killed Harper?" Manny asked.

"Let law enforcement figure it out," Jeff said.

"Possibly D'Angelo," Manny said, "and he probably had help."

"And you had to shoot D'Angelo in that hospital parking lot, so he's not going to trial, that's for sure," Reina said. "That was a horrifying event and one I would not want to see happen again to someone I'm close to—just so you know."

"And the people who were with D'Angelo could have helped to kill Harper," Jeff said. "And they're dead."

"Or the junkies could have killed him," Reina said. "And they're dead, too."

"Rogers had the junkies killed," Manny said. "He didn't tell me that, but I could see it in his eyes the night I killed him. I interviewed Perez when I started this investigation. He had a tattoo on his neck. He picked up Harper from the detox center and a nurse remembered the tattoo. I never got a chance to get her to make a positive ID from a photo, but I'm sure it was Perez. That's the last time anybody I know of saw Harper alive. But I don't think the junkies killed him. I think he was killed because of that tape. And I'm not done looking for who did it."

"Hoo boy," Reina muttered, shaking her head.

"Look into it if you have to," Jeff said, "but do it on your own time. You're still my investigator and I've got a lot of work for you. I do not understand why these people, whoever they are, want that tape so bad. No sensible criminal would take the risks we've seen them take—kidnapping a heroin addict from a hospital and all the rest of it."

"Maybe it's not what's on the tape," Manny said. "Maybe it's what they think is on the tape."

"Meaning what?" Reina asked.

"Harper could have lied to them, told them he had more on them than he did—and maybe there's more evidence and we just haven't found it yet."

"Manny, maybe that's true and I know you want to get to the bottom of this," Reina said. "But the criminal justice system can get a handle on this now. I don't want to go in anymore junkie houses and look under the sinks."

CHAPTER THIRTY-TWO

THAT NIGHT REINA woke up when Manny pitched out of the bed and stood in the middle of the room with his hands up, ready to fight. She spoke to him gently and he came back to bed and slept. The next night it happened again.

"What would your grandmother say about this?" Reina asked.

"How would I know?" Manny said.

That night, lying in bed, not wanting to touch Reina, not even wanting to be in bed with her or anyone, he decided to ask.

"Okay, *nana*, could you help me with this?" he whispered, when he sure Reina was sound asleep.

There was no response, but he slept through the night and woke up the next morning wondering how he could be feeling better—now that he was talking to the hallucinations. He was crazy, he thought. He'd gone to the other side and he was so crazy he felt better over there.

He didn't feel any less crazy when Reina said, on her way out the door to work that morning, "Manny, you look different. You've changed something about yourself. I like it."

"Maybe I put my shorts on backwards," Manny said, pretending to look at his underwear.

"Not a chance," Reina said. "You changed in your soul. We can talk about it when I get back from work."

"Not a chance," Manny said. "I love you, Reina. Have a good day."

They gave each a wary smirk and Reina walked away. Manny watched her take her fabulous body out the front gate.

Ten days later the stitches in Manny's arm began to itch. He let it go on until he'd honored the doctor's orders to leave the stitches alone for a full two weeks. Then he borrowed Reina's sewing scissors, held his forearm up in front of the bathroom mirror, and clipped the black threads out one by one, turning his forearm back and forth when he was done, as if examining a new tool. It was probably too soon for the stitches to come out but he didn't care.

"You're smart, Manny," Reina said to him when she got home that night. "I think you should start reading up on the law and getting some office skills together. You'd make a great paralegal."

"I just talked to Brady Pogue down at the Forensic Center," Manny said, by way of reply. "They're examining Harper's remains again for fibers and other evidence."

"At your request?"

"I knew Brady when he was with TPD."

"You sound like you're ready to do investigations again," Reina said. "I'll tell Jeff."

"Go ahead," Manny said. "I can do two things at once."

"Why Harper? What do you think you'll gain?" Reina said. "This is frustrating and it's scary for me. If you were a cop you'd be off the case because you became part of the case. Why can't you see it that way? You know all of this is under investigation."

"I got fired over this, Reina," Manny said. "I want to know why. I also have a problem with people who try to kill me—and my friends. I want whoever is pulling the strings. And I still want to know who killed Harper."

"Yeah," Reina said, "well, I'll just go feed the cat now before I say something nasty—like go ahead and get yourself killed."

Reina was calm by bedtime but she was quiet and sad, staring at nothing as if she were already in mourning.

"I'll go into work with you tomorrow," Manny said.

"Okay," Reina said. "I feel like saying don't bother but I won't. If you have to keep on with this then I guess you do. I understand why. Just you understand," she poked a long finger into his ribs, "that it's dangerous, I care about you, and I don't want anybody else to get hurt—including Rhiannon—and including me, you idiot."

Manny started to grin, tried to stop, and began laughing.

"Go ahead," Reina said. "Laugh. If I get smacked again over this, or killed, you'll think being haunted by your grandmother is a freaking cake walk compared to being haunted by me."

Manny was sound asleep when his grandmother leaned over him in the middle of a very good dream about the feel of Reina's skin, which felt so fine and thin and silky that he sometimes wondered how she wore it at all.

"*Aie*," he heard his grandmother yell.

Manny also yelled and sat up in bed. Grayboy fled from his position near Manny's feet and stopped at the door, looking at Manny quizzically.

"What is it?" Reina asked.

"Bad dream," Manny said.

"Why am I not surprised," Reina said, in measured tones, and went back to sleep.

Manny began drifting off, trying to stay very still so Reina wouldn't wake up again. He saw his grandmother again as he descended into sleep. She sat at a table. He watched as she opened a box and took a smaller box out of it. She opened that box and took out another box that was even smaller. She opened that one. Manny left her to her game. He had to work the next day.

Jeff had finished just finished briefing Manny on an investigation when Manny's cell phone vibrated.

"Manny, it's Brady Pogue. We sent Harper's head over to the DPS Crime Lab when we ran out of ideas. They found traces of petroleum-based oil. Thought you'd like to know."

"Where was it located?" Manny asked.

"In his mouth," Pogue said.

My grandmother, Manny thought, she didn't yell "Aie." She yelled "Oil." He could feel his heart start whacking the inside of his ribcage. Still, there was one more question to ask, even though his grandmother had already given him the answer.

"What kind of oil? Do you think it could have been gun oil?" Manny asked.

"No idea," Pogue said. "They can tell petroleum from animal fat or vegetable oil but that's all. This was petroleum-based oil in the guy's mouth. It shouldn't be there. People don't eat that kind of oil. It could be gun oil but we can't prove that it is."

Manny ended the call and began wondering if Tony Cisneros was still alive, after reporting to his bosses that he'd failed to get the tape. Tony, the twisted little creep who'd stuck a gun in Manny's mouth.

If he ever caught Tony Cisneros, Manny thought, if Cisneros is still alive, the judge would not want to hear that Manny's dead grandmother gave him the clue about the gun oil. And Manny was definitely not going to tell Reina why he believed Cisneros killed Harper. It would give her too much satisfaction. He thought how hard it would be to leave her again, to go back to Mexico, which would be the only logical place to look for Cisneros. It was December now. He would drive to Mexico as soon as he could. He would look for Cisneros and Adelaida.

Manny and Reina had another routine week together. Then the phone rang as they were settling down in front of the television, prepared to sit through a blizzard of holiday advertising while they waited for the news. Reina picked up the phone.

"I want to talk to Reina," someone said. The voice was male and the man had a thick Mexican accent.

"Start talking, then," Reina answered. "And tell me who you are while you're at it."

"You know me," the voice said. "I want to make a deal with you—for the tape."

"What kind of a deal?" Reina asked.

Manny was already across the room, reaching for the second phone. Reina motioned him to stop, fearing the caller would hang up.

"You give me the tape and I don't kill you or your boyfriend. And I don't kill your grandkids in San Diego. And I don't kill little Rhiannon, the junkie's daughter. We could get to your boyfriend's brother anytime, that *pendejo* who sells the Ford trucks. You understand now I know all about you?"

"Do you understand that I mailed that tape to the Arizona Attorney General's office?" Reina asked.

"Nah, you didn't do that," the voice said. "You got the tape at your house or at your boss's office—and he'll be a dead guy too if you don't give us the tape. You think about it and I call you back tomorrow. You can try to wiretap me but it's going to be hard the way we got it set up. You go to the cops I'll find out right away. You think Rogers was the only friend we got with the cops, you're wrong. And you ain't made up your mind by the time I call you back, we're going to start wasting your little friends and relatives anyway."

The caller hung up and Reina said, "Too bad he rang off before I could tell him I'd hunt him through this world and the next if he so much as touched a hair on the head of anyone I know."

"Where's the tape?" Manny asked.

"I put it under our sink. Same trick Harper used in the junkie house. Why?"

"Let's look at it," Manny said, heading for the bathroom.

Manny found the tape and turned it over in his hands. It was an older design, made of black plastic, and held together with tiny metal screws, the kind used for eyeglass frames. Boxes in boxes, Manny thought. Grandmother and her boxes in boxes.

"We've got a copy of this at Jeff's in case I break it," Manny muttered, and he found a screwdriver, took out the screws, and separated the two halves of the casing. Taped to the inside of one of the halves was a fine quality brass key stamped with the number 100.

"Safe deposit box key," Manny said.

They looked at each other, both thinking: But which bank?

"Poor old Harper," Reina said. "He was smarter than we thought—but not smart enough to keep his mouth shut about the key, huh?"

"Yeah," Manny said. "Now we know why Tony Cisneros is calling us about the tape. I know he killed Harper, too—but I can't prove it."

"How do you know he killed Harper?" Reina asked.

"Harper had traces of petroleum-based oil in his mouth. Cisneros likes to stick guns in people's mouths."

Reina laughed, "And you would know that? God, Manny, you scare the hell out of me. Listen, we have to get to Rhiannon Granger, right now. We've got to call everybody we know and warn them. Then, if we all get through this alive, maybe they'll like us enough to speak to us again some day."

"I don't think so," Manny said. "That would cause a lot of panic. We have to wait to hear from Cisneros again."

"Why? The bastard knows who everybody is. You want your friends and relatives to just get killed without a clue?"

"Reina, this is a negotiation and it's just started. Think about that. He wants the tape. Think about how to give him what he wants and get what we want."

"You mean fake it? Meet with him? Manny, he'll kill whoever meets with him. You can pretty much bet on that."

"We've got something he wants. When he calls back, we let him know we have it."

"I'm calling Rhiannon—and Jeff. We have to, Manny."

"Okay. I understand. We can help hide Rhiannon and Jeff has a need to know."

"Yeah, in case neither one of us get out of this one."

"Jeff wouldn't like to have to hire a new staff," Manny said.

"Do you think they've tapped our phones?" Reina asked, suddenly, "or bugged this house? There are ways to monitor cell phone conversations, aren't there?"

"It's possible," Manny said. "I'll gp around the corner and make a couple calls from the Rincon Market. They'll let me use their hard line."

"Call Rhiannon first, Manny," Reina said.

When Manny didn't answer she said, "I mean it. Call Rhiannon first. Warn her."

When Manny got to the Rincon Market he began to dial Johnny Oaks's number, then changed his mind and called Rhiannon. Her aunt answered.

"She's gone," the woman said. "Somebody took her. Just now. Just before I got home. The window's broken. She fought. The place is a mess."

"Have you called the police yet?" Manny asked.

"No."

"Stay there," Manny said. "I'll be right over."

CHAPTER THIRTY-THREE

MANNY RAN BACK to Reina's, told her what had happened, and told her to lock herself in. Then he went to Rhiannon Granger's home in east Tucson. There was little to see there except a broken hearted woman and a shattered window. Manny looked around for footprints leading up to the back window, tried to see something the kidnappers had dropped. There was no blood and there were no noticeable footprints. He did his best to assure Rhiannon's aunt and told her not to call the police. Then he drove back to Reina's.

"He called," Reina said, as Manny came in the door. "He said he'd call back."

The phone rang ten minutes later.

"Listen, you stinking cop," Cisneros said. "Tomorrow night at midnight you meet me in Skeleton Canyon."

"Where?"

"Look on a map, stupid. It's down by the border—only there are more borders there. One is the border for Arizona and New Mexico. There is a gate when you get in the canyon and they put up the signs on the posts to say you are in New Mexico. You bring the tape, you wait for me there, by the gate. I tell you what to do next. I let the girl go if you are there and you have the tape. Don't bring nobody with you or we mess all of you up and kill the girl."

"You said Skeleton Canyon?" Manny asked again.

"Yeah, and that's what this little bitch is going to be if you screw up, man—a skeleton."

"So you meet me out in the middle of nowhere and then you kill us both and take the tape, right, Cisneros?"

"You give me the tape, I check it out. Then you get the girl."

"I want to meet in Tucson at a public place. Nobody is going to meet you out in the bushes, Cisneros."

"Man, you're lucky we don't make you come to Mexico." Cisneros laughed.

"I would be happy to come to Mexico if we could meet in a public place. How do I know you've got Rhiannon? Let her talk to me."

"No way."

"How can I do what you say if I don't know you have her?"

"You'll have to trust me, *pendejo*."

"If I don't talk to Rhiannon we can't do business."

"Maybe I'll have her call you back tonight, you stupid cop. So you sit in front of your TV and you wait."

Manny heard Cisneros hang up and he put Reina's phone back in its cradle.

"What?" Reina said.

"He says he'll have Rhiannon call us back tonight."

"Well, that's something. What about Skeleton Canyon?"

"He wants me to meet him there."

"What? Alone? Where's Skeleton Canyon?"

"Yes, alone. The canyon's on the Arizona and New Mexico border, east of Douglas, a few miles north of Mexico. It's part of the Coronado National Forest. Rough country, weird rock formations. Good deer hunting. Geronimo surrendered there. In the old days it was a trail through the Peloncillos. Smugglers and rustlers used it."

"How do you know so much about it?"

"I hunted deer there once, with my uncle. And I've talked to guys like Daryl Trainor who like Old West history—and Oaks. Johnny's hunted down there."

"Skeleton Canyon. Such a festive name, Manny. How did that happen?"

"They started calling it Skeleton Canyon after an American gang ambushed a pack train of Mexicans smuggling in silver to buy American merchandise. Nobody buried the bodies. There were stories about pieces of skulls used for soap dishes in ranches around there. These days, they smuggle drugs and people through the canyon."

"So are we going to call the cops now, Manny? This really sounds like a job we can't do by ourselves."

"I don't think I'll have to be by myself for this one," Manny said, "Johnny Oaks still hunts. He knows Skeleton Canyon."

"You and Oaks? You're going up against all these guys? Just the two of you? They're coming from Mexico, right? That's why they want to meet you so close to the border."

"Probably. Oaks and I got Rhiannon together. I can hope he'll feel some responsibility," Manny said.

"So they can have as many guys as they want, Manny, and there's just you and Oaks. What about the FBI?"

"Reina, how many times have you watched a news story where the FBI screwed up? How many times have you laughed about those guys when I was sitting next to you on the couch? The FBI never heard of Skeleton Canyon. They wouldn't know how to act in a place like that. By the time they got organized Cisneros would be tipped off and Rhiannon would be dead."

"But aren't they good at something? Like foiling kidnappers?" Manny just stared at her. "Okay, forget the FBI," Reina said, "but you've still got to call the cops—"

"Reina, the bad guys find out everything. I think we can figure out who's behind all this with the safety deposit box key we have now. But even if we find out, they've still got Rhiannon—and they've got the sources to tip them if we call the cops—any kind of cops—and that includes the Border Patrol, which would be the best agency for the job, but we can't risk somebody tipping off the bad guys. You would be the first to tell me that some cops are corrupt—including some border patrolmen."

"Okay," Reina said. "Look, let's just think about this. If you meet him in the canyon, what's to stop him from killing you and Rhiannon as soon as he gets the tape?"

"I pressured him to meet in Tucson. He wouldn't do it, but he said he'd give us proof that Rhiannon's alive. He needs the tape. When he calls back and we know she's alive, I'll demand another meeting place—a parking lot somewhere in Tucson, down at the Cineplex by the freeway, whatever, but for right now we have to wait to hear from Rhiannon. Then we start trying to match that key to a bank as soon as they open and get in that safety deposit box. If what we find could make any difference for Rhiannon, we could threaten Cisneros with it, but then what would happen?"

"Rhiannon gets killed," Reina replied, "unless we can convince Cisneros and his bosses we're not going to use whatever we find in that bank box—and I'd bet we couldn't do that."

"It's around three hours to Skeleton Canyon from Tucson. I need to call Johnny Oaks and see if he'll go along with this. I don't know what you pay somebody for doing something like this but I'll have to try and talk him into it."

"So what are you going to do?" Reina said. "Oaks sneaks in there first and we all hope Cisneros isn't watching?"

"Only thing I can think of," Manny said. "Go in after dark. I got to know Oaks. Turns out he was Force Recon in the Marine Corps."

"Meaning what?"

"Short answer, it means he's been trained to sneak around in enemy territory. They used him as a sniper."

"Can't anyone else help? Isn't there anybody else you know?"

"No. Johnny and I will do what private detectives do in the movies. We'll commit a crime and try to get away with it. Nobody I know in law enforcement would go along with that—and no other friends, except for Oaks."

"Okay," Reina said, "but it's not only the crime you're committing that you should be worrying about—it's your ass—and Johnny's and Rhiannon's. Just...okay. Call Oaks."

"There's one call I have to make first."

"What's that?"

"Satellite phone rentals. I'll get three so you'll have one, too. Cell phones don't talk very well in places like Skeleton Canyon."

"That's swell, Manny," Reina said glumly. "You think of everything, big fella."

Oaks and Manny Aguilar were going over a topographic map of Skeleton Canyon in Reina's living room when the phone rang.

"I don't want to set up on the north side," Oaks was saying. "The gate's around 1,200 meters from a good position. On the south side, I can work from less than 300 meters—if I can get up there without being spotted."

Reina picked up the phone, listened, and handed the phone to Manny.

"Aguilar," Cisneros said, "you wanted to hear from Rhiannon. Talk, bitch."

"Manny," Rhiannon said, "I'm okay. They say they'll let me go after you give them something."

"I have what they want. Are you okay? Did you get food and water?"

"Yes. Is my aunt okay?"

"She is."

"I'll talk now," Cisneros said. "Get off the phone, bitch."

Manny heard Rhiannon hang up the phone.

"Listen," Cisneros said, "I want to see you tomorrow night at midnight. Bring the tape and you'll get her back, no problem."

"Skeleton Canyon is hours from here. What if my truck breaks down on the way? Rhiannon's not safe out there and neither am I. Neither are you, the Border Patrol comes through Skeleton Canyon—"

"Well, they ain't coming tomorrow night," Cisneros said, "and they can't find nothing anyways. You get me the tape and I'll let you live. I don't care nothing about you one way or the other. I want the tape. You be at the gate to New Mexico in Skeleton Canyon tomorrow night. Don't bring nobody along. And if your truck breaks down on the way, Aguilar, well, that's what you get for driving a Ford when you could of drove a Chevy." Cisneros laughed and hung up.

Manny turned to Oaks. "Looks like we're going to Skeleton Canyon."

"That gate is just under a mile from the mouth of the canyon," Oaks said. "He's probably going to meet you and then get you to come with him if he doesn't kill you right there. And he'll have somebody cover his back to make sure nobody follows you in."

"Yeah, and he'll hide and watch for awhile when I come in. He won't show himself right away. I'll just sit and wait. He might take us down the canyon, farther into New Mexico—or just head south and take us to Mexico."

"We'll have to stop them at the gate," Oaks said. "I have to go in right away."

"Why don't I call somebody I know and see if we can fly Johnny down tonight," Reina said.

"You know somebody that can fly?" Manny asked.

"Yes."

"How do you know him?" Manny asked.

"*Her* name is Hope Wells and I know her from my book club."

"The one you go to once a month on Sundays?" Manny asked.

"Yeah, while you're watching sports."

Oaks looked sideways and hid a smile with his hand.

"Do you think she'd do it?"

"Yeah," Reina said, "she flew medevac helicopters for years. She's got a charter business now. It'll cost us money but she'll understand when I tell her we don't have a choice. She'll keep everything confidential. She's also a mother. She'll understand."

"How does she keep herself out of trouble when she's filing a flight plan?"

"She'll think of something."

"Call her," Manny said. "See what we can do."

CHAPTER THIRTY-FOUR

HOPE WELLS NUDGED the controls and the helicopter lifted off the pad. She made a beeline across the desert, heading southeast toward Skeleton Canyon, almost 200 miles away by car, only 100 miles by air.

Oaks sat behind her, his face greased dark for night work, wearing boots and layers of clothing under a camo jacket and pants. He carried a sniper pack—a belted harness with pouches for gear and ammunition at the sides and back. A lightweight drag bag lay across his thighs. It contained a Heckler and Koch Model 41 semiautomatic rifle, mounted with a variable power telescopic sight and a night vision attachment.

Wells took the helicopter down over a dirt track in flat desert six miles west of Skeleton Canyon and hovered three feet above the ground. Oaks slipped out and ran as Wells lifted off, spun the chopper 180 degrees, and headed out, gaining altitude.

Johnny rolled under a mesquite bush and held his hand broadside between the low sun and the horizon. Each finger counted for fifteen minutes. Forty-five minutes until sunset. He took a piece of camouflage netting from a pouch on the sniper pack, covered himself, and waited. At twilight, he drank from a tube that led from the water bladder attached to the pack, then stowed the netting and began walking east, listening for the sound of a motor, watching for lights, alert for anything that might indicate approaching humans. Twice he knelt or went flat on the ground when brush crackled. Both times, range cattle appeared, moving away from him.

In the 1700s, the Spanish brought the first cattle to this place they had named El Valle de San Bernardino, a desert plain known by geologists as a graben, a down dropped block bounded on both sides by faults, bordered on the west by the Pedregosa and Chiricahua Mountains, on the east by the Peloncillos, the low mountain range through which Skeleton Canyon passed, unobtrusively, in some of the loneliest land on earth, into New Mexico, toward the Animas Mountains.

Near a midnight lit by a full December moon, Oaks sat down and rested while he stared at a low rise of land that lay in front of him like a single, fat coil in a snake's body. He knew he was looking at the final, unremarkable barrier to the western end of Skeleton Canyon. Beyond and above it, he could see the tops of the hills that flanked the canyon on either side—the hills and their outcroppings of welded tuff. Sprouting from the sharp slopes like rows of teeth, these formations of rock had fused together millions of years before during an avalanche of hot lava fragments. A flush of gray splayed across some of the lighter tuff on the outcroppings, a color combination unique, in the Peloncillos, to this canyon.

Snow Moon. December. No snow on the Peloncillos tonight. If it were morning by the river, Johnny Oaks thought, in the days before the Trail of Tears, maybe he would have been the guy to sing the blessing song and start the day for his people. But it was night in Skeleton Canyon—and if a raven rings the doorbell with its shadow in the daytime, then moonlight throws that door off its hinges. Tricky silver light. He would be okay in whatever light there was, Johnny told himself.

He wondered if there was a spirit for the night scope. Geronimo would have thought so. Geronimo had died an old man in Oklahoma—but he had surrendered in Skeleton Canyon, for the last time. Oaks knew that the soldiers who were present had marked the site a pile of rocks, just over the little hill. Geronimo, that sneaky old guerilla fighter, Johnny thought.

Oaks's tribe farmed and took to Christianity and got a death march to Oklahoma. The bluecoats put Geronimo on a train to Florida. Geronimo said he'd got the white man's religion in later years. He didn't, Johnny thought. Geronimo had what Johnny Oaks had—in the blood. Go with all of it. Never approach in a straight line. Honor the curves in the earth. Never overreach, never fear, always pay attention—and always pay respect. Everything's alive. All of it—even the past. Everything you need is already here. It's operating. That's what Geronimo's god said. Worship it and kill your enemies.

After he had rested, watched, and listened, Johnny Oaks took out a current generation night vision scope that Manny Aguilar had borrowed from Daryl Trainor and scanned what he could see of the high ground. The tan hilltops shone blue-gray in moonlight, speckled black with low growing juniper and scrub oak that climbed the high hills as if on a pilgrimage. Some had reached the very top. Others were still coming up, separately or in groups, sometimes massed together, sometimes marching in lines. Johnny drew the night scope over them all, seeing in phosphorescent green, seeing detail no naked human eye could find. He paid particular attention to places where these lines of shrubbery joined each other on the way up the canyon's sides. He would crawl, following the lines that would lead him to the top.

Down the canyon, on the New Mexico side, a young jaguar sensed that the night had taken a bad turn. Black rosettes, tattooed like a wall of paw prints on fur the color of mustard, blew his silhouette to vapor in the shadow of an alligator juniper as he sank, invisible, to wait for the end of trouble in bunch grass cured out by a borderlands winter.

Nothing on those hilltops, nothing hiding in the outcrops or lying in the shrubbery. Oaks stuffed Daryl's expensive tool in the sniper pack and made a cape of the camouflage netting, pulling it up in the middle and clipping it to the hood of his camo jacket, letting it drop a few inches on both sides of his head. He secured the corners of the netting to his shoulders, attached the drag bag to one ankle, and began to crawl over the snake coil that guarded the canyon.

When Oaks could see the other side he lay still. It began only a couple hundred feet away, the woodland along the canyon's bottom, crammed with dark green juniper, oak, and Chihuahua pine, its upturned branches and black bark ridges with their red fissures now invisible in the night shadows. Sumac, grasses, cactus, agave, and hundreds of other plants filled the forest floor and lived in the open spaces.

Bare trees with trunks patterned in white and gray jigsaw puzzle pieces stood out in the dark green mass—sycamores, the deciduous minority, their yellow leaves gone by this or any other December. In the middle of it, twin lines, blue in the shadow, with dark between them, fluorescing, disappearing as they curved—a four wheel drive trail, alien and inexplicable as an Inca road—and, nearly lost in foliage on the other side, the bed of Skeleton Canyon Wash, stuffed with a manic jumble of gray stones eager to turn an ankle and smash a face. Oaks crawled into it all, grateful for the cover.

Concealed, he caught his breath, slowly slung his cased rifle on his shoulder, and took out the night scope again, leaving it in his lap while he dug a Beretta automatic out of his sniper pack. Trainor had provided the Beretta. Trainor had threaded the barrel—and the sound suppressor Oaks took out next. Oaks hadn't carried such a weapon in years—or wanted to. Now, he figured, he didn't have a choice. If anything happened in the crowded vegetation that lined the watercourse, it would happen close up. He kept the Beretta in one hand and Trainor's night scope in the other. His boot knife was there for anybody who didn't see him first.

Oaks started through the woods along the road, pausing again and again to scope in front of him and all around. His boot brushed a virgin's bower where it climbed on a tree trunk and drank from a tank in the wash and then he was suddenly at the edge of a grassy open space, looking at a field of upright rocks on the opposite side—rocks that stood in their sloped shapes like old people hiding under blankets the color of sandstone. Lichen for age spots. Sentient, posed in various attitudes, waiting for the blood time to pass. You cannot try the patience of rocks, Oaks thought. They know how it ends—and men know, too. He saw the dim shape of a square of metal, welded to an upright iron pole, standing in the meadow, wearing the name "Devil's Kitchen" like a mask, the letters cut clean through the steel shingle with a torch, and stars, like eyes, visible behind them.

Oaks floated back into the trees, passing an old fire ring spotted with the skeletons of cord moss, the clumps of twisted stems with the empty spore cases topping them like faces, bent and staring at the ashes. Dead stalks of grass, lost from summer, stood up on all sides.

He caught a faint reek of tobacco when he was fifty yards up a slope on the canyon's south side. He stopped crawling, scanned and listened, realizing the smell had to have come from below him, and to the east, carried on a tiny breeze, the direction of which he'd learned by using a small feather hung from a piece of fishing line.

The big man hugged the ground to avoid being skylighted and kept moving. Any watcher who knew not only to scan the terrain on all sides, but also to look up at the trees and the higher ground, might see him against the horizon.

It was nearly dawn by the time he made it to his firing position on a shrub-dotted hill some five-hundred feet above the canyon floor.

He slipped the drag bag off his ankle. The trail waited below, two pale stripes in the moonlight, the barb wire gate stretched across it, scaled down by the distance, which he already knew was around 200 meters.

Johnny reached for the night scope, keeping the rest of his body still. Like a man moving underwater, he turned his face forward and brought the scope to his eye. A green tunnel of light opened the shadows around the gate. He saw nothing at first. Then, sweeping the monocular down the trail, he spotted a man sitting cross legged in the brush. The man's bored expression belied the Kalashnikov assault rifle lying across his lap. As Oaks watched, the man lit a cigarette, trying to hide the flame with his hand.

Oaks scanned the area again, found nothing, and panned back to the sentinel just as the man drew a satellite phone from his pocket. The man spoke briefly, then pocketed the phone and continued to watch the trail leading up to the gate, a trail that wound along Skeleton Canyon Wash—the trail Manuel Aguilar would come down in his old white pickup truck. Oaks drew his satellite phone, dialed Manny's number, and whispered: "I'm here. There's one spotter with an AK and a sat phone. No vehicles in sight. Later."

Oaks slowly brought his rifle to his shoulder and put the crosshairs of the night sight on the sentry. Then he swung the weapon slowly back and forth, up and down, adjusting the variable power of the scope, testing the magnification and the angle of view he would need to engage multiple targets at that range, turning his intuition loose on what might play out the following night. When he was done, he pushed himself away, backwards, and then crawled in behind a small rock outcropping and got ready to spend the rest of the night and all the day to follow in a hide made by scooping out a shallow pit for his body and covering himself with brush, camouflage netting, and dirt.

By noon the next day Reina was running out of patience. She had one brass key stamped with the number 100. It fit a safety deposit box—somewhere. Jeff had simply told her that she couldn't get into a safe deposit box unless she had a legal relationship with its owner. That wasn't enough to stop Reina from trying and she'd been on the phone, going up against a zombie army of bland bankers from the compliance departments of their respective institutions. They'd all told her they needed a name and proof of a legal relationship. She was cautious about using Harper's name and she was almost sure he would have used an alias to rent a box.

The question in Reina's mind as she curled up in her lair that night, satellite phone in hand was: Would Manny, Oaks, and Rhiannon come back? What was it they called it in AA meetings? Acceptance. Yeah, she thought, this calls for a lot of acceptance. That, and a ritual of protection. She roused herself and began to light the candles and make the circle.

Manny finished dinner at the Gadsden Hotel in Douglas. It was well after dark when he headed east down the two-lane toward Skeleton Canyon. It took him the better part of an hour to reach the turnoff at a place called Apache. He drove south, passing a country school just to the right of the road. He thought about the simplicity of being a child in a country school and forgot about that when he had to brake for a Hereford heifer that popped up in the headlights and then strolled across the trail in front of him.

He came through the front yard of a ranch and the road began to drift to lower ground. Finally, as he left the open range and brush and trees closed around the track, his headlights illuminated an iron gate near in the front yard of another ranch, which seemed, for the time being, at least, deserted.

Manny opened the gate, crossed the Skeleton Canyon Wash, and went through another gate, a wire gate this time, with a sign tacked on a post that said he was entering the Coronado National Forest. He followed the track, turning east again. Cottonwood trees, Alligator Juniper and brush closed in tight on either side. He turned at the wooden forest service signs pointing toward the canyon and toward the Animas Mountains of New Mexico. Shortly, he found himself in a meadow, near a strange rock formation which stood some twenty feet high and to one side. Other rocks, all youngsters in geologic time, jutted out of the gradual slope of the canyon walls like a field of dragon's teeth.

Manny stopped the truck by the metal sign and looked at the words cut by a torch through the slab of steel: "Devil's Kitchen."

He was a half-hour early. Above him, on the south rim of the canyon, Oaks put his night scope on the truck, confirmed Manny's presence, and drew out his sat phone as Manny wandered into the shade of the rock formation, unzipping his pants. There was enough moonlight so anybody watching carefully could have seen his movements—until he stepped into the shadow.

"Two spotters now," Oaks said, "with AKs. No vehicles in sight."

Manny shut off the sat phone, slid it down the side of his leg, let it drop to the ground. They would search his truck—and him. He came out of the shadows, zipping his pants.

The trail shone as twin shafts of silver. The barb wire gate stretched across it, subtle as a spider's web in the moonlight. He opened the gate and pulled through. He left the gate open and sat in his truck.

Twenty minutes after midnight a man with a rifle appeared on the trail ahead. Manny heard a sound to his left. Another thug, holding an AK, and coming toward him.

"Get out of the truck," one of them said.

They searched him. One man pointed a rifle at him while the other searched the truck. One of them used a sat phone, then motioned for Manny to sit on the ground. Another twenty minutes passed before a black Chevy Suburban, headlights off, rolled out of the dark from the south.

Oaks tipped his head away from the scope and concentrated on the Suburban, hoping somebody would roll down a window or open a door.

Cisneros got out of the passenger side, front seat, and approached Manny.

"Have you got her?" Manny said.

"Shut up, *pendejo*. Where's the tape?"

"I need to see her," Manny said.

Cisneros lifted a flashlight and pointed toward the truck. The beam of light showed Rhiannon Granger in the back seat between two men. No bruises on her face. She was pale. One of the men beside her lifted a pistol, pointed it at Rhiannon's head, and smiled.

On the ridge, Oaks did a long, slow inhale and exhale. Now he knew where Rhiannon was and how she was guarded. What he didn't know yet was how to kill her guards without killing her.

Cisneros snapped off the light and turned to Manny.

"Give me the tape," he said.

"It's in the truck."

Cisneros spoke in Spanish to the two men with rifles and they followed Manny to the truck. Manny reached carefully under the dash, brought the tape out and handed it over. One of the men held the flashlight. Cisneros dug in his back pocket and Manny wasn't surprised when Cisneros came up with a knife and began prying the tape apart. One side of the case snapped under the blade.

"*Chingaso*," Cisneros said, and broke the other side.

A key fell out of the casing, glittered in the moonlight, and hit the soft dust of the trail without a sound. Manny put on a surprised look. Cisneros held up the key.

"See what we got? Get in the truck, *pendejo*."

Manny held both arms out, palms up, to signal Oaks.

"Give me the girl," he said. "That was our deal."

One of the men smacked Manny in the head with the stock of a Kalashnikov and he fell.

CHAPTER THIRTY-FIVE

WHEN MANNY WAS able to see and hear again, the two thugs were down and so was Cisneros. The clatter of gunshots still echoed off the canyon walls. Manny stayed down, expecting to be caught in a cross fire.

The men in the back of the Suburban forgot about Rhiannon Granger. One of them bailed and ran. Oaks dropped him. The other one jumped out, trying for the driver's seat. Oaks shot him as he reached for the door handle.

Manny sat up slowly and wiped the blood out of his eyes. He lifted his arm and swung it back and forth, giving a general thumbs-up to the bluffs on the southwest side of the canyon. Then he tottered to his feet and began checking the men lying around him. He didn't want anybody coming to life again when he had his back turned. The two riflemen were clearly dead. Manny kicked them anyway. Twice. He picked up one of their assault rifles and made sure there was a round chambered and that the safety was off. Then he turned his attention to Cisneros. The vicious little boxer wasn't going anywhere but he wasn't dead. He'd been shot through the left lung. The word "exsanguination" popped into Manny's mind. He let Cisneros lie and checked the men who'd been with the girl. Both dead.

When Manny looked into the Suburban, Rhiannon Granger looked back at him from the floorboards. He offered his hand. She took it and scrambled out.

"Okay?" he said.

She nodded.

"Stay here."

He went to Cisneros.

"Who do you work for?"

"Screw you," Cisneros whispered.

"Why did you kill Harper?"

Cisneros gave Manny a look that said he'd enjoyed killing Harper. Then he died.

The three of them, packed in the front seat, stared through the windshield, looking dazed as television addicts on a twelve-hour binge. Manny drove his Ford the fifteen bumpy miles to Highway 80 and turned west on the lonely black two-lane, heading for Douglas through open country, lit by chilly moonlight. No hiding here. No running, either.

Border Patrol trucks passed them from both directions, big four wheel drives, painted white and green. Each time, Manny, Oaks, and Rhiannon waited for the lights and sirens, for the yells and the pointed guns that go with a felony stop—a sure sign they were now known as the folks who'd left a pile of bodies back in Skeleton Canyon. They might never live to see jail if the arresting officers got too jumpy. The trucks passed by.

Town. Four o'clock in the morning. Oaks and Aguilar looked at each other over the top of Rhiannon's head and nodded. If they hadn't been stopped by now they might make it.

They found a restaurant and went in. Ate, drank coffee. Manny dialed Reina on the satellite phone he'd picked up from where he'd dropped it—in the shadows of the big rock in the Devil's Kitchen. While the call was going through he handed the phone to Rhiannon.

"She'll want to hear your voice anyway and I don't want to talk. Keep it short. Don't use anybody's name. Tell her we're all fine. Tell her about three hours, then we'll be home."

They stayed in the restaurant and waited for full daylight. It came, a kind of miracle after the long night. Coffee, truckers, waitresses. The smell of food. The ordinary world, coming back to them. Rhiannon, especially, had almost forgotten it existed.

Manny got more coffee to go. They left Douglas in an anonymous stream of morning traffic. North of Bisbee, in the open country, Oaks slept in the truck, dreamt Force Recon dreams: Fly at night, do the job, then buckle up and sleep in the chopper on the way back.

Manny woke up Oaks in Benson. "You drive," Manny said. "I'm seeing things that aren't there…."

Rhiannon Granger finished calling her aunt and came back to Reina's low slung living room in time to overhear conversation about "the key."

"What key?" she asked.

"A safe deposit box key," Reina said. "Harper had it. We found it. We just don't know what bank it goes to."

"Wow," Rhiannon said. "I couldn't make sense out of it when he told me—"

"Who?"

"My dad. He said Harper said something about the Stock Bank, or the Cow Bank, the Shitkicker Bank…"

"Stockmen's Bank?"

"Yeah."

"Where?"

"I dunno'."

"You didn't remember this before? When we talked?"

"No. My dad said so many things and it was so jumbled up that I couldn't remember it all."

"I know, honey. Makes sense to me. Did your father ever mention a key?"

Rhiannon plopped on Reina's couch, slumped down, and crossed her combat boots at the ankles. "No, just this shitkicker—"

"Stockmen's," Reina said, anxiously.

"Yeah, Stockmen's Bank."

"Was there anything else?" Reina asked. "Did your dad say anything else?"

"I just got, like, the impression my dad and the old guy, Harper, had something going together about that bank."

Manny and Reina looked at each other, both thinking the same thing: Harper pays Granger. Granger rents the box.

By noon the next day, Manny and Reina were driving south in her car, Reina at the wheel. Manny watched the power poles for hawks and ravens as they passed through the grasslands. He glanced behind them from time to time. Somewhere, a real mean somebody was missing a crew of killers and a key.

He couldn't complain about a ride in the wide open spaces. Tucson was fifty miles away and more than two thousand feet lower in elevation. Not a Saguaro cactus in sight here. Sonoita area, ranch country.

Sonoita itself appeared as a dark clutter of buildings hugging four corners of prairie two-lane. Highway 83, meet Highway 82.

The place was growing fast and the Stockmen's Bank had been bought out. The name had changed, but the safe deposit boxes had stayed.

Reina had faxed Granger's death certificate before they'd left town, along with a letter from Rhiannon which Jeff had helped draft, claiming sole survivorship, and asking that the box be opened. Along with that, she'd faxed a letter from Jeff, stating that Rhiannon was his client, as far as this matter went, and that his agents would appear to open the box. Now, Reina and a shaky clerk named Miriam Tremens were turning keys together in the tidy vault of the bank formerly known as The Stockmen's.

Reina put the weighty and sealed manila envelope into a Victoria's Secret shopping bag and Manny walked her back to her black Honda, one hand stuffed in his jacket pocket and wrapped around his snubnosed .38.

It was too early to eat at the Steak Out in Sonoita. They drove out of their way, to see if they'd been tailed, to Patagonia, once a silver mining camp along Sonoita Creek, now a village with a mixed crowd of people who liked the quiet life. Reina checked her rear view mirror all the way there.

They parked near a restaurant called the Gathering Grounds and went inside for coffee and a corner table on the top level in the back. An eclectic blend of locals and tourists populated the other tables.

The manila envelope contained a type written report, documents, audio tapes, and some photographs. All of it looked to have been professionally executed and compiled.

Manny and Reina went to poker face mode, took a breath, and paged to the signature on the report.

"Then, not daring to look at each other—" Reina chuckled, stuffing everything back into the manila envelope. Finishing their coffees, they left the restaurant as calmly as possible and made tracks for Tucson. Time to give it all a good read. Jeffrey Goldman, Attorney at Law, would be looking right over their shoulders.

CHAPTER THIRTY-SIX

NEAR THE OFFICE they remembered they were starving. When Goldman arrived he found them noshing and reading, distracted and dwarfed by a huge pile of paper, audio tapes, and takeout food.

"Christmas for Wiccans?" Goldman asked.

Stuffing onion rings into her mouth, too excited to think of a comeback, Reina nodded and pawed around until she found the last page of the report. She pushed it at him and he took it with one hand, fanning the air with the other to ward off the fumes from Reina's onion rings.

"Signature reads Randall P. Rogers, Detective, Tucson Police Department," Goldman said out loud. "I listened to Rogers lie on the witness stand a lot, so I'm thinking the P stands for Prick."

Reina handed Jeff the rest of the report.

"And you're telling me," Jeff said, after a few seconds of reading, "that Randall P. Rogers gathered evidence on a Mexican drug lord, one Ricardo, umm, "Rico" LaMadrid, and additional evidence that Patrick Dollanger, prominent Arizona land developer, conspired with LaMadrid in criminal activity, to wit, money laundering, human trafficking, et cetera, with said Mexican drug lord?"

"Th—yup," Reina slurred, through the onion rings.

Jeff looked at Manny. "Are you certain Rogers wrote this report? Do you recognize his signature on this report?"

Manny looked at Jeff and nodded.

"And you two believe Rogers put this stuff together because?"

"Blackmail," Manny said, "or for insurance, so he could threaten Rico and Dollanger with it if he needed to. I believe he even thought he could lie to law enforcement. He wrote it like it was part of a Tucson Police investigation he was doing on his own—but we all know he tried to kill me to get to Rhiannon. I believe he was Rico's inside informant with the TPD."

Manny held up an 8x10 photograph of two men. One was tall with sharp, cavernous features. "Rhiannon's father, Granger, gave me the names Rico and Tony Cisneros. I found Tony Cisneros, but this is first time I've understood who Rico is."

Manny pointed at the photograph. "This one is Rico. He was at the party where I wound up dumped in the Nogales cemetery. That's Rico LaMadrid."

Jeff took the photo Manny handed him. "And the man with LaMadrid in this photo is Patrick Dollanger—am I right?"

Manny and Reina nodded.

"I think we know what we'll do with this evidence, don't we?" Jeff looked at his two seated employees like a parent telling his kids they couldn't keep the puppy.

"How did Bernard Harper get his hands on Randy's report and documents?" Manny asked.

"I'm sure it'll come out in the investigation," Jeff said, "and we can read all about it in the papers—"

"But—"Reina said.

"It's time, Reina," Jeff said. His hands were up, gesturing, and his ponytail was flipping. "We've cut a lot of corners. I'm not going to be disbarred over this—and—and," he waved his fingers ferociously to forestall argument, "we'll get some credit for this, maybe lots of credit—if we don't go to jail first. Time for the big talk with staff, meaning you two, over this, this—"

"Mr. Toad's Wild Ride thing?" Reina suggested.

"Yes, Reina, except that Mr. Toad didn't go to jail—nor was he murdered or disbarred."

Reina watched Jeff, loving him for the way he loved the game.

"Jeff," she said, "let's turn the evidence over, but after we've figured it all out. We're so close. Let's finish reading and discuss it before we call the Feds. We've just got a couple more questions—"

"Such as?"

"How did Harper get Randy's report? Randy sure didn't give it to him. Who did?"

"Yeah, okay," Jeff said wearily. "It would help to know the chain of custody for this evidence—that is, before you two got it because you realize you'll have to explain all of this to law enforcement—and then again to the courts, most likely."

"I believe Carole Harper is the link," Manny said. "She identified her father's remains and told me she was leaving Tucson that same day. I saw her later in a car with somebody who looked like Dollanger."

"Let's look at this stuff," Jeff said, taking a seat, "then we'll decide how to proceed with this dangerous, marginally legal investigation. Be mindful of the possibility of unemployment, jail, and disbarment. And, when we're all done, I think you know what else we're going to do before we make any calls to law enforcement."

"Yeah," Manny said, "we rehearse, so we all have the same story for the FBI and the courts."

"Bingo," Jeff said. "It's going to take a lot of work to tell ourselves what happened because we'll be manipulating and withholding some information. If we're caught, all three of us could go to jail. It's that simple. It's that important."

Reina handed Jeff a sandwich. Manny got him some coffee. They read the documents, making as much sense of them as they could, and then Reina put on an audio tape neatly labeled "One." The voices were in Spanish. Reina and Jeff were lost. They looked at Manny. He nodded to indicate he understood every word being spoken.

"Randy's report says those tapes were conversations between Dollanger and LaMadrid," Manny said, after he'd heard the first tape. "If that's true, Dollanger speaks very good Spanish. They were talking about human smuggling. Sounds like LaMadrid procured hundreds of skilled workers for Dollanger's construction projects—"

"Which we all know involve thousands of homes," Reina said.

"LaMadrid shipped these undocumented workers across the border, directly to Dollanger's worksites. It sounds like both men had the power to bribe, or otherwise prevent law enforcement, on both sides of the border, from stopping these loads of workers. It's not said directly on tape, but there were drug shipments in the mix, too, as well as I can make out."

When the listening and reading was finally over, Jeff gave his two employees two days to do whatever they wanted about the details. After that, he would drop the manila envelope and its contents on the desk of the nearest federal authority.

It took some diligent but discreet snooping to establish Carole Harper as Dollanger's mistress. The way Reina's buddy, Bernie "Burns" Sachs, investigative reporter for the local alternative paper told it, Dollanger liked to throw big parties but he didn't flaunt his women. If he showed up in public with an escort, chances were it was a business associate, and not arm candy. The first and only wife had a house in Florida. The kids were grown up and gone.

It wasn't hard to locate Patrick Dollanger's principal residence, a garish three-story house at the base of the Catalina Mountains. Manny drove out there. The building squatted like a golem on the decapitated body of what had once been a hill. Nobody answered the phone. No vehicles in the driveway. No answer to knocks on the door. Time to check out Dollanger's house in town.

The local and legendary land developer had also bought in El Encanto Estates, just a couple of neighborhoods, and a couple of million dollars, away from Jeff Goldman's office in the West University area.

El Encanto Estates was a 1920s vintage, Spanish style community with narrow, tightly curved streets, the whole thing designed like a wheel, a nature park at the center, lined with Royal Palm trees. Thick vegetation everywhere. The neighborhood association fought and gossiped online—and passed along everything they saw or heard, suspicious or not.

Dollanger's place sat at the wheel's hub and it looked big enough to take up a couple of spokes, all the way back to the rim on Broadway Boulevard.

Manny parked Reina's black Honda Civic in sight of the Dollanger mansion and called the unlisted number, got a housekeeper, and asked for Carole. Not there, but at least he now knew she had been there, and recently.

His cell vibrated. "Reina, what's up?"

"Nobody home in Encanto? I just got some skinny. There's a home in Tortolita that's not in Dollanger's name but he owns it. Try up there, but not in my car. I'll call and rent you a jeep, or something. By the way, did you know a lot of the Encanto residents still have their own wells, right in the middle of Tucson? Hey, it's not like we're keeping track of our water use or anything—is it? Anyway, sit tight, I'll call for a jeep. Pick me up on the way to the rental agency."

After the Skeleton Canyon fight Manny had left his truck parked in the fenced yard of a paint shop, part of his brother Reggie's car dealership. When Reggie's boys got some extra time, they were going to repaint it—for cheap. Even Reggie, characteristically easy going, had let Manny know that, for the price, he was getting a favor.

When the story about the bodies in Skeleton Canyon hit the Tucson papers, Manny had been glad to be far away from that truck. But bodies were found, shot full of holes or not, in Southern Arizona, all the time. The incident was a blip in the regional news section and the dead were identified only as Mexican nationals.

Johnny Oaks had seen to making sure that both Rhiannon and her aunt would not be found. He'd called friends in northern New Mexico who'd taken both women in. He'd driven them there himself, leaving his Caddy in his driveway, using a borrowed car. He'd been watching his rearview mirror, too.

Reina called Manny back in a few minutes. He picked her up on the way to a rental agency on Oracle Road.

"Watch out up there, Manny," Reina said. "I'll see you at Jeff's." She pulled out of the lot in her Civic, leaving him with the jeep.

Manny made sure he had a round in the chamber of his Colt and that the weapon was cocked, locked, and loose in the holster. He positioned his camera so he could get to it quick, checked the contents of his briefcase and his PI credentials and started driving.

CHAPTER THIRTY-SEVEN

TORTOLITA WAS AN unincorporated area in mountain foothills northwest of Tucson. It hid itself between two municipalities: the white bread hoodoo of Oro Valley and the identity challenged sprawl of Marana. In Tortolita you drilled your own wells, minded your own business, and guarded your privacy like a bulldog. People had been run out of there with shotguns.

The pavement quickly became dirt roads and the No Trespassing signs were plentiful and detailed, citing the codes under which trespassers could be prosecuted.

Manny finally reached a rise at the end of a track rough enough to tear the bottom out of anything less than a bulldozer. He could see three houses through the zoom lens on his camera.

The house farthest up the ridge looked like an old hippie place, bamboo and corn growing in the backyard. The other two houses were low slung, two-storied, flat-roofed, expensive, and built of stone colored like the high, rocky ground where they sat.

Manny zoomed in on the second floor deck of the house that was straight in front, 150 yards out, and watched as Carole Harper came out a French door and began walking along the deck with a large golden retriever for company.

Calls to his office and a little checking around had revealed that Dollanger was out of town, maybe out of the country, on business. Good. Any contact with Dollanger would have tipped him off.

It didn't look like anybody was home but Carole. Manny cranked up the jeep and rolled into the yard as she stepped into the driveway, dog by her side. Manny got out and held up a badge case with a picture ID.

"Ms. Harper, I was the detective who investigated your father's death. I have something to show you."

"Why didn't you contact me through the telephone number I gave you? Why did you come here?" Her big blue-green eyes were wide and she was hiding behind the dog.

"I found the safe deposit box your father rented. I can show you copies."

He reached into a folder on the seat of the jeep without taking his eyes off the woman, "Look at this, Ms. Harper."

He showed her a wide angle photograph taken from waist level. Dollanger and LaMadrid were seated. Carole Harper stood in the background of the photograph, speaking to Randy Rogers.

"This puts all four of you together. What did you do, give your father the report?"

"He stole it," she whispered, pale now under her tan. The words came out of her as if she'd rehearsed them silently, a million times over.

"What?"

"He stole it. I had lunch with my drunken father out of, uh, kindness—and he stole it. He stole it out of my briefcase. There. Are you happy?"

"How did he know what it was?"

"I don't know. I think he may have thought it was money, or something."

"What was your relationship with Rogers?"

"We were...close. He—"

"Close? He was your lover."

She stared at him.

"He was your lover, and you and Rogers planned to blackmail Dollanger and Rico and disappear."

"I didn't know what was in the packet. Randy gave it to me for safekeeping, my father stole it...." She clutched at the dog leash. The dog stood panting, oblivious.

"Rogers planned on leaving the country," Manny said. "You and Rogers fly away with the blackmail money and live happily ever—"

"No."

"You got the goods on Dollanger. Rogers got the rest. And you thought these guys would never find you? Where were you going to hide?"

"Switzerland." She was whispering again.

"Was Rolf involved in this trip to Switzerland?"

She didn't answer.

"Your roommate, Rolf. I called him, long ago. He wasn't cooperative. He'll answer questions this time, if he's still in this country. Different picture now, isn't it?"

"Don't insult me," Carole said. "You don't know what I've been through. People like you never will."

"Were you unhappy when I killed Rogers? So was I. I went to school with him. He was my friend."

"It was his idea, all of—"

"When your father, Bernard Harper, got drunk and called Dollanger, he wrote his own toe tag for the morgue. You let Patrick Dollanger murder him, didn't you?"

"What was I supposed to do? Tell Patrick? He'd have killed me." She glanced over her shoulder at the house. "I didn't know my father had called Patrick and tried to blackmail him. I was in New York when you people called me to identify his—to identify him. You have no idea what Bernard Harper did to me when I was a child—a child. You don't know my circumstances."

"I know what was done to me," Manny said. "I got shot, rattlesnake bit, beat, cut, left for dead, and called some names. And my best friend got assaulted by the scum your sugar daddy, or his buddies, sent after us. It got very ugly, Ms.. Harper. And there's more: Your lover, Randall Rogers, along with Rico's crew, killed a half-dozen people looking for your blackmail kit."

"I hardly knew Rico. He was Patrick's business associate."

"I don't believe that, Carole. You concealed recording equipment on your body when Dollanger and Rico met. You copied papers that link Dollanger to Rico—and you copied other papers that show Dollanger's dealings with local and state politicians, as well as accounting information that points to money laundering and hidden bank accounts."

Carole Harper gave him an angry, frantic stare. "Tired," she said. "Tired of all you people...."

"I work for an attorney. Let's go to his office. You make a call from there, get yourself some legal representation. Come with me, make a call, then surrender to law enforcement. If you don't go to them, they will come to you. I'll call them right now." Manny held up his cell phone.

"What do I do with Goldie?" she asked.

"Who's Goldie?"

"My dog."

"What are you doing here?" someone said.

Manny looked up to see Patrick Dollanger staring down at him from the railing on the second floor. The billionaire hadn't left town after all. Dollanger was tanned and fit. He undulated slightly, conveying a sense of manic, undifferentiated eagerness. He bared narrow teeth, stuck between a pair of purple Cupid's bow lips, and his eyes were vicious and intent.

CHAPTER THIRTY-EIGHT

"I HAVE BUSINESS with Carole Harper regarding her father's death," Manny said.

"Leave," Dollanger said. "Carole, get back in the house."

Manny looked at Carole. "Come with me. Save your life," he said softly. "It's your only chance."

Carole stood there, frozen. Manny took her arm and put her in the passenger seat of the jeep.

"Buckle up," he said, and took the leash out of her hand and led Goldie to his side of the vehicle and lifted the dog into the back.

"Carole," Dollanger yelled. "Carole!"

"She'll see you in court," Manny yelled back. "And so will I."

Manny, Carole, and the golden retriever headed for Jeff's office. Dollanger kept yelling until they couldn't hear him anymore.

The FBI spent a long time grilling Manny, Carole, Reina, and Jeff. Manny explained that he'd been doing PI work when he came across a suspect, Tony Cisneros, whose present whereabouts were unknown to him.

Manny said he had first heard Cisneros's name through David Granger, now deceased, while working as a Pima County Sheriff's Detective, investigating the murder of Bernard Harper. He'd later discovered that Cisneros also figured in a case his present employer, Jeffrey Goldman, had taken on behalf of a young murder suspect named Larry Armenta.

David Granger had mentioned a tape and connected Cisneros to the tape. Granger said that Harper had been killed because he claimed to have evidence against a powerful person, who, Harper had claimed, was a real estate developer.

Manny said he'd disregarded all of this as a combination of lies and fantasies until he received a mysterious package with an audiotape inside it. He listened to it, heard Harper's statement on the tape, and consulted with his employer, Jeffrey Goldman. In the course of physically handling the tape Manny had noticed that it seemed oddly heavy. Upon shaking the tape, he heard something come loose inside it. He then unscrewed the casing and discovered the key.

Since Granger had mentioned Cisneros, who was himself a key to the defense of young Larry Armenta, Jeff Goldman had sought permission from the courts to locate and open the safe deposit box where the evidence, which turned out to have no bearing on the Armenta defense, was found.

The evidence did, however, show that Randall Rogers had motive to attempt Manny's murder. The evidence pointed toward the solution of Bernard Harper's murder, which was still unsolved. Believing that Carole Harper was involved, Manny had located Carole Harper, who indicated that she was prepared to sing like a bird.

The FBI was not happy with the statement about the tape in the mysterious package. Jeff Goldman and Reina couldn't help the FBI with that one. They said they thought it was an unusual coincidence but, unlike the FBI, they saw no reason to doubt Manuel Aguilar. Apparently, it had occurred to the FBI that Manny was lying his ass off, but it had not occurred to Jeff or Reina.

The phone rang just after the FBI left Goldman's office with Carole Harper. Carole had bent to one knee, put her arms around her slobbering dog, and said goodbye.

"Johnny," Reina said, into the phone, "join us for dinner."

Johnny Oaks appeared a few minutes later, giving Goldie a cautious look as he stepped through the door.

"Whose dog?" he said.

Goldie wandered over and licked his hand.

"Yours if you want him," Reina said. "I promised Carole Harper we'd take care of him."

"I don't think so."

"He likes you, Johnny," Reina said. "Think about it. Manny and I can take him if you don't want him—or Jeff. Jeff? Want a dog?"

"I want food, not a dog."

"Manny, looks like we've got a dog."

"You've got a dog. I've got a cat, Reina."

"We shared the cat and we can share the dog."

"Now we're all happy," Jeff Goldman said. "Let's eat."

"What do I think about the trial?" Nobody had asked Jeff what he thought about the trial, but he knew what they were all thinking and he could guess at what they felt.

"There's no predicting the outcome," Jeff went on as Reina delicately gnawed the last of her fish tacos. Johnny Oaks and Manny were leaning back, impassive as walls, clutching their second beer, their burgers eaten, and the plates already taken away. The three of them had a corner booth in Gentle Ben's. Polished wood, low light, classic rock.

"Patrick Dollanger might do jail time in a federal white collar prison and he might beat the rap completely," Jeff went on. "We know his influence extends all the way to the governor of this state, but that can't be directly proven from any of the evidence we reviewed. All of this will cost him a bundle, but he's got another one hidden somewhere. And he's missing a mistress because Carole Harper ratted him out. I'm guessing Rico LaMadrid will get a show trial and a hand slap in Mexico.

"I've had clients get more time, just for being drug addicts, than these guys will probably get for all the crimes they've committed. We can't give them what they deserve, and the justice system won't. But we ruined their day. We did that. It's about not stopping, even if we can't stop them. Here's to doing all you can do." Jeff raised his glass.

"Here's to not stopping and to keeping faith in magic," Reina said, reaching for her club soda. "Here's to the dignity of that. Here's to virtuous pagans."

Jeff held his glass out in the center of the table. Everybody joined in. Manny looked over Jeff's shoulder and saw his grandmother sitting in a booth. She lifted a long necked bottle. She drank, gave him a wink, and vanished.

Manny and his attorney, Jeff Goldman, showed up a month later for court. The judge ruled justifiable homicide in the shooting death of Randall Rogers. Not long before, the same judge had dismissed charges against young Larry Armenta, making two wins in a row for Jeff.

On a windy day in March, Manny went by himself to Evergreen Cemetery, to a section of graves far behind the others, with their prominent and varied stone markers, where the indigent were buried. Carole Harper had not stepped forward in the matter of funeral expenses for her father's remains. Maybe she'd been too busy, sitting in protective custody, being prepared by a prosecution team to testify against Patrick Dollanger. No one else had stepped forward, Manny included, to pay Harper's funeral expenses, but Manny figured his gift to Harper had been discovering his killers, and seeing them brought, one way or another, to justice, even though no evidence had ever been obtained to prove what Manuel Aguilar and his closest friends knew—

and what Carole Harper knew as well—that Patrick Dollanger had ordered Barney Harper killed.

Harper's head had been buried in a piece of ground large enough for a body and a small metal tag bore his name. The grave next it was just the same, except that the tag read "John Doe." Manny was due to testify in Dollanger's trial the next day. He looked at Harper's metal tag and thought about where you end up, sometimes, because of the things you can't let go—alcohol, in Harper's case—and the idea that somebody else's life is better than yours and that you can blackmail them for it. Manny got in his truck, drove out west of town, and took a long walk in the Tucson Mountains.

CHAPTER THIRTY-NINE

DOLLANGER'S TRIAL HAD been going on for weeks when Manny and Reina settled down, one night, after work and takeout, to watch the 10 o'clock news. Martina Escobar-Hudspeth was wrinkling her pretty brow over a rash of street shootings while her male counterpart sadly shook his head.

The news program shifted to a set of courthouse steps and to Patrick Dollanger, balding, thick lipped, narrow eyed, wearing a lavender tie and a striped suit, ascending those steps for sentencing. They learned from Martina's voice-over that Patrick Dollanger received a three year prison sentence and that most of his known assets had been seized for racketeering. Martina mentioned Carole Harper, who had been spared prison time for cooperation with authorities.

There had been only cursory references to Rico LaMadrid in the American press and there had never been a comprehensive story describing LaMadrid and Dollanger as the international crime lords they were, a pair whose partnership resulted in the deaths of dozens of people, corrupted and exploited many more, and scraped millions of tax free dollars into their hands alone.

Manny read the Mexican papers to keep track of Rico LaMadrid and he had also contacted Eladio Durango, the Pima County Sheriff's Department's interface with Mexico. There was no indication that LaMadrid now cared whether Manuel Aguilar lived or died. He wasn't going to be doing any jail time, either. He'd been painted as a victim of American greed, framed for championing the plight of undocumented workers.

Goldie the dog, dozing on the rug, sighed deeply. Grayboy the cat sat on a counter and watched the bubbles in Manny's beer glass.

"Well, it looks like it's over," Reina said. "He got more prison time that we thought he would. Do you ever think about busting Patrick Dollanger's head—or LaMadrid's? They did an awful lot to you, me, and to a lot of other people."

"Yeah," Manny said, "I'd love to bust their heads. But if I really hated

Dollanger, or LaMadrid, or any criminal, I'd be too burned out to keep going after the bad guys."

"So you're still going after bad guys?" Reina asked.

"Somebody has to."

"Will you try to get your sheriff's job back? Do homicide investigation?"

"Maybe. I could do some work for Jeff on the side."

"If the department won't take you back it's their loss. Just so you know, I'd rather have you around my office, working with Jeff and me."

Reina lit her evening candles. Manny noticed that the walls were changing colors again. They watched the weather report. More sun forecast for Tucson. After that, they headed for the bedroom.

Moonlight came through the window. They could smell flowers of some kind. Even Reina didn't know what they were. The whole house seemed to breathe. Objects seemed sentient, and the walls rippled in colors like the northern lights. They faced each other and stripped.

"I'm going to nail your pelt to the wall," Manny said thickly, struggling out of his underwear.

"Such a poet," Reina said.

Manny mentally swore in the names of Dante Alighieri and his own Yaqui grandmother that, after they had made all the love they could make, he would kiss every scar on her body, let her do the same for him, and never leave her side. In the moonlight her eyes were molten gold. She was whip smart and she could see way better than 20-20 with those eyes, even in the dark. She raised both arms and twiddled one finger on each hand, like a street fighter.

"Come on," she said.

ABOUT THE AUTHOR

CLARK LOHR COMES from a Montana farm and ranch background. He attended a one-room school through the eighth grade. Most of his friends were old men who told good stories. He is proud to have graduated from Arcadia High School in Scottsdale, Arizona. He is a Vietnam vet and a member of Veterans for Peace.

He has drifted considerably in his life, working a variety of dead end jobs. He has traveled in Asia, Europe and Central America. He graduated from the University of Arizona with a BA in Writing and Literature. He is trained as a photographer. He has one daughter, Diana, and a grandchild, Maya.

Made in the USA
Charleston, SC
21 August 2011